# QUEST

## FOR THE

# LOST

# NAME

*a novel*

# QUEST

## FOR THE

# LOST
# NAME

GEORGE MAKRIS

TIMELESS SELF INSTITUTE, INC.

Copyright © 2013 George Makris

Published in the United States by Timeless Self Institute, Inc.
www.TimelessSelf.com

Editing by Dave King
Cover design by Dunn+Associates Design
Book design by Warwick Associates
Set in Garamonde

Cataloging-in-Publication

    Makris, George.
        Quest for the lost name : a novel / George Makris.
        p. cm.
        LCCN 2012948096
        ISBN 978-1-936811-00-7

        1. Psychologists--Fiction.  2. God --
    Name--Fiction.  3. Adventure stories.  4. Fantasy
    fiction.   I. Title.

    PS3613.A364Q47 2012        813'.6
                   QBI12-600188

Printed in the United States of America

10 9 8 7 6 5 4 3 2 1

First Edition

*To my readers*

# PART I

# THE CALL

For terms that may require clarification,
please refer to the glossary at the back of the book.

# CHAPTER 1

**4:25 a.m., Apt. 1C, 214 19th Street NW, Washington, DC**

I woke up screaming. The terrifying feeling of doom that had tormented me for the last few weeks finally yielded its secret.

I sat up in bed, panting, slowly becoming aware of the darkness in the room, broken only by the constellation of electronic devices—phone, laptop, Kindle—plugged in and charging around me.

I had never experienced such a choking sense of looming catastrophe. Not when Vivian and I divorced five years ago. Not when I considered ending my life in a moment of unbearable teenage angst. Not even when I fled from the tanks during the war.

What was going on? Was my premonition true? Or, had my subconscious struggles finally reached a boiling point, causing me to project my own worst fears of annihilation onto others?

I couldn't tell.

I tapped the light on my bedside clock—4:43 a.m. And I had a big day coming up. I rolled over and tried to go back to sleep, but after I heard the campus tower clock strike five, I gave up and went to make myself some coffee. Whatever was coming, I wanted to be awake to meet it. Even Judgment Day.

...

By evening, Earth had not ended, though I wasn't sure if that was a good thing. That afternoon, I had butted heads with my boss over the content of my lesson plans, and I probably said some things I would later regret. Albert Sharpstone, the Psychology Department head at George Washington University where I taught, had complained I was sneaking non-scientific material into my classes. To me, spiritual concepts, such as free will retrieval, the Soul, and the Timeless Self, were the *real* facts of life. To him, they were nothing more than superstition.

Today's verbal warning was my second one, and I was instructed to meet him tomorrow at three for a formal review. A bloody formal review. For all my persuasiveness and determination, I wouldn't stand a chance against Sharpstone's medieval mind. He might as well build stocks in the middle of campus, lock my arms and legs between the boards, and sling real mud.

My headache throbbed, and lack of sleep wasn't making things any easier to deal with. I pushed away all thoughts of my boss, my knuckles massaging my temples until the pain eased. I opened the fridge and peered inside. And there, between the pot of the leftover spaghetti, the bottles of iced green tea, and the pita bread—baklava. I snatched a piece, popped it into my mouth, and enjoyed its almond-honey goodness. The pain faded away. Grandma's advice, God rest her soul, had proven right once again. Food is love, and love can heal anything.

I walked over to the spacious living room. It looked elegant and neat, except for the laundry heap from last week begging to be folded. I hate folding. Greek men don't fold clothes. They just don't.

But I could water my orchids.

Instead, I sank into the blue suede La-Z-Boy. If only Leah were here. She'd make everything right.

The vision of Leah affects me like a statue of Venus. With crystal-blue eyes. It inspires. It exhilarates. It leaves me yearning for another gaze. I appreciate that we can have an intelligent conversation about Plotinus and Bacon, or be awed into silence by contemplating together the beauty of nature.

Of course, the fact that she looks stunning doesn't hurt. And there is something more between us, something magical I can't quite pin down.

I'm also impressed with her work, building Montessori schools around the world for disadvantaged children. So much so, I'm sorely tempted to drop everything and hop on a plane to Boston. Give her a helping hand at the Winslow Hope Foundation.

Right.

Truth is, we never dated as such, never exchanged loving whispers, never kissed. It was love at first sight, yes, but we met only five times at official functions. And there was the problem that her father was a self-made billionaire. Would he give the hand of his only child to a mere psychology professor?

My female colleagues at the university widely acknowledged my good sense of humor. That was always a plus. And the women I had dated before I met Vivian always mentioned my Mediterranean charm as a key point of attraction. I supposed it could have been my thick eyebrows, or my let's-go-sailing gaze, or my accent.

Still, I didn't move in anything approaching the rarified social circle the Winslows inhabited, a world where lunch could include a $500 bottle of wine and the watches cost as much as I usually paid for a new car. There was no way I would ever convince Mr. Winslow I wasn't after his daughter's money, and I had yet to come up with a Plan B.

A sharp knock on the door interrupted my thoughts. "Who is it?"

"Letter. For you." It was Dwayne, a Vietnam vet, the night receptionist at my apartment complex.

A purple envelope slid through the mail slot.

"Thanks, Dwayne. Who brought it?"

Dwayne didn't respond. He was a man of few words.

I scrambled up and ran to the door. Master Theodore's embossed coat of arms held the envelope closed. It was a message from the Inner Order, the spiritual organization I belonged to.

I grabbed the envelope from the floor and broke the seal.

My hand shook with an electric charge. I didn't know what was inside, but this morning's feeling of doom came back with a vengeance.

> Diokles,
>
> Ten days from midnight, a hammer of woe will strike Earth. Continents will shift. Lands will vanish and innumerable lives will be lost—unless an initiate prevails over the four ordeals and retrieves the Scroll of the Lost Name of God.
>
> Cancel all obligations and report to Headquarters at once. Upon arrival, you will discover the scroll's forbidden secret.
>
> The Order of the Red Scorpion intends to stop us at all costs. Watch your movements and speak of this to no one. Your life is in danger.
>
> Challenge: The Mysteries shall be reborn
> Password: The Light shall prevail
>
> Glory be to the invincible Light of Truth,
>
> Theodore
> Imperator, Inner Order of the Masters of Energy

A chill shot up my spine, spiking the hairs on the back of my neck. The premonition would soon come true. Unless—

*Hurry! The tanks are almost here. The soldiers are going to kill us.*

An overwhelming impulse to flee suddenly possessed me.

I clenched my teeth, struggled to fight the flashback. It was no use. A scene that took place in the small town of Khytrea on the island of Cyprus now played on the screen of my mind.

"Hurry!" the mother of the dark-haired boy yells from downstairs. "The tanks are almost here. The soldiers are going to kill us."

The boy jerks, then continues to shove his Captain America and Asterix comic books under his bed. He throws the last one on the pile and sprints to the bathroom, tears flowing freely from his brown eyes. He fills a glass and waters the violet orchid in the corner, spilling half the water on the floor. He crams the cat's bowl with dry food, spilling much of that too.

"My books, my kitty, and my plant will wait till I come back home," he whispers.

"Diokles*, come!"

The boy glances around the stone house one last time, and scuttles down the stairs toward the car, a baby deer running away from hungry wolves. He tumbles into the back seat and latches onto Grandma. The boy's father shifts the forest-green Jaguar into gear and pushes the gas pedal to the floor. It can't be soon enough before they slip out of the noose tightening around Khytrea.

Fields of ripe wheat zoom by. Cars and trucks race along the road as if seized by a sudden madness. Orange tongues of flame leap from behind the mountains and lick the sky. Smoke forms giant, gray-green clouds. The air stinks of dust mixed with pig dung.

Grandma's soothing words to the boy don't help. He continues to stare at shrinking Khytrea through the back window, his olive skin now tomb-pale.

The boy's tears were now my own, my fingers boring into my skull, trying to drain the ugly thoughts that nested there. I sat up on the loveseat. "Enough, *please.*"

The evil was coming again, and Master Theodore said I had to meet it.

---

\* *Diokles [Dī-oh-klees]: Greek for "Glory of Zeus"*

Twenty-three years ago, the war didn't just rip away my child-hood and my vast inheritance from the family's factories and land. It also took my peace of mind.

During my high-school days, I tried to heal my soul wounds by drinking myself numb and experimenting with drugs. My teenage rebellion didn't help much, nor did it banish the inner demons that surfaced to drag me down.

In spite of it all, I never gave up. Because of my high grades, I earned a full scholarship to Columbia University and escaped to America. I chose to study psychology, mostly so that I could understand how my own mind worked. After earning my doc-torate at George Washington University in Washington, DC, I was hired as a professor there. The flashbacks continued on and off, especially when real or imagined stress made me feel I had to flee in order to survive.

One fateful day, a fellow professor introduced me to the Inner Order of the Masters of Energy. I had visited the Headquarters in Wyoming for a month every summer since then. Mainstream psychology is useful and wonderful. Yet, it wasn't until I put my heart into the spiritual practices Master Theodore taught me that I managed to wrestle those inner demons and find some peace. He said I was getting better at managing my energies and mani-festing my goals.

It was this focus on spirituality that cost me Vivian—she was more interested in the hard-partying Diokles. Apparently, we had gotten married for the wrong reasons.

I stared at the crumpled letter in my hand. The planet was falling apart and Master Theodore wanted me to help save it. Sure, I *was* progressing steadily through the levels of the Inner Order, but I also knew how far I had to go. Many initiates were miles ahead of me, spiritually. No way was I up to such a task.

An echo of the Inner Order's teachings rose up in my thoughts. *A Master of Energy never caves in when the sea of his negative emo-*

*tions rises up to drown him. Liberate the inner power and defeat the Great Forgetfulness. Remember your unconditional soul identity. Trust the Timeless Self.*

I drew in a calming breath. Maybe this was an opportunity to repay my debt to Master Theodore. I would obey the summons.

A rattling of the windows shocked me out of my reverie. Half-dazed, I looked at the rain pounding against the glass. A bolt of lightning cut the clouds in two, like the flaming sword of an archangel.

I began the count almost automatically. One . . . two . . . three. Thunder penetrated the walls and jarred my ears.

Wait. I had that formal review tomorrow afternoon. What would I say to Sharpstone? "I need to be excused because I have to help save the world?" No, I'd say I was sorry. I had been a little rough on the man. I called his office, intending to leave a voice mail. "Dr. Sharpstone, this is Dr. Philaretos. Please accept my apology. I was out of line, and—"

I hesitated. Why should I play nice if I didn't really mean it? I despise pretending. "Dr. Sharpstone," I said in a manner that would have landed me a failing grade in an anger-management exam, "I have a life-threatening emergency out of town and need to reschedule our meeting. And my class. Please don't try me in absentia."

I accessed the Internet to book my morning ticket for Jackson, Wyoming.

Then, I leaned back and squeezed my eyes shut, my body going numb. Life as I knew it was over.

# CHAPTER 2

**6:30 a.m., Day 1, Foyer, 214 19th Street NW, Washington, DC**

I reached the foyer of my apartment complex and paused. The buff walls, the Lady Palms, and the art deco pieces were all supposed to work together to create a warm, friendly space. Today, the foyer felt like the entrance of an upper-class funeral home.

Dwayne slumped behind his desk. He was a large man, red faced, with short white hair and grey eyes. A retired welder, he worked the night shift to supplement the peanuts he and Mable collected from Social Security.

"Morning, Dwayne," I said.

"I'm not your delivery boy."

"I didn't say you were."

"You have a package."

"From whom?"

"A cupcake. She brought it this morning."

It must have been the woman my racquetball buddy, Tony, had been trying to fix me up with, even though I had told him I wasn't interested. This morning, it seemed, the woman in question had decided to take matters into her own hands.

I crossed over to Dwayne's desk. "What'd she look like?"

"Tall. Blond. A looker." Dwayne instinctively straightened up and made an effort to suck in his pot belly. He came up short. "Made me wish I was young again."

"When was this?"

"Twenty, thirty minutes ago."

"No way."

"Yes way."

"Save it for me. Got a flight to catch."

"Here. She made me swear I'd give you the package. You take it, or you don't go through that door."

The package had my name on it and a lipstick-kiss impression. I tore off the wrapping and opened the little box.

A white puff lurched.

I held my breath, threw the box away.

Too late. The chloroform vapor skulked into my nose, catapulting me into a stupor.

Arms falling limp, legs buckling, I tumbled to the carpeted floor. The foyer spun. My ears buzzed. Psychedelic images bumping against each other in a blizzard of bright colors smothered my brain. Soon, I knew, all would go dark.

"Leaaaaaaah."

The image of Leah's face emerged through the hallucinations.

I seized it with my mind and held on. Only one thought, the thought of losing her, kept me from sinking into unconsciousness.

I struggled to roll onto my side. Couldn't. Struggled harder. Could not. "Dwayne—"

Dwayne's eyes had bugged out like those of a soldier spotting a roadside bomb. "What the hell is going on?"

"*Help.*"

Dwayne walked over and gripped me by the forearms.

When I tried to stand up, I almost passed out. I needed fresh air. "Dwayne, *do* something. Slap me."

"Huh?"

"Slap me."

*Smack.*

My cheeks stung. Blood stormed to my head and shut the giant door of the abyss.

Dwayne made the sign of the cross.

I stumbled to my feet and made it to a chair by his desk. Master Theo had warned me, and he wasn't kidding. I knew better. I shouldn't have let my guard down.

I stretched my limbs to regain feeling, trying to anticipate the next trap.

# CHAPTER 3

**6:17 p.m., Day 1, 5,000 Feet over Wyoming**

The SkyWest Airlines Bombardier CRJ700 began its descent above the western edge of Yellowstone National Park. Out of the window, I spotted a herd of bison stampeding toward a hill. Steam billowed from the bubbling geysers, rising in massive clouds. The living magma chamber of the colossal volcano that is Yellowstone was letting off pressure safely.

For now.

*A hammer of woe will strike Earth.*

The small plane landed with a jolt. Only nine miles separated me from Jackson and Master Theo. If I were the Order of the Red Scorpion, how would I kill me in that space?

I wrapped my scarf around my neck, grabbed my carry-on bag, and ran to the Hertz rental booth. The blond young man attending the booth wore an extra-large cowboy hat that looked incongruous above his boyish face, as if he were trying on his father's gear. "Howdy. What can I do for you this fine evening?"

"Diokles Philaretos. I need my Jeep and info on road conditions."

The young man stood and hung his hands from his belt, fingers pointing down, John Wayne style. "You mind saying that in English?"

I had forgotten to speak slowly. When I get excited, my accent can be pretty impenetrable. I planted my American Express Platinum Card and reservation note on the counter, and enunciated every word. "You have a Jeep for me, I believe."

He tapped at his keyboard, processed the card, and produced the keys.

I located my car and opened the door to get in when a cold sensation skittered across the back of my thighs. A premonition—a more normal one than I'd had yesterday morning, but I wasn't about to ignore it. If someone wanted to take me out the easy way, they would hotwire my car with a bomb, sending me on a no-return journey to the Other Side.

I made my way through the snow, back to the rental booth. After some loud Greek persuasion, the young man succumbed and gave me the keys to a different car.

I turned the key and floored the accelerator. The white Grand Cherokee growled like a lioness and leapt forward. Though the road was plowed and sprinkled with sand, black-ice patches lurked everywhere, forcing me to keep to a cautious forty-five miles per hour.

The sun, setting below the peaks of the Teton Range, saturated the sky with golden-pink brush strokes. A swarm of whirlwind-like snowdrifts chased each other and my car. My eyes scanned the road for stray elk and suspicious vehicles.

None showed up and finally, the white-marble Headquarters of the Inner Order came within sight. Seconds later, my fingertips tingled as I crossed the mansion's field of protection, sustained daily by the sacred invocations of Master Theo.

I loved this place.

I pulled up to the wrought-iron gate and lowered the window. The tall, muscular guard examined me closely, his gaze fierce and unyielding. "State your business."

"I am here at the invitation of Master Theo."

"The Mysteries shall be reborn."

"The Light shall prevail."

The guard's gaze softened. "Please walk from here to the main entrance. We will park your car." He opened the gate.

"Thank you. And can you call the local police, anonymously, and let them know there might be a bomb in a Grand Cherokee at the Hertz booth at the airport."

I gave him the information on my first rental, left the Jeep running, stepped out, and traced the clean-swept, red-brick walkway to the front door.

The mansion sat at the foot of a soaring mountain, surrounded by a tall railing secured by blue-granite posts. Within the yard, mature pine trees, aspens, and willows strained under the weight of the snow.

The structure itself personified sacred geometry. Its Ionic pillars, pediment, and massive portico observed the golden ratio. With its external walls parallel to the cardinal points and its thirty-three rooms aligned to the cosmic grid, the building maximized the flow of auspicious energy. This edifice was not built to be a simple residence or a meeting hall. It was built to be a *living* temple.

The pair of lion statues guarding the entrance greeted me with their abiding silence. A lean Hindu man in his middle fifties dressed in white, turban and all, opened the door.

"Follow me."

Ranjit was much more than Master Theo's assistant. They had met decades ago in India, where Master Theo had served as the US Ambassador and Ranjit as a translator. When Ranjit was caught stealing to pad his sister's dowry, Master Theo forgave him and resisted calls to prosecute.

Since then, Ranjit and Master Theo were inseparable. Master Theo offered Ranjit his unconditional freedom time and time again, but Ranjit always refused, choosing instead to stay. Over the years, they had become friends, confidants, Brothers.

We crossed the entryway without speaking and stepped into a long corridor. Pilasters in light-blue marble adorned the doorways on both sides. Portraits of past imperators of the Inner Order, spanning the centuries, hung on the walls. Men and women of great spiritual realization, some famous, most of them unknown. Each, a humble servant of humanity behind the scenes. Each, a guide of spiritual seekers to the Higher Way.

We paused in front of a heavy door.

Ranjit took my carry-on bag. "The Master knows you are here. When he is ready, you shall know."

So once again, I was left alone to face what I was being called upon to do. And ponder why I was the one called to do it.

I paced in front of the door. With every passing second, my muscles tightened, as though I were a defendant about to receive the jury's verdict. Yet the thought of seeing Master Theo again set off gentle tremors of joy within my heart. He was more than a teacher, more than a mentor. He was the very embodiment of loving Father.

One minute went by. Then three. Five. At last, Master Theo opened the door.

At six feet six, he towered a half head over me. His long white hair along with his aquiline nose matched his imperial bearing. Bearded and austere, he carried himself with a dignity normally found only in four-star generals and royalty.

He placed his left hand on his heart and made the Sign with the right, bringing it straight down and then forward at a ninety-degree angle.

I responded likewise.

"Welcome back, Diokles," he said in that resonant baritone voice.

"It's good to be here."

Our footfalls echoed off the wood-paneled walls. The three-tiered crystal chandelier shed shafts of soft light. The study smelled of lilacs, with a hint of smoke from the fireplace.

Master Theo walked to the end of the room and stopped before his enormous rosewood desk. He sat in a chair and motioned me to do the same. "Tea?"

"Yes, please."

"I see a white hair in your left sideburn," he said, as he poured tea in my cup. "You're getting old."

I couldn't resist a smile. The tension in my shoulders eased.

"You must have questions," he said.

"Any *good* news?"

"Sadly, no."

I shifted on my Queen Anne chair. "Then give me the bad."

"First, the catastrophe. If the hammer of woe hits Earth, America will become unrecognizable and fall into chaos. Europe will lose its coasts. Much of Southeast Asia and East Africa will sink into the ocean. Billions of people, literally billions, will perish."

A dagger of dread dug through my ribs. This was far, far worse than I had imagined.

"If this catastrophe comes to pass, life will. . . ."

Master Theo's discourse faded into a distant murmur.

I slouched in the chair. Haunting scenes from my past paraded before me. Fumes of gunpowder made me dizzy.

"Diokles!"

His call slashed through my mental fog like a scythe. My head jerked up, and hot blood burned my cheeks. "I'm sorry. I meant no disrespect."

"I understand."

"I can't figure out what to do about these flashbacks. It's some form of post-traumatic stress disorder, a kind of dissociation. Flares up under stress."

"You've had the flashbacks since the war, correct?"

"Right."

"Do you know why?"

"I should, but no . . . though it sounds like *you* do."

"I do, and I would have helped you lance that soul wound when you were a bit further along the Path. We are going to have to move that schedule up, which is going to be hard on you. But we can't do it today. It will distract us from our work."

I nodded. I wasn't in any hurry to stir my inner demons.

"Can you concentrate enough for me to finish?"

"I'll bite my tongue if I slip out again."

Master Theo took on a distant look, as if he were accessing tablets of history secreted away in his memory. "Men and women of goodwill can invoke the Revealed Name of God to wield the powers of creation and transformation. The Name *I AM that I AM.* But not enough among mankind have reclaimed their divine birthright. So, to stop the descent of the hammer of woe, we must unleash a greater force. A force all true adepts know and respect. The force of the *Lost* Name of God."

A holy stillness descended in the large room.

"There is an object of great power," Master Theo said, "the Scroll of the Lost Name. Whoever can access the scroll and recite the Lost Name of God has tremendous authority over heaven and earth. Enough to prevent the hammer from falling. Of course, they must be pure in heart. And more."

"I see."

"We must locate the scroll in the next ten days. There is one problem, though." Master Theo anchored his blue eyes into my own. "No one can speak the Lost Name without attaining a level of spiritual strength that only a small number of humans have in the past. If you are not strong enough, if the ordeals haven't sufficiently tempered you, then you will bring instant annihilation upon yourself."

A chill passed over me, as if the angel of death rustled his wings nearby.

"Never fear," Master Theo said in a manner that stirred my Soul's deepest hopes. "If we all stay true to our inner calling, and *we will*, Earth shall be spared. But . . . someone else is interested in the scroll—the Dark Master, head of the Order of the Red Scorpion."

"You had mentioned the Red Scorpions. They tried to kill me."

"You need some background," he said. "The Inner Order works to build an Era of Universal Enlightenment on Earth. The Red Scorpions work to counter it. We master energy to bring freedom to all. They manipulate energy to bring about tyranny. We appeal to mankind's higher impulses. They appeal to selfishness. Do you understand?"

I was finding concentration a bit easier, as long as the conversation stayed away from what I knew was coming. "I think so."

"The Dark Master sees the upcoming disaster as an opportunity. He wants to misuse the power of the scroll to rule whatever world is left."

"Better to reign in hell. . . . Wait, didn't you say something about being pure?"

"It's not his plan to unleash the power of the Lost Name. He knows he never could. He wants to draw upon the resident energy of the scroll and misuse it as a dark talisman. Like Hitler is reputed to have done with the Spear of Destiny."

My right hand clasped into a fist. "So we stop them."

"Indeed." He rested his elbows on the armrests of the chair and steepled his fingers. "I have battled the Dark Master in the past. He and his henchmen will lie, maim, kill, whatever it takes to prevent you from getting the scroll."

It took a moment for what he had said to register. "Prevent *me* from getting the scroll?"

"Yes. That's why I have called you here. You are the best candidate to retrieve and use the scroll."

The thought of self-annihilation came to mind, but oddly it paled before other considerations. I was willing to sacrifice myself to save the world. My problem was believing I was able and worthy to do it. "But . . . I thought you said the scroll could only be accessed by someone pure in heart. That's hardly me."

"The standards of purity might not be what you expect. Lancelot was hardly an innocent, yet he was able to heal Sir Urre and see the Grail at Carboneck."

"Surely there's someone in the Inner Order better qualified. I've only been with you for the last few years."

"That is true. In *this* lifetime."

"What? Oh."

"Yes, Diokles, there were a number of things I was planning to tell you quite soon. I'm sorry to surprise you with them all at once. But I'm certain beyond doubt that you are the best candidate for this mission."

I was reeling, but the peace of Master Theo's study and the calm, collected voice with which he said all of this made the undertaking somehow plausible. "Where is the scroll?"

Master Theo walked over to the marble fireplace and gazed into the embers. He threw in a pine log and returned to his chair. "The Scroll of the Lost Name is hidden in a secret cave at Mount Kailash."

"Tibet?"

"Yes. The scroll has been kept there, lost to the world, for twelve thousand years. The four of us saved it before the sinking of Atlantis."

I focused again on the peace permeating the room, gripping it like a life preserver. "Okay. Who's us?"

"Myself, you, and the Secret Master."

"*The* Secret Master? Our Secret Master?"

"One and the same. The founder of the Inner Order."

"And the fourth?"

Master Theo hesitated. "A woman, a Sister. I'm afraid you two have karmic issues."

"Oh?"

"More on her later. Now back to the scroll. . . . One of the greatest temples of Atlantis, the Temple of the Inner Name, stood close to its northern shores. The Secret Master officiated as the Chief Priest and I was the second in command. You and our Sister were members of the priesthood. A crypt under the central altar held the scroll. No one knew how old it was or who wrote it. Even then it was ancient.

"We left a few months before the waves of the ocean swallowed up Atlantis. We journeyed by land and sea, and carried the scroll to the secret cave at Mount Kailash. For twelve thousand years the scroll has rested in that silent abode, protected by a force field that would kill anyone who entered the cave.

"When mankind arrived at the brink of a great catastrophe, one man or woman would receive permission to recover the scroll. That time is now, and the Powers of Light will remove that force field in forty-eight hours. But . . . the traps and obstacles guarding the passageway will remain, and only a high initiate can navigate them and stay alive."

"You should send someone else to get the scroll. Someone better qualified."

Master Theo lifted his index finger and pointed at me. His signet ring glimmered with the light of the waxing moon coming through the south windows. "The Secret Master has *also* chosen you to go after the scroll."

"I don't think I can do it."

"That's where you are wrong." Master Theo's fierce eyes fixed me to the chair. "I'm confident you can recover the scroll for a number of reasons, and here's one of them. In that ancient time, as now, the Dark Master had lusted after the scroll. He and a small army of his minions—they weren't called Red Scorpions then, of course—caught up with us at the foothills of Mount Kailash. You, Diokles, volunteered to stay behind to defend a narrow pass by yourself. The delay gave us the time we needed to reach the cave and complete the mission."

"I can feel I died there."

"Unfortunately, you did. You accumulated merit, though, good karma. That is why you must be given the first opportunity to recover the scroll now."

"What if I fail? In *this* life, I'm just an absentminded college professor. Not Indiana Jones."

"This is no time for jokes."

I swallowed the lump blocking my throat. "I meant no offence, but I'm not joking. Surely you have people who are better prepared."

"Outer circumstances can deceive the untrained eye," he said, stroking his deep white beard. "Over many lives, you have accrued spiritual attainment far beyond your present earthly years. When you tear the veil of the Great Forgetfulness, you can reclaim it. And you served the Secret Master well in many past lives. Others betrayed him. You never have."

"Master Theo, look at me. You of all people should see through my tough exterior. It's just a facade—a defense mechanism that helps me survive. . . . Deep down, I'm still the troubled Greek boy you rescued from the rubble. I'm not the one you want."

"So your human personality is a little burdened? So what?"

I crossed my ankles and arms.

Master Theo stood. "If you have already decided, let's not waste any more time."

I put on my brave face. "Please go on."

He didn't look reassured. "Four ordeals, each more terrifying than the one before it, stand in your way. First, you must pass through probation. Because even if you accept, I can't allow you to proceed unless you are tested first."

"The ordeals are necessary, I suppose?"

"You know they are. Only when you are proven worthy can you receive the next level of empowerment. So if you accept this mission in the name of humanity, over the next ten days you will descend to the deepest levels of hell and ascend to the highest heavens. You will encounter fiends and Beings of Light. You will know terror and ecstasy. Be ready."

I tightened my lips, trying to keep control over the alarm and disbelief raging inside of me. Master Theo paced in front of the fireplace, hands clasped behind his back. I knew he could smell my self-doubt.

Distant, rippling howls from a pack of coyotes yanked my attention away. Dark clouds hid the moon.

"Only the very best can stand up to the Dark Master and his minions, and win," he said. "Woe to you if you fail. And woe to Earth. Consider your choice well. If you are afraid, you can still withdraw without dishonor."

My hand leapt over my heart. "I'm indebted to you and the Inner Order and I'm prepared to do my duty. You know I would sacrifice everything."

"I do. You often have in the past."

I dragged in a deep, steadying breath. "The scroll is different. We're talking billions of lives here. My biggest fear is that I'll blow it. I'm not sure I can handle such responsibility."

"Now *you* look at *me*," he said, his countenance ablaze, voice booming across the room, drawing might from unshakable conviction. "You are not a bag of bones. You are not a human weakling, though you may think you are when the winds of suffering toss you around like a helpless dry leaf. You are the emanation of the Timeless Self on Earth. You are made of divine fire. You have access to great power. *Are you listening?*"

"Yes, sir."

"You are important. You count. Life needs you. Now, straighten up your spine and pick up the pieces of your broken self-esteem."

Goosebumps blanketed my skin as the self-evident truth reverberated through my consciousness. However long this state of childlike faith lasted, in that blessed moment, I believed. Yes, *I believed.* "Thank you."

"No need to thank me. I have confidence in the divine potential of every man and woman." His gaze scanned my aura. "An average man with your soul traumas would break. Instead, you are growing stronger each day. Not like your father, who never recovered from the war. Pity he died before I could help him release his grief."

"I feel guilty for coming to America. Not staying behind with the family. Not accepting my karma . . . I just couldn't take it anymore. America was the Promised Land. I had to escape. And I did."

Tears stung my eyes. My mind fluttered away.

I bit my tongue and the pain brought me back to the present. "What are the ordeals?"

"How's your mother?"

I scratched my head. His question seemed as puzzling as a Zen koan. "My mother's a trooper. She lives with my sister and her husband. Does her best to deal with Parkinson's. I call her every Sunday."

"Good."

"The ordeals? I'm getting anxious here."

"In a moment. There's something else we need to discuss first."

I braced myself, though I couldn't imagine what could be worse than what I had already heard.

"The fate of Earth is at stake, and you must devote all your energies—body, mind, and soul—to the victory. Before you face the first ordeal, you must sever any romantic interests you have. You must take a vow of celibacy."

My self-imposed, non-dating hiatus of the last few years had effectively rendered me a celibate, so this didn't seem worth the buildup. "Is that all?"

"For now."

Thick silence moved in, the only sound in the room the crackle and hiss of the burning logs.

Master Theo walked over and towered before me. Two small wooden objects lay within his palm—a red cube and a white triangle.

"You have till dawn to decide whether or not to accept the challenge. You know what to do when you make your choice. If your answer is 'Yes,' your training and testing will start right away. If it is 'No,' you will return to Washington tomorrow morning, first thing."

"If I choose 'No,' can anyone else take my place?"

"The Inner Order never pins its hopes on one person. There is an alternative."

"It's the priestess of the ancient temple, isn't it?"

No answer.

"Master Theo, who *is* she?"

Ranjit opened the door.

"Please show Diokles to his room."

I took the triangle and the cube, bowed my head, and followed Ranjit. I had only a few hours to decide the course of my destiny.

# CHAPTER 4

**5:15 a.m., Day 2, Private Room**

I could count on the fingers of one hand the moon rays that managed to sneak through the closed curtains. Darkness wanted to rule in my room. And in my heart.

The logs in the fireplace had turned to embers. A merciless chill penetrated my flesh. After a sleepless night, I curled into a fetal position with the covers pulled over my head.

I loved Master Theo. I owed him. And I wasn't afraid to die in order to pay that debt. Yet I was willing to consider giving it all up because I couldn't stand to lose Leah. A woman I didn't really have in any sense that mattered. I hadn't realized until I was alone in this room, contemplating the possibility of a life of celibacy, how deeply I loved her. Yearned for her. It just struck me. Taking this mission could kill me, but it was the prospect of giving up Leah that really tore at my Soul.

Still, I had to do my duty. It wasn't right to desert Master Theo.

But he had given me a way out, hadn't he?

I cried out, clutching my head, forcing the stale, under-the-sheets air down my lungs again and again. It helped some. My brain was clearing up.

I had to go after the scroll. I would just have to trust in God. God, who had abandoned me in the past.

Maybe I should just stop pretending I was some kind of hero. I was weak. The only thing that would happen if I took this mission on is that everyone would die.

A metallic aftertaste invaded my mouth. Icy sweat crawled down to the base of my neck. My fingers and toes grew numb. It was the same reaction I always had when something critical was out of my control. The same feeling you get when the lip of a loaded handgun kisses your forehead and you see the killer pulling the trigger, putting an end to it all.

My nails dug deeper into my skull. The dawn would break soon and I still hadn't made my choice.

I fumbled for the brass bedside lamp. Its dull-yellow light flooded the room. I sprang out of bed and collapsed on my knees. My brow touched the tile floor.

"God have mercy. What should I do? Give me a sign. *Please!*"

A tingling sensation came from the bottom of my feet. It lingered there for a few seconds, charged upward through my legs to my spine, and all the way to the top of my head. A weight lifted off my shoulders. For the first time in hours, I experienced a touch of relief and even the faint whisper of hope.

Then, my third eye quivered, accelerating my inner vision. On the screen of my mind, I saw seven Beings of Light, both male and female, sitting on ornate golden thrones. Radiant white robes covered their translucent bodies. Golden halos shone around their heads. Their benevolent eyes were fixed on a young man.

Me.

Somehow I knew it was a scene from my karmic review, an event that took place in a celestial temple right before my birth.

"Son of Earth, hear my words and mark them well," the Being sitting on the tallest throne said. "A time shall come when duty calls and you are asked to sacrifice. Sacrifice that which you hold most dear."

I realized his voice made no sound. I was hearing him in my head.

"As always, you will have the choice to accept the quest or reject it. Everyone who passes through the door of life has a divine plan. And everyone can call upon the power from above to fulfill it."

The blue diamond on the top of his scepter flared. "Remember this truth when the clouds of karma block the sun of your Timeless Self. Command Light in the Name *I AM that I AM* and you *shall* have your victory."

The younger version of me bowed his head. "I vow to do my duty as asked."

"So be it."

"I have a petition to make."

"Speak."

"The veils of flesh are heavy. I ask that I receive a sign to remind me of my vow."

"Your request is granted. The restoration of this memory shall be your sign."

"I thank you."

The image faded away, a sense of triumph wrapping around me. My hands flew up. The Being of Light had kept his promise.

Now it was my turn.

I strode over to the fireplace, tossed a handful of pine kindling onto the coals, and fanned them to life.

I picked up the bag where I had placed the wooden objects Master Theo had given me. The red cube—a symbol of the ego, the synthetic ego. The white triangle—a symbol of the Timeless Self, the divine Ego. I caressed the triangle and pressed it over my heart. Then I cast the red cube into the fire.

"May that which you represent be transformed. Be redeemed. Be liberated."

I watched it burn. "In the Name *I AM that I AM*, I accept the quest set before me." My lips trembled. "I surrender my human will to the Divine and vow to return victorious or die trying." I hesitated, pretending for one last moment that I really had a choice. "And I pledge to be celibate like a monk. So help me God."

My insides shook in equal measure with tension and excitement. I walked over to the bed and sat at the edge. The die was cast. No more fooling around. No turning back.

Inexplicably, I was overwhelmed by an intense urge to go out for a walk and breathe some fresh air. It was odd. I should have been searching out Master Theo, not going to the woods.

I enjoy hiking and the great outdoors, but I haven't made peace with the frigid weather. I'd much rather sunbathe on a secluded, sandy beach somewhere in the Aegean Sea. When I came to America thirteen years ago, they told me my blood would thicken up and the cold wouldn't bother me. I'm still waiting.

I pulled open the curtains and looked out the window. The sky was clear and the light of the dawn had just burst over the hills. New-fallen snow covered the ground, the trees—everything. The thought of going outside iced my bones but I couldn't resist.

I bundled up and crossed the corridor to the backyard. The west wind flogged my exposed skin and even bit through my down parka. The moisture in my nose froze instantly.

Better get moving. I wrapped my scarf around my neck and scanned the yard for Master Theo's golden retriever. "Zara, Zara. Come *here* . . . Zara."

An elongated yelp came from behind a tall pine twenty feet away, and Zara bounded through the snow toward me. She stuck her whitened snout between my knees, all the while swaying and wagging her tail.

I knelt down and gave her a big hug. "Hi, Zara." I pointed toward the mountain. "Want to go for a walk?"

Her body strained against my hands like a coiled spring. I let her go. She led the way and I followed.

We reached the plateau above the mansion in about twenty minutes and, by then, I could feel all my fingers and toes. I decided to rest on a fallen blue spruce. Zara spied a pair of pheasants and gave chase. A mule deer and her two fawns, nibbling on dried-up silky Phacelias that poked through the snow, didn't seem bothered by my presence.

I closed my eyes and breathed in the beauty of nature. Silence. How beautiful was the silence.

A piercing wail jolted me out of my reverie. Two hundred feet away, Zara sprinted toward me. Behind her, an enormous grizzly bear almost had her within reach.

Then the bear spotted me. In a surprisingly swift move for something so massive, she halted her advance.

My heart lurched as if it were trying to escape through my chest. My hand jerked toward my coat pocket.

I had forgotten the pepper spray.

Zara reached me and cowered behind me, trembling.

"Zara, go. Go, girl."

Still wailing, she raced toward the mansion, following our footprints in the snow.

In a split second, I checked out the terrain. Running was useless. The bear would catch and maul me in no time. My only options were to play dead or climb the nearest tree.

The grizzly reared up on her hind legs, stretching almost nine feet tall. She took short steps forward, baring her sharp, yellow teeth, growling as she moved.

"Back down! Turn back!"

My commands didn't impress her. I imagined those teeth sinking into my flesh.

Far behind her, two cubs, *her* cubs, huddled by a sage bush.

That was it. I was dead.

With a bone-crushing roar, she dropped on her forelegs and charged.

My mind commanded my legs to run, but then a deep inner voice, the voice of Master Theo, came from the center of my head.

*Stand your ground.*

I could still run for the nearest tree. But I obeyed.

The sound of the bear's massive paws hitting the ground was the only sound in the world. The wind carried the stench of her fur and foul breath. Her savage black eyes grew bigger and bigger.

Just before impact, the bear swung to my right.

I spun around. The bear galloped toward a small pack of gray wolves, their fangs bared, less than a hundred feet away. It would have been an epic battle to watch if I hadn't already been running toward the trail.

I managed to reach the back gate without stopping. I opened the gate, and let a panting Zara through. I secured it and let myself fall on my back in the snow. My lungs gulped in the cool morning air. Zara jumped on my chest and licked my chin.

"Zara, that was so close."

After we had both recovered our breath and our dignity, I rushed toward the mansion. Thick snow pressed down on the gabled roof. Hundreds of icy stalactites hung from the copper gutters that encircled the walls.

Ranjit stood by the door. As always, he wore a flawlessly pressed white suit and his shoes had a perfect shine.

Pushing my willpower to the limit, I regained my composure. "Ranjit, I need to see Master Theo. Now."

"He is expecting you," he said. "He will meet you in the dining room for breakfast."

"Thank you."

I waved goodbye to Zara and walked inside. In the cloakroom, I shed my coat and brushed the snow from my pants, then hurried to the dining room. Magnificent mystical paintings hung on its cream walls. About a dozen Brothers and Sisters had just finished their breakfast and were heading to the sanctuary for their morning devotions.

Master Theo sat at the head of a rectangular table drinking tea, surely Darjeeling with a touch of honey—his favorite. My breakfast waited next to him, a plate full of steamed vegetables and a cup of miso soup. I would have preferred an omelet with tomatoes, kalamata olives, and feta cheese, but I didn't have much choice. The staff at Headquarters followed a strict vegan diet.

"A bear almost ate you, and you're whining about food?"

I always suspected he could read my mind. Now I knew. I made the Sign, took my place, and waited.

Master Theo offered his hand. "Congratulations."

From the extra-firm squeeze, I could tell he was pleased. "For not being eaten?"

"For passing the outer test of fear. If only overcoming your abandonment issues were that easy. Later today, you will face that inner test at the Hall of Mysteries."

I stared into his unblinking eyes. "Nearly getting mauled by a bear was a *test*?"

He didn't flinch. "You were forewarned."

"I didn't expect it."

"A Master of Energy expects the unexpected. He sees with the eyes of the Soul. He hears with the ears of Eternity. He discerns the Voice of the Silence. Besides, you never really were in any danger. I was hovering above you in my ethereal body and could control the bear's mind at any moment."

"I should have known."

"Diokles, the bear incident was a trifle compared to the ordeals."

"Yes, the ordeals. When will you tell me about them?"

"When the time is right."

"I get the impression you're trying not to scare me off too soon."

He took a slow sip of his tea. "Perhaps."

"So these ordeals are more frightening than a charging bear?"

"Easily. Oh, one more thing. If you hadn't stood your ground as I commanded you, I would have dismissed you from the mission on the spot."

I let loose a whistling sigh of relief. "That *would* be a disaster. You know this, I'm sure, but I have to tell someone." My voice grew louder. "Last night by some miracle, I got the inner sign. I remembered the great Being of Light who reminded me of my vow to serve. To do my duty against all odds. I'm so grateful."

"Very good. Just don't let your guard down."

"From now on, I don't think much will surprise me."

"Don't count on it."

"If you can't fill me in on the ordeals, can you at least tell me who would replace me if I had failed?" The salty aroma of miso drifted into my nostrils. I filled the porcelain spoon and brought it to my mouth. "It's the ancient priestess, isn't it?"

"Yes. She has a karmic tie to the scroll as well, being one of the four. Now that you've passed the test, I can tell you her name."

"Good."

Master Theo held my gaze. "It's Leah Winslow."

The hot liquid slid into my windpipe, and I began to hack.

"Something wrong?" Master Theo asked.

As if he didn't know. His lips betrayed him.

"I'm . . . fine," I said.

"You know Leah."

I did my best to keep my feelings for her in check but he could read my mind. "I met her a few times at the official functions of the Inner Order. I've felt from the first that there was something about her. And . . . there was, wasn't there?"

"Indeed. This very day, she passed the outer test of fear herself. In her own way." He set the teacup on the table. "John Winslow has been a Brother since before she was even born. Like you, she's also thirty-three years old and on the Third Level."

"Seems our paths are similar."

"More similar than you know."

"What do you mean?"

"You really must develop patience, Diokles."

There's a time to speak and a time to shut up. A time to ask questions and a time to nod along. The wise ones discern the timing perfectly. "What now?"

Only the weak become exasperated, and Master Theo was an adept. But I could have sworn I saw him roll his eyes.

"Collect yourself and go to the Hall of Mysteries right away. Something important is about to happen."

# CHAPTER 5

**7:45 a.m., Day 2, Hall of Mysteries**

The images on the stained-glass doors leading to the Hall of Mysteries seemed to come alive in the streaming sun. I entered and settled on a chair at the very back, taking care to make no noise so I wouldn't disturb anyone's concentration.

The chanting generated a sea of electrically charged energy that pulsated through the room. This was no common sanctuary. It was a chamber of spiritual renewal. A chamber of regeneration. A chamber of Light.

The stress of the last twenty-four hours melted away, and I crossed over to the inner worlds, the Secret Temple of the Heart forming on my mental screen. I saw the image of myself kneel before a golden altar, hands raised in adoration. Bordered by golden columns crowned with arches, the altar rose against the inner temple's back wall.

At the center of the altar I beheld the Timeless Flame. Its three plumes, electric blue on the left, bright yellow in the middle, and rose pink on the right, sprang out of a small white sphere. The living flame pulsated, as though it were breathing. Its glowing light filled the secret temple with a transcendent radiance.

*What magnificence, what heavenly glory.*

My consciousness merged with the holiness of the Flame. My chakras realigned and throbbed with new life.

A motion drew my attention to the left of the altar. The Secret Master was walking toward my image. He reached the altar, positioned himself in front of the Flame, and faced me. He wore a magnificent violet cape over a gold-trimmed purple tunic that reached to his ankles. His light-brown hair was short, and his shining eyes burned to the bottom of my Soul. His entire presence radiated with the majesty and power possessed only by a Lord of Eternity.

Reverently, I saluted him.

"Diokles, I received your vow," the Secret Master said. "Your mission is sealed in my heart, and the Light from above shall help you fulfill it."

Though I heard no sound, I could clearly perceive his words in my mind, and I welcomed each one of them, precious jewels of ancient friendship and holy love.

"Arise."

A luminous angel, carrying a purple, gold-trimmed cape, approached.

"This mantle is a concentrated force field of my energy," the Secret Master said. "Through it, I grant you a measure of my power. Do you accept it and solemnly swear to use it only for good?"

"I do, I do."

The angel placed the cape around my shoulders and fastened it.

A current of liquid fire rushed through me.

"You now hold the spiritual office of Friend of the Secret Master."

"Thank you for this great honor."

"You are welcome indeed." The Secret Master stepped closer. "Know that if you would fulfill your noble quest, you must become a fully realized Master of Energy." The amethyst-studded medallion over his breast discharged a lilac blaze. "This inner journey and the freedom it brings can take two decades, two centuries, or two millennia. But time is running short for planet earth. And I have need of you today, not tomorrow.

"Thus I have secured a dispensation on your behalf. Your cycles of initiation shall accelerate, compressing a lifetime into the next nine days. Beings of Light eager to see you render your service to life will grant you powers and spiritual gifts.

"And you will pass through the gates of the Deeper Mysteries. The Baptism by Water. The Baptism by Fire. The Deep Purification. And the Crystallization of the Light Body."

I tried to respond, say something. Anything. But I could not.

"Brother of old, rejoice. Forever, we shall be One." He touched his chest with his left hand and with his right saluted me with the Sign. "Glory be to the invincible Light of Truth."

The image of the inner temple on the screen of my mind faded.

I opened my eyes. I could sense a sphere of Light had formed around me, and though my body was still in the Hall of Mysteries, I had lost all sense of time.

The door creaked. Ranjit peeked in, beckoned me to follow, and led me to Master Theo's study. The scent of lilacs still lingered in the air. The second movement of Beethoven's Seventh Symphony captured me in its melody.

Master Theo sat on a Queen Anne chair in front of his desk. A worn-out scroll, tied with a leather string, lay on the round coffee table before him. Four yellow pins now marked locations on the huge world map hanging on the wall behind him—Washington, DC, Varanasi in India, someplace in western Tibet, and central California.

I opened my mouth to ask what it was all about. Just in time, common sense prevailed and I held my tongue. It was less than an hour since he had told me I needed to develop patience.

I took my position on the chair across from him.

"Anything to report?" he asked.

"I saw the Timeless Flame. And the Secret Master came to me. I'll remember his words as long as I live."

"I knew he would come." He gave me a nod of approval. "I trust you understand the requirements of the mission."

"Not totally."

"Well, through the training you've already undergone, you have gained access to a measure of the power of the Timeless Self, and you know how to wield it. But the ordeals before you are Herculean, the most difficult being to defeat Death itself. Only when you have permanently banished the hold of Death over you can you speak the Lost Name without instantly dying."

*Whoa!* "So I can only survive by conquering Death?"

"Yes. Which means you must massively increase your access to the power of the Timeless Self over the next nine days. Otherwise, you don't have a chance. Is that clear enough for you?"

I moistened my dry lips with my tongue. "Crystal."

"Energy follows free will. The more locked-up fragments of free will you retrieve from your false beliefs, the greater your access to the limitless power."

A double knock on the door interrupted our conversation.

"Come in."

Ranjit crossed the room and whispered something in Master Theo's ear.

A crevice marked his aged forehead. His face turned grave.

I gripped the padded arms of the chair. Whatever the news was, it wasn't good.

"An earthquake killed ten thousand people in the western Mediterranean," he said without prompting, his normal confident tone subdued.

A spike of agony tore through me, nailed me to the chair. This was what was really at stake if I failed. I buried my face in my palms.

"As I suspected," he continued. "Smaller but growing catastrophes are preceding the hammer of woe."

Images of carnage I had witnessed during the war dropped like bombs in my brain. I resisted the images and kept my awareness pinned to the here and now.

"We must proceed with our plan," Master Theo said. "Tonight, at seven o'clock sharp, you'll face the first ordeal in the Hall of Mysteries."

"I'm ready." I hoped.

"Meanwhile, I want you to learn thermoplasis."

"Control of my body heat? Why?"

"I have a premonition you'll need it in Tibet. Ranjit can generate body heat at will. He'll teach you."

"I've heard of yogis sitting naked outside. Melting the snow."

"I'm not expecting you to reach that level in a day. Do a few trial runs in your room first. Then go over to the old hunters' cabin and practice. See how long you can stay warm."

"No bears coming after me this time, right?"

"Always expect the unexpected."

Something in the way he looked at me made my shoulders jump.

I spent an hour with Ranjit, learning the breathing and visualization practices of thermoplasis. After thirty sleepless hours and counting, I had little stamina left, and my feet dragged on the red-brick walkway to the front gate.

Something wet licked my right hand.

"Zara, you scared me." I stroked her snow-sprinkled, aged head, her tail wagging like a puppy's.

She scampered right behind me until I reached the front gate. "Go back. I can't take you."

A black Mercedes SUV drove up the plowed road, probably one of Master Theo's VIP guests.

Zara stuck up her tail and growled. Either the coming car disturbed her or she sensed an unseen menace lurking. My hand felt the bulge in my parka pocket to make sure the pepper spray was there. "See you soon."

The guard opened the gate and let me out just as the Mercedes pulled up. The driver's side window rolled down. A stylish woman sat behind the rental-car wheel.

Zara let out a happy bark.

I stared at the woman, torn between the desire to run and embrace her, and the urge to disappear. She had a take-charge face, with narrow, elegant jaw and wider cheekbones. A touch of freckles complemented her fair skin. A short ponytail, secured at the nape of her neck with a silver clip, pulled back her strawberry-blond hair.

Leah returned my gaze, equally stunned.

It was one of those magical moments when the two halves of the white-fire core of life become one.

But . . . I remembered the ten thousand dead and that they were just the beginning. I steadied my wobbling knees, waved at her with a straight face, and walked. Actually, I more or less ran. Had to stay focused. Had to send any thoughts of her to the back of my mind.

I failed. Her crystal-blue eyes blinked at me with every step.

Fifty feet above the road, I came to the log cabin hidden among aspens and lodgepole pines. I trudged through knee-deep snow up a deer trail to reach it. Built in the late 1800s, the cabin seemed ready to crumble with the next gust of wind. Moss and lichen grew within its rotting, brown logs. The front porch had caved in. A bleached buffalo skull, horns intact, crowned the door.

I stepped on the porch, taking care not to fall through the boards, and pulled at the rusted doorknob. The door creaked open and my eyes swept the cabin for any signs of danger. Nothing. Just cobwebs in the corners, logs on the floor, and a rickety rocking chair. No more than three hundred square feet, reeking of black mold even in the cold.

Mold I could handle. Leah, I wasn't so sure.

Shoulders sore, muscles numb, I sank into the rocking chair, lowered my wool sock hat over my eyes, and pushed gently back and forth. I saw my body turn into a giant white balloon with a yellow fire burning at its base. My breath stabilized into a measured sequence.

*In. I am magnetizing the Inner Fire.*

*Hold. I am absorbing the Inner Fire.*

*Out. I am. . . .*

With each passing second, the cold faded into the background and my eyelids became heavier. Unable to resist their weight, I let go and fell into a dreamless sleep. . . .

From the center of my head, the voice of Master Theo echoed like a screaming siren. *Wake up!*

Chemical signals jarred my body off the chair. A sound came from across the room at my left.

"Who's there?" Fully alert, I pivoted on my feet, ready to handle the attacker.

No one. The room was bare, as always. Then I caught sight of the enemy—a dark-red scorpion on its back, legs flailing, trying to find its balance.

A tremor galloped up and down my spine. The scorpion had just fallen off of me. I grabbed the closest log and hurled it at the scorpion. I missed.

By now, it was upright and crawled toward me, pinchers open, stinger ready to attack.

"You little fiend." I edged closer to the deadly creature and brought down my boot with a vengeance I didn't know I possessed. Brown-yellow fluids spurted from the scorpion's crushed body onto the pine floor. The odor of sulfur assailed my nose. Its legs kept wiggling.

One more hit and I sent it where it belonged. The darkest corner of hell.

I rushed back to the mansion and tiptoed into Master Theo's study. He sat behind his rosewood desk.

Master Theo's countenance was drawn tight. "My apologies."

I stopped midway. "Master Theo, please. *I* need to apologize. Not you."

"I tried to spare you from the first ordeal, make it optional."

"What are you talking about?"

"You passed the test of fear when you didn't run from the bear. You failed the test of vigilance when you slept on assignment. If you had passed both tests, you could have skipped the first ordeal." He pressed his palms on the desk. "Now it's inevitable."

"Is it *that* bad?"

"You'll dive into your unconscious to wrestle with your greatest inner demon. I pray you come out sane."

I shook my head to dispel the descending shadow of foreboding. "So the thermoplasis was a ruse?"

"No, my premonition was real. It could save your life in Asia. It's just that . . . I shouldn't have risked sending you to the cabin."

"I'm missing something here."

"Diokles, we don't have scorpions at the Tetons. Didn't you wonder about that?"

"It crossed my mind and—"

"It has to more than cross your mind." He pointed at the chair before the desk. "Take a seat and don't interrupt."

I sat and held his gaze.

"The Dark Master has sent an assassin named Arashi* to kill you. Arashi followed you to the cabin and released the scorpion through the window. One sting and you would have died. I al-

---

* *Arashi [**Ah**-rah-shee]*

lowed him to do this, of course. I chose to give you this test. Tests can always go either way, but you never get one you are not able to pass. That wouldn't be fair." Regret still lingered in his words. "This is the last time I intercede on your behalf, Diokles. For any reason. You have to rise or fall through your own inner power. I can't hover over you forever. If I did, it would weaken you in the end. And you would fail."

"I'm not afraid of them."

"*Of course,* you shouldn't be afraid, but you must act wisely. This is real life, not a movie. The good guy can die. Remember, you have in the past."

I knew better than to respond.

"Underestimate Arashi and you'll end up in a back alley with a dagger in your back."

I remembered what was at stake and steeled my spine. "I won't fail."

"Your proclamation of strength is admirable."

"Thank you."

"And inadequate. Intentions are good. Actions even better."

"Who *is* this man?"

"He was handpicked by the Dark Master to stop you from securing the scroll."

I pressed my jaws together until they hurt. "Why him?"

"Of all the Red Scorpions, Arashi is the most cunning. And he hates you with a passion."

"Why? What have I done to him? I don't even know him."

"He feels you stole something that belonged to him a very long time ago. He never forgave you and carried the anger in his Soul lifetime after lifetime. He's frothing with revenge."

"What else do we know about him?"

"He grew up in San Francisco and operates from Mount Thamserku in Nepal. The lair of the Dark Master and the Red Scorpions."

"How'd they track me?"

"The Dark Master has attained a remarkable level in energy manipulation. It's easy for him to know your every move and communicate it to Arashi."

"I'm getting a pistol."

"Absolutely not."

"I was a conscript officer in the Greek army. I know how to use a gun."

"You can't stain your hands with blood and speak the Lost Name. Arashi will never lift a gun against you himself. He abides by the code of the ancient warriors. He can only use poisons, daggers, and energy manipulation."

"So how will I defend myself?"

"The Timeless Self is the solution to *all* your problems. The master key that unlocks all doors. Recognize this eternal law and apply it, and you will never lack for anything, including protection from your enemies."

"I hear you, I really do. I just don't grasp the message fully yet."

"Get some rest and meet me at 6:45 p.m. sharp . . . in the Underground Chamber."

"I saw Leah."

"I know. And now you need to forget her."

I nodded, though I wasn't sure that was possible.

# CHAPTER 6

**6:40 p.m., Day 2, Stairway to the Underground Chamber**

I crossed the corridor to find my way to the Underground Chamber, my mind beating back anxiety.

Ranjit stood at the top of the stairway. "Put this hood on."

I gave him a Greek bear hug, mostly because *I* needed one. "Thanks, Ranjit, for everything."

I pulled the black hood over my head, initiating my symbolic descent into the darkness. Ranjit led me by the hand down two flights of stone steps. The dull echoes from my shoes raised a haunting memory from a childhood visit to Egypt—going down the stone passageway to the pit of the Great Pyramid.

We reached level ground, walked another thirty feet, and stopped. Ranjit knocked at a door three times.

"Enter."

"The Master is ready," Ranjit said. "No one will disturb you. I shall stand guard here and recite mantras for you."

"Thank you, Ranjit."

The door creaked open. Ranjit nudged me in and shut it behind me, sealing off my only escape route. I had reached the pit.

Cold nipped at my skin. My nose wrinkled. The room smelled of musty air and neglect.

Master Theo pulled off the hood. He wore ceremonial purple robes and a gold medallion over his chest.

I took in the Underground Chamber. The small room had a single lamp hanging from the low, oppressive ceiling and a cobblestone floor. A mirror covered much of the basalt-rock wall to my left, and a black curtain, the wall to my right. A tall baptismal font, filled to the brim with water, rested at the far end. Everything seemed to issue a challenge and whisper in unison that I wasn't welcome.

My gut tightened, preparing me for the trial.

Master Theo lit the two pole-mounted candles on each side of the incongruously ordinary fold-out chair, which stood at the center of the room. He walked in front of the baptismal font and faced me. "Candidate for the Deeper Mysteries, what is your given name?"

"Diokles Philaretos."

"What is your unconditional soul identity?"

"I am the emanation of the Timeless Self in the matter spheres. I am an immortal Flame of Life traversing through time and space. I am. An electrode. Of Light."

"Are you prepared for the coming ordeal?"

"I am."

"Do you swear to use all new powers you obtain only for good?"

I raised my hand. "I do."

He motioned me to sit.

"Tonight, your task is to retrieve fragments of your free will. In particular, those fragments which are imprisoned in the clutches of your false belief of abandonment. To prove you are worthy, you must awaken your slumbering faith. You must trust in the Timeless Self to come through for you in the hour of your greatest need."

I suppressed the rumbling in my solar plexus. "I don't understand."

"Unless you do, you cannot cross the threshold of initiation from which there is no return."

I narrowed confused eyes. "I thought I trusted God."

"We see what we want to see. Faith is believing all shall be well. Faith is trusting God to take care of you when you don't know how things will turn out. Faith is knowing you can liberate the power of your Timeless Self to manifest the abundance you need when times are rough. To take care of your family. To overcome every limitation so you can serve others."

That was more like it. "What do I have to do?"

"I need to test your knowledge first," Master Theo said. "Explain belief genesis. Briefly."

I sighed like a student overly prepared for an exam. I preferred the role of the professor, not that of the freshman reciting his lesson by heart. "We create an energy pattern by building a mental form and empowering it with feeling. A right belief is an energy pattern of perfection."

"And a false belief an energy pattern of *im*perfection."

"Yes."

"Good." Master Theo glanced at the mirror as though he could see the past through the glass. "When you lost your home and ran from the tanks, you created a false belief." The volume of his baritone voice had come down a few decibels and grew soothing, a blanket of Light sheltering me from the cold. "A false belief that God had abandoned you and took away the things you loved. What does that mean?"

Soothing voice or not, I didn't feel like answering.

"It means you used primordial energy coming down from the Timeless Self through your silver cord to build a mental form," he said. "Thinking over and over 'God has abandoned me, I can't trust God to take care of me' built this mental form. Then, you used fresh primordial energy again to empower the mental form with your feelings. You gave it life with feeling-energy. A car can't run without fuel. A seed planted in the garden of your consciousness can't grow without water, without feeling-energy."

"Master Theo, no offense. I *know* these teachings."

"Then apply them. That's what counts. And the Ancient Landmarks oblige me to spell everything out for you so you can make an informed choice. It doesn't matter if you are an advanced initiate or a neophyte."

"I see."

"Every time you felt frustration, anger, or fear about the injustice done to you, more of your energy converted to negative feeling-energy and nourished the mental form. It made it more potent. The act of empowering this mental form with enough feeling turned it into a false belief. A belief that lives in your energy field. A belief that locked up a large fragment of your free will. A belief that robs a portion of your daily allotment of primordial energy, since energy follows free will."

I had stopped listening halfway, nearly overcome by the urge to cry.

Master Theo placed a hand on my shoulder. "This soul wound has festered in your consciousness for too long. We can't postpone puncturing and healing it. Can you handle the pain?"

I nodded in agreement. I lied.

"Would you like a glass of water?"

"No, thank you." I would have said "Yes" to a stiff drink, though.

"Beliefs are sentient," Master Theo said. "Beyond being mental forms empowered with feelings, beliefs have consciousness, vibratory frequency, and intent. Your right beliefs are altruistic. They seek to serve. Think of them as energy flowers that radiate beauty and attract blessings. Your false beliefs are selfish. They seek first to survive. And once they have assured their survival, they want to grow. At your expense. Think of them as energy weeds that radiate ugliness and attract suffering. Repeated thoughts become seeds. Feelings are the water. Your positive feelings water the flowers. Your negative feelings water the weeds."

"I know what I need to do. I'm just not sure I have the strength."

Master Theo studied me, a father eagle about to witness his eaglet's first flight out of the nest. "This is your last chance to withdraw without dishonor. Leah is prepared to take your place and go after the scroll."

I ignored the quake rattling my body and squared my shoulders. I had taken an oath. Plus, if I went, Leah would stay in America, away from danger. "I'm ready."

He picked up a leather tube leaning against the wall and pulled out an old ivory scroll. "One of the Timeless Scrolls from the archives of the Inner Order. It's reserved for initiates of the Seventh Level. The Scroll of the Lost Name is, of course, the greatest of the Timeless Scrolls."

I reached over and took the scroll with both hands. I didn't dare open it without permission.

"The Secret Master accelerated your cycles of initiation. That is why you can jump from the Third Level to the first sub-degree of the exalted Seventh."

I opened my mouth to respond. Not a word came out.

"Perfection transforms imperfection. When you speak the words on the scroll with passion and conviction, you will create a mental form and empower it with your deep feelings. This pattern of perfection will then transform your false belief by raising its frequency."

"I understand."

"Don't let the simplicity of the invocation deceive you. It's powerful. Any questions?"

"None, thank you." I hoped he would stay in the room and watch over me.

He must have heard the thought. "This is a battle you must fight alone." He reached the door and looked back. "May you be victorious."

"I will." *I hope.*

"Remember the feeling, Diokles. The quality of feeling is the real secret."

He turned the single light off and exited the room. Only the tremulous flames of the pole-mounted candles resisted the blackness.

My fingers traced the length of the fragile scroll, arrows of doubt assaulting my resolve.

I wondered about the age of the scroll, its country of origin, who wrote the sacred words. Anything to distract myself from opening it.

*Enough.*

I raised the shield of my courage and loosened the scroll's leather string. I held the scroll open and silently read the words by the dim candlelight.

Pinpricks needled the back of my legs. My hands tightened at the edges of the scroll. My muscles stiffened with resistance, and a long-suppressed memory rammed through my head.

I crossed swords with the flashback and lost. I crushed the scroll and hurled it to the floor. My body sank on the chair. The room now had the feel of a prison.

On the screen of my mind, I saw the dark-haired boy as in a three-dimensional movie.

He sits motionless on the balcony of a high-rise apartment. His gaze is locked in the direction of a small town ten miles away. His shoulders droop below his grey winter coat. His hands clutch a newspaper and he reads the headline. *Failure. Negotia-*

*tions between Government and Invading Army Collapse. Refugee Families Cannot Return to their Homes.*

The boy jumps up and kicks the metal railing with the toe of his black boot. "It's hopeless," he says between his teeth. "Hades is closer than Khytrea."

A storm on the horizon rolls over the small town. The boy tears up the newspaper and flings the pieces over the balcony.

"Stop littering," an old man from below yells.

The boy ignores him and slogs into the seventh-floor apartment. He pauses for a moment to take in the soft holiday music and look at the familiar ornaments on the Christmas tree.

"Diokles, where are you?" Grandma calls. "Food's ready."

Her raspy voice irritates him and he doesn't respond.

The tang of boiling egg-lemon soup and garlic bread scents the air, but the food doesn't tempt him. He makes his way to a tiny bedroom and locks the door. The room is sparsely furnished, the light-brown parquet floor coming apart, the tan wall paint uneven and chipping.

Perfect stillness reigns. Nothing makes a sound. Nothing moves. Nothing except his icy gaze that scours the icon above the bed—the icon of the Holy Trinity.

The boy's fleshy lips twitch. "How could you do this to me?" he says, venom infecting every word. "Why did you take my happiness away?"

His fingers bore into his skull. "You didn't take care of me. You let them take our country, our factory, our *home*." He drags his fingers down the sides of his head. "How can I believe in you? *Tell me!* How? Do you care if I live or die?"

Indignation simmering in my solar plexus erupted. I stomped my right foot. God didn't just abandon me back then. He betrayed me. He sold me out. He left me helpless to fend for myself. How could He be so cruel? So uncaring? *How could He?*

He ruined the country I loved. The country I escaped from, hoping I'd escape from my pain.

Cyprus, Cyprus. Gold-green leaf floating in the sea. Island of Venus, Saint Hilarion, and Jacques de Molay. How the dark-haired boy adored you with a tender love.

But you are still torn in two and so is his heart—my heart.

The scene with the boy faded, replaced by a pandemonium of later memories, coming one after the other like camera flashes from paparazzi.

*Flash.*

My father's company rebuilt from scratch after the war—bankrupt. He sits at the kitchen table, mumbling to himself. His eyes, sunken and shadowed with sorrow, dash around like terrified sparrows. I want him to take me in his big, hairy arms, give me a hug, and tell me everything will turn out okay, but he doesn't even notice I'm there. I run outside for fresh air, wanting to escape my own sorrow.

*Flash.*

My mother—a seamstress, having to work for the first time in her life at age fifty-five. Just so we could eat. It's her first day at the clothing factory. She wears a plain green dress and flats. Her right hand clutches a brown lunch bag. A bandana covers her head, her graying hair tucked in a bun. She waves goodbye and rushes to the elevator, trying not to cry.

I stand on the apartment balcony and watch her on the city pavement. Cars honk, motorbikes rev. She doesn't look back. I don't know if I should feel proud or mad. My hands fist.

*Flash.*

My grandma—dead. A simple wooden coffin sits in the middle of a domed Greek Orthodox church. The sun pours sad rays through stained-glass windows and skylights. The bearded priest shakes a censer around her rigid body and chants.

She took care of me, comforted me. I long for her to come back but I know she won't. I shed no tears and bury my grief.

*Flash.*

My search for a cool teenage identity—doomed. I lurk at the neighborhood disco, trying to find my place, trying to fit in. The hanging disco-ball shines silver light on me as I shake my body. From the glances, I can tell it didn't work very well. I pull out a Lucky Strike, light it up, and take a puff. It doesn't help much with the overpowering angst.

*Flash. Flash. Flash.*

A realization struck me with the force of a spear lancing a wound, turned my indignation to panic.

Throughout my adult life I had lived a big fat lie and *pow*—suddenly I knew.

I had lost to the Great Forgetfulness and spent my life in fear.

I had paid lip service and pretended I placed my faith in God.

I had fought my battles, clinging to my precious illusions of duality, thinking *I* was the doer.

And now I realized the futility of a human existence separate from God. Now I realized I chose—was still choosing—to remain abandoned and alone.

Panic threatened to drown me. Sweat gushed through my pores.

Even as I struggled to stay afloat, a coil of unfathomable sadness rose up from the very core of my being. Then from that same core, the silent, mournful voice of my Soul cried out. *I'm cold. I'm scared. I'm lonely. No one loves me. No one takes care of me. I want to go home.*

"O God," I said, "*please,* help me."

Before I had time to react, an angel became visible on my mental screen. The angel wore radiant azure-and-gold garments reaching down to his feet and held a lapis lazuli orb in his right hand. His wings rose above his shoulders.

"Son of Earth, the choice is upon you." Though I heard no sound, I could clearly perceive his words in my mind. "Brace yourself. I now part the veil to reveal the mental form of your false belief."

The vision of the angel gave way to a soldier standing in the middle of a dim, misty dungeon. He wore torn camouflage fatigues. A rusty AK-47 hung from his shoulder. An army helmet with bullet holes covered his head. His face was unshaved and harsh. Vertical slivers of green flame burned in the two empty sockets that passed for eyes.

The soldier suddenly jerked as if he sensed he was being watched. His predator eyes darted to the dungeon's corroded metal door.

I winced. Shivers scurried up and down my body. I knew that beliefs have mental form and that they reside in my energy field. But mere knowing didn't prepare me for actually seeing one, especially a *false* belief—my own belief of abandonment in the form of a soldier.

The angel returned, rings of fire rippling his aura. "The time has come. Dare to summon the Light. Dare to liberate the imprisoned fragments of your Soul's free will."

Consumed with hatred, I let out a low growl. Yes, I should smite this soldier form with everything I had. Send it back to nothingness. Settle the score for all those years it sucked me dry.

But . . . it was part of myself, energy of my energy. And I loved it. Day in and day out, I nursed it with my feelings. It was ugly and dirty and maybe a little scary. But it was family. And family was everything.

Had I lost my mind? This soldier form had no business existing. It was the invader who took over my consciousness. It *stole* my energy to fatten itself. It wrecked my creative potential. It weakened me. No way would I let the soldier form go on. It was time to burn it up with the Light.

The voice of the soldier form sounded within my head. *No, no. Don't listen to them. Don't abandon me. You're my father and my mother. I'm your child. I'm you. It's not my fault you created me. I have a right to survive. A right to live.*

Indecision paralyzed me.

And there was the issue of trust as well.

Real-life experience taught me over and over that God did *not* show up at the hour of my greatest need. Why would it be different now? How could they expect me to suddenly erase the past and believe?

Bile snaked up from the pit of my stomach, brought my awareness back to the underground room. A shred of reason managed to sneak through the daze.

Was I a psychologist or *what?* Healing psyches is why I got paid the big bucks. If I couldn't process my own stuff, what good was I? I should be able to clear my head, get a grip, and get rid of the soldier form once and for all.

I clenched my jaw and pushed back the daze, calling upon every erg of willpower I possessed. I was done letting a false belief run my life. I reached for the crumpled scroll on the floor.

*Have mercy. Pleeease.*

"Enough is enough. You deceived me for the last time." I plunged into the depths of my heart, and addressed my waiting Soul. "Blessed Soul, I hear you, I know you. Be strong. I'll never abandon you again. I'll never let you face life alone. I swear, I swear, I swear. May you forgive me for burying you away to avoid my pain. Draw close to me and let my love heal your wounds. Let go now of all sorrow. And may you forgive God who loves you too and has never abandoned you. Karmic debts must be paid. All energy we send out must and *will* return to us for redemption or reward.

"Let the Truth make you Free."

I paused to reclaim greater control of my faculties, my sanity returning by degrees. I set aside my guilt for wrinkling the precious scroll and unrolled it. The words of the scroll jumped out at me as if they were made of living fire.

"O most sublime Timeless Self, Fountain of Life Divine,

"I seek you in the heavens and in the earth. My arms yearn for your Divine Embrace. My ears long for your Heavenly Voice. My mouth thirsts for the nectar of your Love."

I straightened my spine. With my voice growing from a whisper to a roar, I poured my feelings into the invocation.

"In your Name, *I AM that I AM,* I declare:

"Today I choose Life,

"Today I choose Faith,

"Today I choose Victory.

"I now summon your limitless power, the power of Light.

"I command—and I am—the transformation of all imperfection,

"I command—and I am—the liberation of the imprisoned fragments of my free will,

"I command—and I am—the Soul that is Free.

"It is done. And I accept it as done at all levels of my being.

"Receive and multiply my invocation.

"Purify and amend it by the flawless geometry of the Divine Intent."

Crackling energy surged through my tissues. My third eye quivered and my eyes bolted.

The soldier form scrambled to the iron door, thrusting forward the bayonet-topped AK-47, spewing howls from its mouth. A rumble shook the dungeon.

In that moment, the screen of my mind went pitch black. The seconds marched on, every inch of my being on edge.

The vision stormed back. A river of violet fire knocked down the door and flooded the dungeon. Flames engulfed the struggling soldier form, bubbling and boiling, transmuting this pattern of imperfection into sparkling light.

A newfound freedom took possession of me, as though I were Atlas and the weight of the world had been removed.

The gentle voice of my Soul spoke again. "O my Beloved, long have I waited for you to rescue me from the pit of despair. My silent tears have filled oceans. Countless times my lips have drunk from the cup of sorrow. But at last you are here.

"The chains of duality no longer hold me down. I am Free to love. Free to serve. Free to Be. I climb the spiral staircase, and in the Secret Temple of the Heart I take my abode.

"And I forgive. I forgive.

"Love me, guide me, protect me. Never let go of my hand. We are One. All Life is One."

Relief mixed with gratitude choked me. After decades in exile, my Soul's free will fragments had come back Home.

"The Timeless Self awaits," the angel said. "Meditate upon it now."

Without any time to fully understand what had just happened, I switched gears and visualized a white-fire sun.

In response, innumerable points of energy cascaded into the room. The energy cloud enfolded me, swirling until it crystallized into a pyramid without a capstone. Its square base reached two feet around my chair, its top reaching up to the lower part of my neck. The capstone hovered above me.

"The pyramid is the key to infinity," the angel said, "and you are about to place the capstone on the pyramid of your being."

"I can do it," I said without thinking, surprised at my confidence.

Under the guidance of the angel, I willed the capstone to come down. Foot by foot, it descended until it rested only inches above the pyramid. Blue electrical sparks streaked between the two.

With a final mental command, I pulled it down. The capstone enveloped my head, crowning the pyramid in perfect symmetry.

The angel raised the lapis lazuli orb. "Activate the spiral at the base of the pyramid and you will travel safely to the octave of the Timeless Self."

"Thank you so much."

"It is an honor to serve."

My inner gaze shifted to the base of the pyramid around my feet. A coil of white fire sat flat within its square base. As I watched, it seemed to come alive and stir.

I seized the coil's outermost tip with my mind and visualized it rising clockwise within the pyramid walls, in circular, ever-shrinking rings. The movement unleashed a great force. Every muscle vibrated, quaking as though I were holding a jackhammer. My breathing accelerated. My fingernails dug into the chair to keep me from toppling over. Ring by ring, the white coil charged upward to the top of my head.

An explosion of energy within my brain and my consciousness shot toward the sky like a missile. This was no vision. It was an out-of-body experience.

A tall, golden staircase came into view and I glided to its base.

I took a second to examine my ethereal form. I wore a long purple cape and sandals. The form itself was semitransparent and emitted a soft white glow.

With millions of distant stars twinkling all around me, I walked up the golden steps and encountered the most sublime, the most holy vision I could ever behold—the Timeless Self standing on a platform at the top of the steps, in all of its glory.

He was slightly over six feet tall and wore a long, scintillating white garment that seemed to be made of liquid fire. His golden hair touched his shoulders and a yellow, elongated flame burned in the middle of his brow. A white halo shooting white beams crowned his head.

I dropped to my knees and lowered my gaze, unable to look at such stupendous power, such blinding divine beauty. Yet obeying an urge far more compelling than any will of my own, I lifted my face to meet his blazing blue eyes.

An angel approached and presented him with a flaming sword.

The Timeless Self lifted it with his right hand and touched my right shoulder, then my left. A current of cosmic energy set my chakras aflame. The field around my form flared.

"Hear, O Universe, this *is* my beloved Son." The voice of thunder reverberated through space. "I live in him and he in me. Forevermore."

Divine love, the infinite love of the divine parent, filled my heart to overflowing, and I entered into a state of ecstatic bliss.

"Now, O Holy King, you grant my divine inheritance.

"Now, O Great Hierophant, you unveil the Deeper Mysteries.

"Now, O Divine Cupbearer, you fill my chalice with fire.

"I am the knower and the Known.

"I am the spark and the Flame.

"I am the ray and the Sun."

A crown glistening with jewels appeared in his hands. The Timeless Self came close and placed the crown on my head. "Receive the Crown of Life as a sign of our union. It is a starry crown, each jewel representing a point of your attainment on the spiritual path."

A tingling sensation raced around my forehead.

"Go now, Beloved," the Timeless Self said, "for you cannot yet stand in my presence for long." He opened his arms. "Cleave unto me and remember—you are loved, you are worthy, you are powerful. And all is well."

I returned to my body in the underground chamber, possessed by a boundless sense of victory. I opened my eyes, marveling at the spiritual encounter.

What grace.

The fires of love filling my aura warmed the room. The flames of the candles trembled, as if they too wanted to cheer me on, share in my divine joy.

Someone knocked at the door.

"Come in," I managed to say.

Master Theo flipped the switch on, and darkness was dispelled by the light.

I stood and looked in the mirror. I liked what I saw.

Master Theo's aged face glowed with hope. He pulled open the black curtain to unveil a mural of spiritual symbols surrounding open gates, the gates of the Deeper Mysteries.

"I have this sense I've always existed and I always will," I said. "I see my life as an endless spiral of Light traversing through the cosmos. The human personality of 'Diokles' seems . . . insignificant."

"It's always a cause for celebration when an initiate attains the mystical ascent," Master Theo said. "When he or she tastes of gnosis, the experiential knowledge of the Timeless Self."

He paused for a few moments and allowed me to cherish the holiness of that exchange. Then he said, "Come."

Our steps led us before the baptismal font.

"Kneel."

He dipped a twig of acacia into the baptismal font and tapped the top of my head three times. The water trickled over my face.

"By the authority vested in me, I seal the Baptism by Water. As above, so below." He set aside the twig and placed a gold signet ring on the index finger of my right hand and a medallion over my chest. "By the sacred emblems of the Inner Order, I confirm your entrance in the first sub-degree of the exalted Seventh. Wear these emblems with the dignity and humility of the office you now hold."

I fought back tears. "I accept them with gratitude and shall do as you command."

"Do you vow to uphold the Code of Conduct?"

"I do."

"I now reveal to you the banishing command," he said. "Speak it when you face danger." He uttered the command. "Arise."

I stood.

"I offer my hand as a token of love. The love that forever binds all Masters of Energy from all nations, races, and creeds. May you extend them your loyal friendship, pure and free from any thought of personal gain."

"I will."

He whispered a password in my ear. "Trust everyone who has reached the Seventh Level. Their lives are dedicated to bringing in the Era of Universal Enlightenment. I now call upon a Brother to witness."

"I witness," Ranjit said, still guarding the open door.

"It is done."

"I pray your trust in me is rewarded." My words tumbled into each other, the importance of the occasion finally sinking in.

"I have good reason to trust you," Master Theo replied. "Because you have rebonded to a greater degree with your Timeless Self, the Flame on the altar of your heart has expanded. The Flame is the magnet of the primordial energy coming down through your silver cord. The greater the Flame, the more energy descends. The more energy descends, the greater your access to the limitless power. Do you follow?"

I seemed to have lost the gift of speech.

"I'll make it easy for you. Timeless Self Rebonding is the practice of uniting with the *I AM that I AM*. By degrees. To unite with the *I AM that I AM* is to vibrate at its frequency. Radiate its Divine Feelings. Put on the *I AM* Mind. It can be as simple as placing your attention on the Timeless Self and sending upwards your love and adoration. Or as complicated as undergoing initiation—preparing, passing a test, and receiving the ensuing empowerment. As you just did. The more you rebond with the Timeless Self, the greater your access to its limitless power."

My speech returned. "Thank you."

Ranjit cleared his throat. "Master, it is time to meet your other guest."

*Leah.*

"Thank you, Ranjit." He turned toward me. "We still have some unfinished business. Meet me in the library in two hours."

"I'll be there, and my apologies for wrinkling the scroll."

"You are the energy of the Timeless Self in manifestation. *You* are more important than any object."

# CHAPTER 7

**11:33 p.m., Day 2, Library**

I spent the next two hours practicing yoga and meditating. When it was time for my meeting, I made my way to the library, hoping Master Theo wouldn't make me wait much longer before he revealed the next ordeals.

I pulled open the arched door. Master Theo sat behind a table to my right, writing something under the light of a bronze lamp. Though he seemed more approachable than usual, I still had to follow protocol. He'd be the one to speak first.

I gave the Sign.

He reciprocated and motioned me to come.

I walked over. Shelves brimming with embossed leather-bound books, some with heavy metal clasps, lined the walls, their smell rising over the delicate scent of rose incense. Local-flavor mementos from Master of Energy centers around the world complemented marble busts of philosophers in niches and a lighted globe under the window that overlooked the grounds. All together, the room had an atmosphere of universal brotherhood sustained through wisdom.

Zara, lying flat on her side below the table, welcomed me with three tail flaps on the oriental rug. I sat and gave her a quick pat on the head.

Master Theo put his pen down. "All right. Your second ordeal is to discover the Adept's Password. You'll need it to secure passage into the cave of the Scroll of the Lost Name at Mount Kailash."

I leaned forward in my chair.

"I can give you no clues except this," Master Theo said. "You'll find the key to the puzzle in Washington. I would tell you more, but that's as far as my intuition can see. You'll have to rely on your own inner guidance."

"I think I have the first clue. The Library of Congress kept popping up in my head while doing my asanas."

"Just now?"

"Yes. It was so vivid, I thought I was standing there. Could be a map, an ancient text, who knows?"

"It sounds like you're on the right track. Go after the clue. On another note, do you realize your voice isn't loud anymore?"

"No, I didn't."

"It's not surprising. For twenty-three years, the little boy inside you yelled for someone to hear him, to protect him. Finally, you, as the Adult Self, listened and took action. So the boy no longer has reason to yell. It's the first time I've ever heard you speak in a normal voice."

"Amazing." I paid attention to my voice. "It sounds like a whisper to me."

"As a Master of Energy, you wear the mantle of authority from the Timeless Self and bear its aegis. You are responsible for managing the other self-states—the Soul, the Instinct, and the ego." Master Theo studied a pale rectangle the moon stamped on the carpet. "Transforming their resident false beliefs is one of your key responsibilities, and today was a good day's work. And it's not just through invoking. You can use any number of spiritual practices to redeem the energy of a false belief. From our tradition and others."

An overpowering inner stillness took hold of me and I responded with silence.

"Your flight for Washington, DC, leaves tomorrow morning at eight-thirty. Be forewarned. Away from Headquarters, you must work harder to keep your energies from dropping in frequency." He sealed a yellow envelope with his embossed coat of arms and passed it over. "This is a letter for Mataji, the High Priestess at the Temple of the Mother of the World."

"I'm meeting Mataji?"

"After you find the password."

"I see."

"You will go to Varanasi in North India and present her with this letter. She'll give you the directions to the cave and provide any help you need."

I dropped the letter in the inner pocket of my corduroy blazer and buttoned it shut. "Are we letting the Feds know about the coming catastrophe?"

"A member of the president's cabinet is a high-level Master of Energy and a long-time Brother," he said. "If you fail, I'll ask him to inform the White House."

"Who is he?"

"You don't need to know," he replied in a tone that would force a general to stand at attention. "And you're forgetting a key rule from the Code of Conduct. Any discussion of politics is strictly forbidden at all centers around the world. We are Brothers and Sisters and we allow nothing to divide us. What unites us is infinitely greater. Brotherhood and Sisterhood in the Light transcends all labels."

"I apologize."

"Apology accepted. This doesn't mean you can't belong to a party, work for a cause, or run for office. But that is *your* business, and you don't bring it here."

The grandfather clock at the far end of the room chimed. It was midnight.

"What about the Red Scorpions?"

He steepled confident fingers. "Yes, about them. The moment you exit the front door, you are a target."

I lifted my chin. "I'm ready."

"It'd be smart not to face the Order of the Red Scorpion alone."

"Leah?"

"Yes."

Goosebumps rose on my skin. "I'd love for her to come along."

"You have ancient ties of karma and more," Master Theo said. "She'll complement your strengths. Plus she speaks Hindi and three other languages."

"When can I see her?"

"She can't join you just yet. If she passes her inner test, she'll meet you in Washington."

The image of a woman appeared in my drifting mind. She stood on a mountaintop surrounded by fields of wheat, her gaze fixed on a distant road. A headdress held her black hair high, and her ancient Greek garment billowed in the wind.

Then it struck me, and the karmic record revealed its secret.

This was Cleomene, Leah's embodiment in the time of ancient Sparta. Every day for the past week, she had climbed the mountain, hoping to welcome her husband returning victorious from the battle against the Persians at Thermopylae.

He never returned. And he had been me.

His blood, my blood, had watered the hungry tree of freedom that was Greece. It was one of the many times I had lost her in our past lives together.

Sudden, intolerable grief overpowered my senses, knocked the breath out of my chest. In a heartbeat, the grief morphed into a primal fierceness, churning in me like a cyclone.

No one would take her from me, not even death. I *would* spend my life with her.

"She's my twin soul," I said, through clenched teeth. "I want to see her. Tonight."

His changed expression dampened my hopes. "Not until she passes her test, Diokles. And even then . . . I don't know."

I stood up. "Master Theo, you don't understand. I *have* to see her."

"Nonsense, I understand perfectly. Your memory brought the karmic record to the surface. You're experiencing the thoughts and feelings of that time *now*. In this body. But this isn't Sparta, and I need you to get your bearings fast. And be nonattached."

I shook my head, bringing myself back to the present. "Okay, I understand."

The fierce fire burning in his eyes intensified. "You speak a good line, but I have my doubts. I may forbid her from coming with you. Many missions fail because of undisciplined hearts. I can't take that risk."

"Will you tell her who I am?"

"No. Like you, she took a vow of celibacy. There's no need to introduce temptation."

My shoulders and spirits sank.

"Yes," Master Theo said, "this seems right. Plan to go on the mission alone."

I swallowed my disappointment and wore my composure like shiny new armor. "Master Theo, thank you. I won't let you down."

He offered me a hand. "You were born for this moment. I have full confidence in you."

I released all last-minute doubts in his firm grip.

"One more thing," Master Theo said. "Be prepared to face unknowns more terrifying than any terrors you can imagine. Terrors not of this world. Trust your skills. Trust the Timeless Self. You can be victorious. You are a Master of Energy."

# PART II

# ALLIES AND ENEMIES

# CHAPTER 8

**5:30 p.m., Day 3, Delta Terminal, Gate 85C, Denver International Airport, Denver, Colorado**

The airport speakers announced it was time to board the plane. My journey to Denver to catch my connecting flight to Washington had been uneventful, but that in itself had me worried. I examined the gate surroundings for suspicious activity and showed my boarding pass to the airline agent. All seemed well. I entered the Boeing 747 and sank into seat 17D. I picked up the airline magazine, looking forward to a few hours of mindless rest before my struggles began, when I caught sight of a femme fatale in stilettos.

She strutted down the aisle as though it were a catwalk. Hips swaying, breasts threatening to barge through a black-leather jumpsuit, she absorbed the salivating stares of the males and the death glares of the females with equal indifference. My eyes grazed on her assets. I know I should have stopped myself. I just didn't. I estimated her age as late twenties, and she was easily six feet tall. Short, raven-black hair, coming to the center of her forehead in a widow's peak, capped her oblong face. Hoop earrings and a choker necklace complemented the killer look.

The femme fatale towered over me and cleared her throat.

I pointed to the seat next to me. "Please." From close range, I explored the chiseled features, the black bedroom eyes, the pale skin. A gorgeous woman. But not Leah.

"You have any gum?" she asked. "Takeoff makes my ears pop."

The accent was French Canadian, and the voice sensual, unhurried, the incantation of a priestess of seduction.

I handed her a stick of Wrigley's Spearmint.

"Merci. I'm Medusa."

My mouth froze in an open "O" position, as if I had seen the mythical Gorgon in the flesh. "Your parents named you Medusa? Do you have a brother called Perseus?"

She chuckled. "All right, that's my stage name. I prefer it to Claudine."

A handshake followed and she held my hand a little too long. She knew I knew and didn't seem to care.

An icy rope went up through my spine, raised a red flag in my head. I put my hand on my lap.

"Nice to meet you," I said, unable to keep the awkwardness from spilling into my words. "I'm Diokles. Stage name, you said. You an actress?"

"A model. Some say a super model."

"I see why." The words slipped out before checking in with my head.

Her big, bad smile bit me back. Hard.

But then, the world was ending. I had better things to do.

I picked up the blended aroma of oriental rose, tuberose, and bergamot that tickled an entirely different part of my brain. "I thought Lancôme discontinued Magie Noire."

"You can still find it on eBay. How come you know so much about perfumes?"

"I do brain research with my students, memory recall through smell."

"A professor?"

"Psychology."

"I could use a good shrink."

"What's on your mind?"

"Not here," she whispered. "We should talk in private."

"Riiight." I nodded several times. "You live in Washington?"

"Visiting for a photo shoot."

The plane took to the air and the small talk continued on and off for the next few hours. Ditto for the mating dance.

...

Reagan National Airport came into view. Illuminated and proud, the Washington Monument dominated the skyline, a stone sentinel standing watch over the city. The Boeing 747 landed and taxied to the gate. Without warning, Medusa leaned toward me and inhaled, as if she wanted to indulge in the fragrance of my skin, bathe in the pool of my pheromones.

"Want to ride together, save some money?"

I never scrimp and I don't like sharing cabs. "Sure."

Throughout the drive, Medusa talked my ear off, edging closer with every bounce of the cab. I kept my responses to a polite minimum, even tried to come across short and cold, but she would not be denied. By the time we reached my apartment, her leg touched mine, hot as a blowtorch.

I also kept an eye out for any cars following me. I was out in the open, vulnerable. I would have expected the Order of the Red Scorpion to take advantage of that. Nothing looked out of the ordinary. "Over there," I said, pointing to the front entrance.

I rolled down my window, using the movement as an excuse to move my leg. The blue of cobalt dust colored the night sky. The light of the moon glinted off the cars lining the curb, and a jazz tune hummed from the bar across the street.

Medusa wetted her blood-red, thick lips and tilted her head. "I'm feeling kind o' lonely. Care for a drink at my hotel? We could have our first session."

After my previous false starts with women, I had become incurably monogamous, and lovemaking without deep soul connection just didn't cut it for me anymore. Not to mention that vow of celibacy I had taken only yesterday. "Sorry, long day tomorrow. Thanks anyway."

"You sure?" she responded, her tone so girlish, so vulnerable, so drenched in forbidden promise, I almost squeezed her in my arms. To comfort her, of course.

I braved a glance. Her unzipped jumpsuit revealed more of her cleavage, toned stomach muscles—

—and the stinger of a half-hidden scorpion tattooed in red ink.

I locked down my reactions, keeping my face as friendly and bland as it had been the whole trip. I had been looking behind the cab for Red Scorpions. I should have looked a little closer. I tried to imagine what weapons she might be carrying.

The cabbie pulled up. I handed him a twenty-dollar bill and motioned him to keep the change.

"See you later, Medusa."

I hauled my bag from the trunk and all but sprinted to the entrance, sneaking a discrete glimpse behind me. Medusa wore a scowl of pure nastiness, a predator ready to pounce. I moved quickly, aware of how vulnerable my back was, and felt a flood of relief when the door closed behind me.

"Evening, Dwayne," I said. "See anything strange tonight?"

"Like what? Flying pigs?"

"That would qualify. Seen any?"

"No."

I made my way to 1C and shouldered through the door, happy to be back home. The apartment reeked of stale air mixed with a salty tang. I opened a window to let in some fresh Washington smog.

The unfolded laundry heap and the piles of books seemed undisturbed. "Aslana, come here . . . Aslana." She was probably angry at me for deserting her.

A red number "2" blinked on the answering machine.

*Beeep.* "Hey, remember me? Name's Tony, known among the ladies as *da* maan. Give me a buzz right away. The girl I found for you is dying to meet you."

*Beeep.* "Dr. Philaretos, this is Dr. Sharpstone. Sorry to hear about your emergency. Dr. Jones is unavailable so *I* have to teach your class. And by the way, your file will go to the Dean today with my recommendation. Too bad you couldn't make your case before he makes a decision. Goodbye."

Great. Save the planet, then get fired.

"Aslana, come out. I won't be happy if you're sleeping on my bed."

Aslana and I found each other at the local animal shelter within a week of my arrival to America. She's something warm and fuzzy to pet when I work alone at night. What's more, I hold her in high esteem for having reached the pinnacle of worldly success—that of a *fat* cat.

I walked to the bedroom, and for a surreal moment I gaped at the bed. Aslana's white-orange corpse languished on the comforter in a puddle of dried blood. Her severed head perched on my pillow, glassy eyes staring into the void.

My body shook and I flashed back to another cat I had lost.

The little boy fed his kitty, not knowing this time would be the last. He stroked her, and told her he'd come back soon. Aslana raised her back and thanked him with a purr. The boy raced to the waiting forest-green Jaguar.

I scrambled toward the bathroom and threw up in the sink. Then I cleaned my mouth and stalked out to the living room, fists clenched, teeth chewing the edges of my lips. This wasn't an attack meant to make me afraid. This was just needless cruelty, a ploy to throw me off. Arashi's idea of a joke.

I wondered if Medusa's attempts at seduction were another. Get me all worked up, have me charging up to my apartment for a quick change of clothes while she waited in the cab. Having me find Aslana. . . .

I tried to concentrate, to kick her image out of my head. And that's when I saw with my inner eyes the mental forms Medusa had built with her sick mind, empowered with her anger and hatred, and sent after me. A string of energy grenades seething with Medusa's rage charged from across the room.

Shock stole precious seconds I should have used to react.

The first one struck, exploding as it passed through me. Invisible shards stabbed my arms and legs, hurtling stinging pain into my flesh, bleeding out my strength.

I ordered myself to leap off the couch, my mind to fend off the attack.

I couldn't move.

Shock mutated into a shroud of panic, swathing me in its dark embrace, choking my will to fight.

Energy grenade number two, five feet away from impact.

I could sense Medusa's escalating frenzy. She felt sure she'd prevail, sure she'd knock me unconscious, sure she'd soon be doing a happy dance around my coffin.

My lips unlocked, labored to utter the banishing command.

Nothing came out. Dazed, I watched the grenade advance.

*Boom.*

My scream ricocheted off the living room walls and I doubled over under the weight of rising pain.

The third energy grenade floated toward me, six feet away from impact. If I was hit again, it was game over.

A desperate determination, shooting up from the core of my being, fueled a whisper. "Holy Presence of *I AM that I AM, you* are the only power that can act."

The grenade slowed.

An increment of strength bounced back. My blood pressure shot up, my lungs filled. I sat up straight. "Holy Presence of *I AM that I AM, you* are the only power that can act."

A river of cool fire, the return current of the limitless power from above, cascaded down my silver cord, coursed through my nerves. My limbs loosened up. The stinging pain eased.

A beam issued from my heart chakra, bore through the grenade hovering in front of me, and stopped it in its tracks. The beam hit the floor. Its tip swelled, formed a spinning white coil that stood four feet tall.

One by one, the mental forms zoomed into the top of the coil like genies being sucked into a bottle. The coil consumed Medusa's ghastly energies as it whirled, turning them to golden sparks that sprayed in arcs around the room. The coil finished off the grenades and vanished.

*Perfection transforms imperfection.* I sat back and enjoyed the inundating feeling of victory.

But only for a second. Even as I marveled at my ability to wield greater power from the Timeless Self, I thought it wise to waste no time and run. I could handle another energy attack from Medusa, but Arashi surely prowled nearby, and I could feel that compared to him, Medusa was as skilled in manipulating energy as Betty Boop. Not to mention I didn't like the odds of facing them both at the same time. I wasn't ready yet.

I jumped off the couch and ran toward the door, choosing to believe prudence motivated my retreat.

In the foyer, Dwayne sat behind his desk, hands folded on his stomach. The front exit beckoned me. Beyond it awaited freedom. Or a lurking trap.

I stopped before Dwayne and held his bored stare. "Listen to me and stay calm, okay? Take a deep breath." I took one myself. "There are people who want me dead."

"You stoned?"

"Don't do drugs."

"Who are these people?"

"Can't tell you."

Dwayne's hand struck the desk. "You lying to me?"

"I wish."

"Who the hell are you?"

"Dwayne, shut up and listen, okay? We're dealing with some really nasty dudes here. Killers. Get out of here. *Now*."

Dwayne grabbed the receiver. "I'm calling the cops."

I leaned over the desk. "Go man, *go*. They'll show up anytime. You don't want to be here asking for IDs."

Dwayne didn't budge.

I scoped the door. "Any way to sneak out?"

"Not unless you're Spiderman."

"Bingo. I owe you."

"I'm calling the police."

"Fine, do it. Then get the hell out."

I hurried back to my apartment. Arashi and Medusa guarded the exits, but if I made them think I was still in the room, I'd have a chance to get away. I ran around the apartment, setting things up. Lights on, blinds down, shower running. Done.

I bolted down the corridor and up the emergency stairs to the roof. The wind buffeted my face. By the light of the moon, I could see the heating and cooling equipment, solar panels, vents, and—*yes, the ladder.*

The siren from an ambulance coming down Nineteenth Street pierced the air.

Perfect. I dropped on all fours and crawled to the east side of the roof. My eyes scanned the area. Everything looked normal—

the bluish glow permeating Washington, the top of the White House, the Washington Monument. Except for a figure crouching behind a bush to the left of the front entrance.

Medusa. Arashi must be covering the west exit.

I darted back, snatched the metal extension ladder, and carried it to the north side of the roof. The twin building across rose to the same height as my apartment complex, only ten feet away.

I checked out the west side and saw no sign of Arashi, but no doubt he knew how to blend with the shadows. If he figured out my plan and caught me on the ladder, he'd have fun bumping me off.

I waited till the ambulance bulleted by, the siren now blaring to the max. I pushed the ladder across the gap and hooked it to the opposite ledge. I mounted it and edged forward inch by inch.

One third of the way, I realized the ladder slid along as my body moved. I hadn't planned on slippage.

Fear tightened my fingers around the rungs. It'd be foolish to move on until I knew how far off the ledge the ladder had skidded. I could only hope I wouldn't pay with my life for being unprepared.

I forced down a few gulps of cold air. They didn't calm my frazzled nerves.

I turned my neck ever so slowly. One wrong move causing the slightest loss of balance, and *boom*. I'd plunge to the pavement from the eighth floor with a one-way ticket to the Great Beyond.

The ladder shook and squeaked.

I clasped it harder. If I looked back again, I deserved to fall. I had only one option left—to move ahead. To take the risk and trust I would survive.

I advanced, each motion a struggle. After what seemed an eternity in an out-of-body state, I crossed over the ledge and my feet touched the roof. One more inch and the ladder would have plummeted.

I took note that Fortune indeed favors the bold, even when they're meek and scared inside.

The siren died away.

I took my shoes off and dashed toward the fire escape. Either Arashi wasn't as smart as I thought, or he was waiting at the bottom of the stairs, ready to knife me.

...

It took twenty-five minutes to reach the local center of the Inner Order on foot, looking behind me both physically and spiritually all the way.

Built in the Renaissance Revival style, the three-story mansion had a taupe-colored brick facade and a low-pitched hip roof. Terra cotta ornaments along with wrought-iron balconies evoked old-world grandeur.

I unlocked the tall door and muscled my way through. All members of the Board of Directors, including myself, had a key.

My fingertips tingled. It could have been the sight of the spiritual paintings in the vestibule that calmed me down, or the familiar Persian rug and the gold-trimmed chandelier. Or it could have been the sense of timelessness permeating the place. The Washington Center, like all centers of the Inner Order of the Masters of Energy around the world, was a haven, a refuge of Light.

I walked up the grand staircase to the sanctuary on the second floor. Absolute silence, the silence whose presence takes you to the arms of God, enfolded me in its holiness. High-frequency energy filled the room. The sanctuary worked its divine magic in full force.

I cherish solitude, long for my daily meditation, take delight in traversing the inner planes. I should have become a hermit or a monk, sheltered in a monastery, chanting and meditating twenty-four hours a day.

I settled on a chair and invoked divine assistance for finding the password that would secure my entrance into the secret cave.

First, I practiced advanced rebonding with the Timeless Self, now that I knew how. I saw my ethereal form scale the golden staircase, kneel before the presence of divinity at the platform, and offer my adoration. With every passing moment, my consciousness merged with its sacred essence, and I drank deep from the cup of ecstatic bliss.

Next, I visualized myself in possession of the Adept's Password and animated that scene on the screen of my mind with feelings of fearlessness and gratitude.

Then, I sent my empowered mental form up to my Timeless Self for purification and multiplication, and called to the Powers of Light for help.

Arashi had become a faint memory when a white light flashed, and now I could see the image of myself in a celestial temple. A light with no visible source filled the space with radiance. At the farthest end across from me, an enormous amethyst crystal, situated on a golden altar, glimmered with life. An arched ceiling crowned the windowless, marble-like walls. Imposing tapestries and evenly-spaced white pillars added to the temple's magnificence.

The Secret Master stood in front of me, solemn and noble. "Welcome.'"

Joy flooded my Soul.

He faced the rectangular altar and lifted a sword lying on its surface. The amethyst discharged a purple stream of fire, the tip of the sword absorbing it like a lightning rod. The Secret Master bowed in reverent acknowledgment of the One, the Universal Timeless Self. Then he turned to me. "Kneel."

I knelt on an intricate mandala drawn on the floor.

"By the action of the inner fire, I now make you my spiritual son. Do you accept?"

I took a moment to collect myself. "Yes."

The Secret Master touched each of my shoulders with the sword.

Energy coils spiraled up and down my chakras, clearing their accumulated dross, raising their frequency.

He stepped closer to me and placed the flaming sword into my right hand. "This is the sword of Life. Use it to defeat the consciousness of Death." A scabbard had appeared on my right side. The sword glided out of my hand and sank into the scabbard as if it had intelligence of its own.

"I call upon the angelic host to witness."

Two angels materialized, one to my left and one to my right. "We witness."

"It is done. Speak of this to no man."

*Thank you.* "I hear and obey."

"Get some rest. Tomorrow you shall commence the search for the password."

"I could use a clue." My forthrightness surprised me.

The Secret Master waved his hand and the vision of the temple gave way to a glyph, a pediment sitting on three columns. Three numbers appeared within the pediment and the columns themselves stood on a base containing one word—"wisdom."

It was more than I expected to receive. Just being handed this clue meant that the Powers of Light were accelerating the process for me, and I was grateful.

The silence of the sanctuary received me back. I pulled a piece of paper from my inside coat pocket and sketched the glyph. A number of possibilities hatched. I hoped at least one of them would lift the cloak concealing the mystery.

# CHAPTER 9

**7:57 a.m., Day 4, Vicinity of the Library of Congress**

I had slept through the night as best I could. The beaten-down Chevy Malibu taxicab now taking me to the Library of Congress limped along Constitution Avenue.

Something was giving me the creeps. Was it a premonition, or simply the grime on the taxi seats? I couldn't decide. But the feeling of imminent doom I was nursing was so tangible, it may as well have grabbed me by the lapels and yelled in my ear that I would fail.

On the sidewalk, tourists took pictures. Children walked to school. Men and women in business suits beelined to their jobs, in hot pursuit of their monthly paycheck and their American dream.

A part of me wished I were like them. An anonymous city dweller after my own human dreams. Not some amateur tomb raider chasing after lost passwords and scrolls. The occupation was a lot less exciting than you saw in the movies, and I'd be glad when this whole undertaking ended and I went back to my boring, predictable life—teaching college students, fending off Tony, and adoring Leah in my fantasies.

I took a moment to hold Leah in my heart and send her strength to pass her own tests. Then, I swatted my thoughts and focused on the morning news that came on the cab's radio.

After the obligatory review of the day's politics, the female announcer switched topics and tones. "In other news today, a homicide on Nineteenth Street, four blocks away from the World Bank headquarters. Officers were called to the area in the early morning where they found an elderly man with a slit throat. The victim, whose name has not been released, was described as retired. Police have not made any arrests and are—"

The address was familiar, and there was only one person it could be. I cradled my face with both hands, and silently begged God to bring back Dwayne.

Burying our emotional pain actually works, even though it's only a band-aid. The suppressed energy will erupt sooner or later, yet we do whatever it takes to survive, physically or psychologically. So I repressed my guilt over Dwayne's death. I'd grieve later. Right now, I had to press on with a clear mind.

The anger, I didn't repress. I could forgive Arashi for wanting to assassinate *me*. He's a Red Scorpion, and I'm his enemy. But killing Aslana, a harmless, innocent animal, a friend I loved, I couldn't forgive. And Dwayne? Arashi clearly killed for pleasure, for sport, enjoying the pain he caused me.

The taxicab took a right turn on First Street SE, and the Library of Congress came into view. Three stories of close-grained granite capped by a dome, the massive edifice dwarfed its surroundings. Busts of great men, including Emerson and Goethe, each profiled in front of a round window, graced the portico of the main-entrance pavilion. Massive pillars, arched windows, cornices, and bas-reliefs blended together in a loud echo of neo-classical glory.

The cabbie pulled over with a screech of brakes. I handed him a ten dollar bill, stepped out, and slammed the door. Anger was heading me in the wrong direction. The cabbie was innocent. The guilty party was Arashi.

The morning chill prickled my skin. I skipped around the ice puddles by the roadside, surveying the area for anything suspect. Nothing obvious. I swaggered up the concrete steps along with the other early birds. If I at least *looked* confident, maybe Arashi would think twice before attacking. I reached the pavilion at the top of the staircase, paused to glance at the figure holding the torch of knowledge over the central portal, and headed to the entry door.

"Watch out, *behind* you."

I pivoted, hands clenched.

Something soared toward me.

I ducked to the right. Too late. The ninja star bore into my chest.

I collapsed on my side and rolled on my back, yellow dots appearing before me. I gritted my teeth and pulled out the dripping star. Extracting it didn't ease the pain in the slightest. Poison.

Footsteps approached.

I craned my neck. "Help."

The man coming toward me was a small mountain of muscle. He had a handsome oriental face with a small nose and a cleft parting the chin. His black eyes stared at me the way you'd look at a bug on your arm, right before you killed it.

He stopped and stood tall. "I'm afraid the pain will only get worse," Arashi said in the calm, detached tone of a professional assassin, as he drew a curved dagger. "I'll bring you relief."

He jumped to my side, the folds of his black trench coat billowing like the wings of a condor. "I win. Again."

I fought to regain control. Had to roll away. Had to push back. Had to survive. For Master Theo and for my father and for Leah.

Fat chance. The bloody poison had paralyzed my muscles and siphoned my strength.

I felt no fear. Maybe that just meant I was going through the motions of a defense mechanism, a final rationalization. Then again, maybe I simply submitted to the inevitable. I told Master Theo I wasn't up to the task. But I had done my best and fulfilled my promise—to get the scroll or die trying.

Arashi's lipless mouth broke into a self-congratulating smile. The ropy scar on his left cheek bulged. "Say hello to the devil."

The blade seemed to come down gradually, as though I were watching a slow-motion movie.

I kept eye contact. Didn't want him to think I was scared. Didn't want him to have that last satisfaction.

The dagger glinted, an inch away from carving out my heart.

*Baaaaam.*

The dagger flew. Arashi jerked back, but lost neither his balance nor his chilling cool.

"Freeze," a woman said. "Let him go."

Could it be? No. The poison was making me delusional.

Arashi sneered. "I don't take orders from women."

"Not even when they have a gun on you? Someone call security. Quick."

A man among the stunned bystanders peeled off and disappeared behind the entry door.

The New England accent and the sophisticated enunciation left no doubt. I managed to tilt my head to the right.

Leah held a pistol with both hands, feet spread, crystal-blue eyes on fire.

Something akin to the happiness of a dying man having his last wish fulfilled flowed through my numb limbs. At least I saw Leah one last time.

Arashi swung around.

She didn't shoot.

Then, Arashi recoiled, blushing all the way to the roots of his thick, black hair. "It's you," he said, in a voice that was oddly tender. "I know it."

"On your knees, or I swear I'll pull the trigger."

My body spasmed. *Leah, turn around.* The warning petered out on my lips.

"Put the gun down, darling. Nice and slow."

Medusa, standing behind Leah, wore a brunette wig, super-tight blue jeans, and a ruffle blouse with a deep V-neck.

Arashi stood.

Leah crouched and placed the pistol on the porch floor, chin high, eyes unblinking.

"Stay there," Medusa said and switched her attention to Arashi. "Finish her off?"

"If you touch her, I'll kill you," Arashi said.

Medusa bent over and dug her revolver into Leah's back.

"You deaf? I said don't touch her."

Medusa said something in French. It sounded nasty.

More pain, more blood. Less strength, less awareness. Still here but not for long.

"Kill him, Dusa. We take the woman."

Medusa fumed, didn't reply, pointed the revolver at me.

I prepared for the end.

A police whistle distracted Medusa.

"Take him out," Arashi said. "Now."

Leah twisted, struck the side of Medusa's face in a classic tae kwon do kick. Medusa tumbled to the concrete floor. Her wig and revolver followed.

Leah grabbed her pistol and trained it at Arashi. "Freeze. Both of you."

A commotion of boots approached.

Arashi buttoned his coat, ignoring Leah. "I'll call the hearse for you." He kicked my ribcage. "We'll come back for Naisis."

Pain boomeranged. The yellow dots waxed into novas. Then my eyes rolled back and I lurched into the blackness.

# CHAPTER 10

**8:33 a.m., Day 4, Library of Congress**

I hovered a few hundred feet above the library in my ethereal form, my physical body left behind.

Waves of guilt pounded against the crumbling rock of my self-esteem. I buried my face in my hands to hide the shame in the darkness. No consolation there. My hands were transparent and I could see right through them.

Why did I let Arashi clobber me? How could I have been so naïve?

I tried to find excuses, find something to hold onto, shift the blame to some scapegoat. No luck. It was bad enough the Grim Reaper had snatched me at my prime, far worse that I had failed to carry out my mission.

I had believed that you don't experience bad feelings when you cross the river to the Other Side. That you're automatically absorbed into some kind of nirvana. Well, apparently you feel the same as you did before you drew your last breath. You have the same exalted thoughts and the petty. The same noble desires and the low.

Mental note for my next incarnation—get serious about the business of living. Rise above the human condition. Make that embodiment your last. Win your victory.

"Come," a voice in my head called.

I obeyed because I trusted that voice with my . . . well, life.

My ethereal form accelerated. Everything below—the people, the cars, the buildings—shrank to distant specks, and I landed within the Secret Master's celestial temple. The crystalline light cast its soft glow everywhere, and the amethyst on the golden altar shone with a greater brilliance.

I battled to cork the agony in deference to the presence of the Master. "I'm dead, right?"

His regal demeanor remained undisturbed. "Arashi certainly thinks you are."

"I . . . wait, are you saying he's wrong?"

"You have thirty minutes. It is all in Leah's hands. If she gets you the antidote in time, you will live."

The facade of my forced decorum broke. "I'm so sorry. I can't believe I let Arashi beat me."

"Do not cave in to self-pity and hatred."

I wished his mastery over every human emotion had rubbed off on me. It didn't. "Why does he hate me so much?"

"Fair question." He made a circular motion with his right hand. "The answer lies in your past lives."

A curtain at the back of the temple parted, revealing a flat, milky-white surface that resembled a movie-theater screen. "The records of your past lives reside within your Soul and in akasha. When you understand the causes, you will understand the effects." He signaled me to move closer. "Fix your attention on the Timeless Self, and as a Master of Energy, project the distant past on the Cosmic Screen."

I did as he instructed.

A pink light glowed in the center of the screen and a scene in Elizabethan England came alive as in a three-dimensional film. I'm standing in a room that looks like it's in a castle. Francis Bacon is leading a meeting of the Knights of the Helmet, his secret order. He reports on our work to safeguard the highest occult teachings in underground vaults across Europe and the New World.

The screen flashed and the scene changed. A fellow knight of the order stands before Queen Elizabeth accusing me as a spy of the Spanish Court, and my wife as an unwilling accomplice. He presents forged evidence and asks that the queen make an example of me but spare my wife. The queen issues an order for my immediate imprisonment in the Tower of London.

"Who do you suppose is the wife?"

"Leah."

"And the accuser?"

Guilt became a bitterness that threatened to choke me. "I'm guessing it's Arashi."

"Correct. Go further back."

Now I see the Soul of Leah in the body of an oriental queen. She wears an ornate gown, her hair in a complex coiffure held together with bejeweled pins. She stands by a golden casket that holds the corpse of the poisoned king. Though her shoulders sag and sorrow sculpts grooves on her veiled face, she holds onto her proud composure.

"Arashi used cunning and sorcery to become your vizier. He abhorred you and envied the love you shared with the queen. Instead of serving you, he laced your food with poison."

Dark vapors swarmed in my solar plexus chakra, a mass of combustible fumes ready to explode. It wouldn't take much to ignite them, just a tiny spark.

"Leah and you adored one another as only twin souls can. You came out of the same white-fire core energy, as all spiritual twins.

You were born to be together, to cultivate the garden of Love. To serve life. To be Free. Losing each other over and over scarred both of you deeply. Each time, right before you passed away, you swore no one would take her from you in future lives. The wheels of karma turned. Reincarnation took its course. Arashi kept coming after you. Duty to country called for sacrifice. And you lost her again, and again."

I wanted to scream, let the pressure out. I wanted to hold Leah, find comfort in the harbor of her arms. I wanted to see Arashi caged in a dungeon, flogged daily for his crimes.

"Further back, Diokles. Atlantis."

I braced myself.

The image of an ancient temple replaced the Asian palace on the screen. Four stories high and circular, it sits at the foot of a mountain. Doric columns hold up the gold-plated, domed roof. Two young priests, Arashi and I, stand on opposing sides of a gigantic purple flame burning on the central altar. Clad in white robes, hands raised in adoration, they—we—offer sacred chants to sustain the manifest presence of Divinity on the physical plane.

The screen skipped to a new frame, years later.

In a building next to the temple, the Chief Priest teaches a class on mastery of energy. I recognize him as the Secret Master. Twenty initiates of the Atlantean Mystery School attend the class, all candidates for probationary membership in the Order of Melchizedek. Leah and I sit next to each other, our focus on the Chief Priest. Arashi sits two rows behind us, stealing glances at Leah.

The Cosmic Screen flashed, ushering forward yet a new scene. Arashi stands before Leah in a narrow corridor, his feet spread apart, his left arm blocking the way. She doesn't turn back, doesn't flinch.

Her defiance doesn't discourage him. He confesses his love and asks her to become his secret lover. With the full power of her dignity, Leah, whose name in that life is Naisis, rejects the offer. She declares that her love, her *pure* love untainted by the temptations of this world, belongs to another. That as long as she lives, she will never betray the sacred bond.

Arashi pins her to the wall and rips off her white dress, but Leah knees him between the legs. He tumbles to the ground, groaning while she flees.

Arashi recovers and searches out the Chief Priest. He accuses Leah and me of violating our vows of celibacy, and demands we be punished. The Chief Priest sees through the lies and delivers the sentence. Arashi is banished from the temple and the Mystery School.

The Cosmic Screen froze.

My solar plexus morphed into a crimson wound, oozing beads of hatred. My hands balled into fists. My aura swayed with a dark power. I didn't care if he hurt her twelve minutes or twelve thousand years ago. I'd had enough of Arashi.

"Peace!" the Secret Master said.

Violet shafts shot off the Secret Master's aura, his countenance the epitome of absolute control. The force behind the single word jarred me back to a semblance of sanity.

"Arashi did not ask for a second chance," the Secret Master went on. "Instead, he empowered his desire for revenge with ever-potent dark feelings until the desire possessed him. And he continued in this way embodiment after embodiment."

"Justice must be served. If I live, I'll deliver his due punishment."

"It is not your job to mete out justice. To Arashi or anyone. Karma is flawless and will perform its perfect work in due time. Your duty and privilege is to forgive."

"I . . . I can't. After all he's done? I just want to get rid of him."

"A Master of Energy surrenders his anger and forgives. The world drinks from the fountain of his mercy."

I took a step backward, wishing I could shrink. "Some Master of Energy. I'm not worthy of the name."

"I hold a vision of perfection for you and give no power to your human weakness," the Secret Master said, eyes beaming with the fervor of a Lord of Eternity. "When your negative feelings overtake you, do not indulge in self-pity. Pivot *above* the frequency of turmoil. Rise to the *I AM* State, the state of bliss."

"It's not that easy."

"You can make excuses, or you can act."

I kept silent. I had nothing to add.

"I repeat. It is critical you forgive Arashi. Much depends on your choice."

The ugly voice of my ego demanded recompense. *Forgiveness is for the spineless. You need to retaliate.* "I can't do it. I just can't."

"I bow to your free will," the Secret Master said.

My thoughts whipped between compassion and revenge with dizzying speed.

*Sure, I'll forgive him. Didn't someone say to forgive is divine?*

*Never. You must exact revenge.*

*Think, think.*

I scoured the walls of the celestial temple for a hidden door, a secret escape route, when Arashi's words zeroed in, each one a hand grenade.

*We'll come back for Naisis.*

The thought of Leah kidnapped tipped the scales. I imagined Arashi writhing on the ground helpless. Defeated. Humiliated. I stood over his body, my boot on his throat. He begged me for mercy and I laughed. I told him what a loser *he* was and that I'd cut off his dirty hands with a chainsaw before I let him put them on Leah. And I enjoyed every moment of that conquest. I did.

The ego did. The voice of conscience begged to differ. *Don't turn into Arashi. Even* he *is worthy of mercy.*

Unconvinced, I looked at the Secret Master, pleading for some sign, an honorable way out of the choice. None came.

The voice of conscience continued to speak. *Forgive him. Liberate the locked-up fragments of your free will imprisoned in your hatred. Reclaim your power.*

How gratifying it would be to take revenge.

But at what cost? The Secret Master had asked me to forgive Arashi, and I was listening to the ego instead. *How absurd.* My failure to honor the Secret Master's admonition was more than foolishness. It was lunacy.

I grappled with my unruly emotions until one by one I corralled them into the fold of divine reason. "I forgive him," I said, and I believe I meant it.

The Cosmic Screen stirred. A ray shot from my heart chakra, grew into a violet fireball, and engulfed the scene of Arashi attacking Leah. The flames crested and ebbed until the images dissolved.

Frame after frame of my ancient encounters with Arashi rolled on. The manifest power from above pulverized the karmic boulders of past lives, transforming the patterns of imperfection into light. Then, with a final rumble, the flames collapsed upon themselves and evanesced. The curtains closed.

My solar plexus pulsed, a miniature sun. A blissful sensation of freedom overpowered me, the ball and chain of my anger removed, my mind healed from the desire to wound, my free will restored.

"Had you failed to forgive Arashi," the Secret Master said, "I would have immediately dismissed you from the quest. None who fails to forgive can advance to the higher levels. None who willfully imprisons his energies in lower frequencies can be entrusted with the secrets of creation and transformation."

I rejoiced in quiet relief, my thoughts turning to Arashi. He was still out to kill me and kidnap Leah. I had to vanquish him, and I would. But rather than hating him, I now felt compassion for his predicament and even a strange desire to turn him back to the Light. He was an ancient Brother. A blinded, misguided Brother, but a Brother nonetheless.

"Arashi's name is fading from the Book of Life," the Secret Master said. "His chances for redemption have diminished."

I pushed away all concerns about Arashi. Worrying about his spiritual welfare was a luxury I couldn't afford when my life hung by an increasingly thinning thread. "Am I going to make it?"

"Leah is pulling up to the hospital. Any minute now, either your silver cord will snap or consciousness will return—"

The world went dark.

# CHAPTER 11

I pried my eyes open. I lay on an elevated hospital bed, an IV needle funneling something into my bloodstream, a rhythmic *beep beep* pestering my ears.

The blended waft of rose, jasmine, and ylang ylang sliced through the smell of disinfectant—Clive Christian No. 1. I combed the room for the source of the perfume.

Leah stared out the window, lost in her thoughts. Sans the cashmere coat, her hourglass figure stood out. She wore a grey business suit, along with an elegant, high-neck white blouse and a pearl necklace. Her sun-caressed, strawberry-blond hair shimmered with flecks of gold.

A heat wave flared in the center of my chest, radiated to all my limbs. I was alone in the same room as Leah. She came for me.

She turned around, no doubt having felt the surge of my adoration. I risked another look.

Something seemed to flare. Energy streaked between us like two bolts of lightning, striking each other halfway.

Leah held my gaze, a shiver giving away a small crack in the wall of her confidence. "Diokles, are you okay?"

My tongue refused to work.

"Something wrong?" she asked in her take-charge, Boston-preppy tone.

*Relax.* "I'm . . . fine. Considering. How long was I out?"

"Couple of hours."

"In a coma?"

"What coma? At one point you gestured and mumbled so loud I thought you'd get up and sleepwalk."

*Uh-oh.* "Did you make out anything I said?"

"Why do you ask?"

"Hope I didn't say anything stupid."

A light blush highlighted the freckles of her cheeks. "You called my name." Then, her jaw muscles tightened. "I almost put a bullet in Arashi."

"No way. A Master of Energy doesn't do evil that good may come and—"

She cut me off with a silencing palm. "I know the Code. I'm saying that something in me, something powerful, wanted to nail him. Stop him from harming me. Stop him from harming other women. Not to mention killing you."

"I thought we couldn't use guns."

"We can't spill blood. I shot his knife, which doesn't bleed. But if Arashi came after me, I'd pull the trigger, Code or no."

"I don't blame you."

"So glad I listened to Dad and brought the pistol. He made me take shooting lessons after—"

The pink gave way to a washed-out pale. She covered her mouth and looked away, distress burgeoning under the tough, Harvard-lawyer persona. There was a secret there. I'd give anything to know what it was. Not only to satisfy my curiosity, but to put a healing balm on the hurt. "I'm glad too or I'd be watching over you from the Other Side. Thanks for saving my life."

"Any time," she said, keeping a polite emotional distance.

"Lives depend on you."

My spirits sank. Was I as special to her as I thought? Or was it strictly business?

"You'd be long gone if the medallion didn't stop the star."

"Thanks again anyway."

I studied Leah's fingers. She wore the signet ring of the initiates of the exalted Seventh. "You passed."

"Feh. Not by much."

A wisp of hair dropped out of her ponytail and onto her heart-shaped face. She twirled it, then tucked it behind her ear. I had a sudden vision of the first time I met Leah at Headquarters, curls tumbling loose on her lightly freckled shoulders.

"I can't believe Master Theo let you come," I said.

"I talked him into it. I couldn't stay behind. Did you find the Adept's Password?"

"I have a hint."

"What is it?"

"A glyph. It's in my—hey, where's my coat?"

"Calm down, it's by the bed."

"Phew. Can you get it for me, please?"

"Sure."

Leah strode toward me, pumps clicking on the linoleum floor. She handed me the coat, settled into a chair by the bed, and tugged her grey pencil skirt down to her knees.

I sat up in bed and put out a blaze of temptation. "My apologies for the gown look."

"I've seen worse."

Ouch.

I dug out the paper. "Here."

"How did you get this?"

"Secret Master."

"Seriously?"

"He's trying to help as much as he can."

She fished a Cross pen from her Gucci black leather purse. "I think better with a pen in my hand." She went on to scrutinize the glyph with the carefulness of a jeweler examining a diamond.

"Anything?"

"Patience, Grasshopper."

Except for the beeping of the medical equipment, the hospital room became temple-still.

"Ah. That's it."

Her victory smile drenched me in its excitement, hung me out to dry, and left me craving for more. "Tell me."

"You're supposed to go to a library and you have three numbers. What else could it be?"

"Duh. Book pages. I got that far."

"Exactly. We get the book, we crack the code."

"Should be simple. There are only twenty million books at the Library of Congress."

"Ha. Ha. Ha. I wasn't done. You have three columns, and three page numbers. If you add the numbers up, and then the digits of the sum, you get a three. You also get a three by adding 2, 3, 6, 0, 7, and 3. The glyph screams the number three."

"Wait, I'm confused. Run it by me again."

She scribbled the numbers on the back of the paper and passed it over.

Three page numbers: 23, 60, 73

$23 + 60 + 73 = 156$    $1+5+6=12$    $1+2=3$

Or

$2+3+6+0+7+3=21$    $2+1=3$

"Get it?"

"Yep."

"So, you have the number three and the word 'wisdom.' I'm thinking if we search for threefold wisdom, we'll locate the right book."

"You did all this in your head?"

"Uh-huh."

"Smart."

She fixed me with those crystal-blue eyes. "I don't like it when people butter me up."

"If you don't want the compliments, stop being so smart . . . dear."

"*Please*, don't call me 'dear.'"

"Sue me."

She crossed her arms. "Fine."

"We have work to do," I said, "we can't be acting like teenagers for much longer."

"Agreed."

We exchanged a glance that confirmed the truce.

"I'm thirsty."

"I'll call the nurse," Leah said.

A few minutes later, a nurse entered the room, a middle-aged woman who broadcasted a don't-mess-with-me vibe. Pink scrubs, a size too large, covered her heavy-set body. "How we doing, professor?"

"The pain's manageable, but I'm thirsty."

"Yeah, there was some blood loss. Not to worry. The wound's minor." She strolled over and handed me a plastic cup. I put the straw between my lips and sucked down the water.

The nurse grabbed my free hand without asking and stuck one of the fingers in a portable blood-pressure monitor. "Looking good. You could leave tonight or in the morning."

"Or now."

The nurse pushed her glasses up. "You're not going anywhere, hon. Doctor's orders."

I feigned indifference. "If you say so, no prob."

She gave me a "good-boy" nod and left.

I checked on Leah, surprised she hadn't chimed in. She was doing something with her smartphone.

"Get me the rental car *now,*" I said. "I need to hit the library before Arashi sniffs out I'm alive."

"Done."

"I'll be out front in twenty and drop you at the airport."

Leah brought together her long, manicured fingers. "No you won't."

"Yes, I will. Arashi's out to kidnap you."

"And he's out to kill *you*. Now stop arguing and put on some pants."

...

No one stopped me on the way to the front exit. I opened the door and climbed into the white Mercedes SUV. The walnut burl wood and the premium ash leather added the unmistakable upper-class touch. Looking superior is, of course, the principal motive behind the money the wealthy fork over for luxury cars. Advanced engineering is only the excuse. I was born into a rich family and learned early how to play the game. I took a whiff of the new car smell. I enjoyed my Jeep Grand Cherokee. Mercedes, I prized.

Leah floored the gas pedal.

The SUV hurtled up New Hampshire Avenue, my back flattening against the seat. "Slow down."

"Who's the woman with Arashi?"

"She goes by Medusa. She's a Red Scorpion."

Leah arced around the Washington Circle roundabout on to K Street. "Not the smartest hen in the coop," she said. "We shouldn't underestimate her, though."

"Why do you think she's so dangerous?"

"In addition to a taste for darkness, Medusa loves Arashi and she's jealous."

"Of whom?"

"Me," Leah said.

"Did I miss something?"

"It's not that. Women can sense passion."

I scratched my head and attempted to decode Leah's answer. Was she opening up to me? "I read in the Post you put in fourteen-hour days at the foundation. Is it true?"

"Dad pressures me to let up, but I love my work. I can't stop."

"You know, sometimes we keep busy to block emotional pain from surfacing. Basic defense mechanism."

She kept her eyes on the road without responding, the only sound in the car, the muffled engine hum.

"Speaking of family, are you leaving any significant other behind?" I had hoped the question came out in a non-threatening way.

Leah shifted in her seat like a hyperactive child confined in a corner. "I'm not a patient on your couch, Diokles."

A sudden impulse took over my right mind and prodded me on. *Show her who the boss is, Big Guy. Women like a strong male.*

I turned to face her. "Tell me." It wasn't a request, it was an order, coming straight from my ego. And I hated it as soon as it marched over my tongue.

"It's none of your business." Her volume had gone up by several notches.

Her rebuke mutated into a familiar put-down, boomed within my brain in my mother's voice. *You failed the family.*

I saw the dark-haired boy, now a teenager, cowering on the living room couch. He didn't want to watch his parents fight. He didn't want to hear the same accusations and the same excuses. When the mother you adore humiliates the father you idolized, because he can't put food on the table, your world collapses. *You failed the family.* Each word grinds the bones of your fragile self-esteem into dust and shoves it down your throat.

"*Do* accept my apologies, Your Highness," I said. "I didn't have your royal childhood."

"My childhood wasn't as charmed as you think."

"You grew up like a spoiled princess."

"Money didn't raise my mom from the dead."

The bitter words doused my hostility. "I'm sorry. Really. I didn't mean to be a jerk."

She took a far-off, melancholic look. "I miss her."

"I understand. I lost my grandma when I was fifteen."

She slowed down the SUV and exited on Fourteenth Street. "Appreciate it."

I chained my ego down, and, in a sudden stroke of brilliance, kept my mouth shut.

"Dad never remarried . . . made me the center of his world." The whisper drifted out so soft, I stretched to hear it. "I'm his daughter and the son he never had."

Sadness stirred within my Soul, sinking me lower in the car seat. I imagined her as a child shedding endless tears, asking God why, trying to wake up from the bad dream. I placed a comforting arm around her shoulder.

Leah flinched away. "Don't touch me."

I pulled my arm. "I meant nothing by it."

Her chest heaved. "Inhaler," she cried through choking coughs.

"Where is it?"

"Purse."

I rummaged her purse, beginning to panic. "Can't find it."

"Side pocket," she said, lips turning blue, each gulp of air a struggle.

An oncoming driver blasted his horn.

"Pull over!"

She pumped the brakes and slid the Mercedes by the curb of the nearby park. She tilted her head back and fought to breathe.

I found the inhaler. "Open your mouth." I squirted the medicine in.

Leah's recovery reflexes kicked into gear while I took cover in the uneasy silence.

Leah's breathing slowed. Color returned to her cheeks. She checked herself in the rearview mirror and fixed her hair.

Forget sending for flowers. I should just ask for the keys to the doghouse. "I apologize."

No answer.

"Want to talk about what happened?"

"We're late."

"Leah, I'm begging you, go back to Headquarters. You'll be safe there with Master Theo."

As an answer, she started the SUV.

...

I held open the door leading to the Library of Congress rotunda. Leah stepped through and paused. I followed. "Anything suspect?"

"No."

Our echoing footsteps dissipated in the colossal Main Reading Room. Surrounded by massive marble Corinthian columns, the rotunda ascended over one hundred fifty feet. Classical archways and clerestory windows led to its dome. Statues of prominent historical figures, set on the second-floor balustrades, stared at each other's bronze immortality.

Imposing in every way, this timeless monument to the quest for knowledge was my second favorite spot in Washington.

"Over there," I said.

Backs to the wall, we took seats by a table, keeping a safe three-foot distance between us.

I pointed a finger at the computer. "Type 'threefold wisdom' in the search box."

"Thanks. I had thought of that."

I ignored the dig. Someone here had to be the adult.

Leah tapped the keyboard. The monitor circled back over twenty entries. I browsed the top three. *The Jyotistoma Ritual: Jaiminiya Brahmana. The Writings of Origen. Dzogchen: The Heart Essence of the Great Perfection.*

"What do you think?" I asked.

"It should be in the title—'threefold wisdom,' I mean. Not in the body of the book."

"Exactly. Let's keep looking."

None of the remaining entries fit the bill.

Leah massaged the bridge of her nose. "Let me see that glyph again."

I handed her the piece of paper.

"What are we missing here? We used the numbers, the word. . . . Hmm."

"What?"

"Are you sure you're Greek?"

I could swear I caught a smirk under those well-defined lips with the rounded tips and the matt lipstick, but I couldn't be positive. "*Trelathikes?*"

Instead of responding, she observed me with piqued curiosity.

"Look," I said, "if you're going bonkers, I think I can find a spot on my client list."

"Gratis?"

"You wish."

"Trino. Sophia."

I smacked my forehead.

"Precisely. The columns and the pediment tell us we should translate 'threefold wisdom,' into Greek."

While I was busy feeling stupid, Leah's hands flew over the keyboard.

"I got it," she said, voice high-stepping.

"Seriously?"

"See for yourself."

Only two entries had come up. *Divine Trinosophia through the Ages* and *The Most Holy Trinosophia of the Comte de Saint Germain.*

"You *are* good."

Leah permitted herself a half-smile. Maybe I imagined it, but her perfume suddenly waxed more potent, embracing me in its allure.

I held onto the chair and managed to keep myself from melting. "You stay here. I'll go get the books."

"No, you stay."

"Fine, let's go together."

Twenty minutes later we returned to the desk with the two books. Still no sign of Arashi.

"Page numbers again?" I asked.

"23, 60, 73."

We took our time perusing the volumes, I *The Most Holy Trinosophia of the Comte de Saint Germain,* and she, the other.

She shut the book and wiped off the film of dust it had left on her fingertips. Spirituality clearly wasn't a big topic in Washington. "No connection among the pages. How *you* doin'?"

I loved the classic New York accent she had put on to amuse me, though I still preferred her natural Boston, JFKesque enunciation.

"I'm doin' mighty fiine," I replied in my best Texas drawl. "It's three drawings, no text. I think there's a pattern."

[23]                [60]                [73]

"Let me see." Her auburn eyebrows tightened and curled downward. "Maybe each picture holds a clue. If you put them together, you'd solve the puzzle."

"Doesn't feel right. I say the clue is an element common to the three drawings."

"The crown."

"Yes. But what does a crown have to do with the Adept's Password?"

"Maybe it's like the Tzitz."

"What on earth is a Tzitz?"

"It's sort of a crown. Actually, more of a tiara. Aaron, the high priest of the Israelites, tied it around his miter, you know. When he entered the tent to commune with the Presence of God in the Ark of the Covenant."

"And?"

"It had the words 'Holiness unto the Lord' embossed on it." She rocked the Cross pen between her thumb and index finger. "The password could be carved on a crown, like the inscription on the Tzitz."

A quiver in the center of my heart told me she was right and I raised my hand. "I agree. High five."

She gunned me down with a look.

"Sorry," I said, donning a grin so sheepish, so remorseful, it must have compelled her instant forgiveness. Problem is you never *really* know what women think, and more importantly what they feel, unless they volunteer the information. And Leah wasn't volunteering.

"Okay," I said. "What kind of crown are we looking for and where?"

She quieted down, sifting through the possibilities.

I looked at her out of the corner of my eye. *Just three feet between us. Three bloody, barbed-wire feet.*

A scene of our future happiness together paraded before me. We held hands at Santorini's most secluded beach and watched the sunset, letting the fizzing waves caress our feet. Next to us a little boy with strawberry-blond hair and a girl with black curls built a castle in the sand—

"Hey, come back. I need you."

"What? Oh, sorry."

"You space out a lot, don't you?" she asked.

The familiar emptiness inside came to the fore. "Long story."

"Shrink, heal thyself."

"Phooey."

"Seriously. On the way here, you alleged I keep myself busy so I never take time to explore my emotional pain."

"Right."

"I suspect you produce these trances to cover up your own pain."

*Click.* Sudden awareness unlocked a steel door in my brain. Ever since the war, I had held the root cause of my disorder captive in the room's lightless gloom. At last, I had set it free, brought it to the light of day. A gentle warmth flooded my insides. The awareness coursed through my consciousness and brought a long due cathartic release.

"Un. Be. Lievable," I said. "I harangue my students to lead the examined life and I fail to see my own defense mechanism."

"You didn't fail to see it. You didn't *want* to see it."

"You read my book, didn't you?"

"Sure. I know a lot about Diokles Philaretos." She gave me a level gaze. "So you had an 'aha' moment. You want to share?"

I considered bowing to her and rolling my hand three times in the chivalrous manner of the medieval courtiers, then decided against it. "Gladly, my lady."

She sighed, but in a lighthearted way.

"Most people can concentrate. *My* attention ping-pongs all the time. No focusing on my soul wounds, so no problem. It's a pretty strong illusion."

"Is it all better now?"

"You know it's more complicated than that. Emotional traumas get hardwired in the body and block the flow. It probably needs more work."

"I'm sure you'll deal with it at the right time," Leah said. "Let's get back to business. We're searching for a password carved on a crown. Whose crown? Where do we find it?"

"Kings and queens?"

"I doubt it. We know nothing about Atlantean royalty."

"How 'bout a historical king with a relic that survived the flood?" I asked. "Like the scroll."

"Can't see it. A crown like that would either be famous or securely hidden away."

An insight surfaced. "It's not a human who wears this crown. It's a Being of Light."

"A Lord or Lady of Eternity," she added. "A being existing for long ages. If we could find a statue or a painting."

"No, no. I sense we have to scout the inner planes. Make contact with the Being of Light. Don't know how yet." I stood. "Let's go back to the center."

...

Leah maneuvered the SUV on to Independence Avenue. "No touching, okay?"

I had already figured that out, though I felt shackled to the leather seat. I'd said that emotional wounds get hardwired into the body. I could tell that somewhere in her past, Leah had been touched in inappropriate ways that had left behind trauma.

I nodded. "I'll keep my distance, I promise. But do you want to talk about what's bothering you?"

A barricade of tension split the car right in the middle. This was a hot spot. I had to proceed carefully.

"Please," I said.

Her fingers gripped the wheel. "Why should I?"

"I could say because I want to help you the way you just helped me. I could say because we're a team, and we both have to be at our best now. And all of that would be true. But the real truth is, I want to know because I care. And have cared for—"

It occurred to me that she might not be aware that in past lives, we had been lovers, husband and wife, parents together, intimate on all different levels over and over. She was already emotionally delicate, and I didn't want to throw a new shock at her.

"—for years," I said.

She looked at me, nostrils dilating. "You are *so* clueless."

"What?"

"I know you're my twin soul," she said, her tone colored in equal measure with contempt and longing.

"You saw our past lives together?"

"No, I recognized you from day one."

"*What?* Why didn't you call? Write to me? I weep for the years we wasted."

"I couldn't," she said.

"Why?"

Her hands tightened on the steering wheel, fingers turning white.

"Leah, please," I said, "I want to help. I'm tired of begging."

"You're not begging, you're pushing."

"If you hurt, I hurt."

Her face continued to send a silent distress signal.

"We're on a suicide mission," I said, "two lentils boiling in the same soup, as Grandma would say, God rest her soul. This is no time for secrets."

Still the tension-riddled silence.

"I can't stand to see you suffer. Don't you get it? You'll feel better if you release the shame. Who am I going to tell? A yak in Tibet?"

"No, *you* don't get it," she said with a trembling smile.

Ah. Progress.

"Diokles, get real. Our relationship is hopeless."

A primal ferocity aped up, gathered strength, and growled. "No. No. No. I won't lose you again. No."

She let out an incredulous gasp. "Have you lost your mind? We're supposed to be celibate, here. We're on a mission."

"I didn't ask you to . . . I'm happy with a platonic relationship. Just to be in the same room. Talk to you, laugh with you. That's enough for me."

She took a right turn to Fourteenth Avenue. "I wish it were different. There are so many roadblocks. The mission. The vow. The issues I can't talk about."

"You can do something about that last one, you know."

"Listen, Diokles, we can't be messing around. This is no time for romance. You have to sacrifice *everything* to get the scroll. Even leave me behind if I become a hindrance."

"Forget it."

"No, we need to settle this. Promise me right now."

"No."

"Would you sacrifice billions of people for a woman?"

"*Stop it.*"

"I'll never forgive you if you compromise the mission for my sake."

"You're driving me nuts. I can't—"

Out of nowhere, a ripple of energy darted right through me. My shoulders fell back as though someone pulled a lasso.

"What's wrong?"

I studied the surroundings, listening to my feelings. "The Washington Monument," I said, pointing at the edifice five hundred feet away. "Something's pulling me there, some kind of force. We need to get there. Now."

"Are you sure?"

"Positive."

"It could be Arashi pulling you there."

"It's not that type of energy."

"What about the password?"

"It will have to wait. Make a left to Madison Drive and get as close as you can."

She took the turn and drove around the block.

"There," I said.

Leah tucked the SUV between a Cadillac and a Prius with the precision of a pro.

# CHAPTER 12

**1:17 p.m., Day 4, Vicinity of the Washington Monument**

We bailed out of the car and marched up the walkway to the Monument.

The giant white obelisk soared heavenward, showing the way to God. The usual throng of tourists strolled about the vast grounds. Park rangers in green-gray uniforms passed out pamphlets. The smell of hot dogs, the giggles of children, the drone of the traffic—everything seemed normal.

But I could feel it wasn't. We crossed the circle of flapping flags surrounding the Monument and reached its base.

Leah buttoned her coat. "What are we doing here?"

"No clue."

"Let's leave before we regret it."

"No, there's. . . . Look around for a sign."

"What kind of sign?" Leah asked.

"Wait, check out the third lady on the bench, black hair."

"Can't tell much from the back."

"Huge aura," I said.

"You see auras now?"

"Feel them."

The lady stood up and looked behind her, sensing she was the subject of our conversation. The authority behind her brown eyes seemed familiar. We sized each other up until a smile of recognition softened her flawlessly groomed, oval face.

"She's the sign," I said.

The lady walked toward us in short, purposeful strides. She wore navy-blue slacks and a double-breasted, beige coat with a vintage jewel pin on the right lapel. I gauged her age at early forties. She had olive skin, an elegant nose, and wore her hair in a formal chignon style. Her countenance projected spiritual power, self-mastery, and benevolence—a quintessential adept.

She stopped in front of me, acknowledging Leah with a nod. I had at least six inches over her. "I didn't expect you to answer the call so soon."

The lady's finely modulated, low-pitched voice had a California tinge and matched her classy looks. She was a complete stranger, yet I felt I had known her for ages. "Have we met before?"

She stretched her hand, the signet ring of the Inner Order adorning her index finger. "I work for Master Theo. Incognito."

We exchanged a handshake.

"The sacred fire shall purify all," I whispered.

She edged Latino close, cupped her palms, and brought them to my right ear. "The Light shall manifest the Victory."

"I'm Diokles. This is Leah."

"I'm Agata, nice to meet both of you."

"Pleased to meet you," Leah said.

We moved away from base of the Monument to a spot with fewer people around us.

"Did you find the Adept's Password?" she asked.

"We're following up on a clue. What's going on here?"

"I'm to build an energy pyramid over the White House," she replied with the natural aplomb of someone who possessed the forbidden secrets of creation. "Per Master Theo's orders, a pyramid must be raised in every major country before the end of the week."

"What for?"

"Speaking the Lost Name of God will release an energy mass. The pyramids will receive it and radiate it out to counteract the catastrophe."

*Wow.*

"This will give us the opportunity to bring in the Era of Universal Enlightenment."

"Why Washington?" I went on.

"It's the throat chakra of America, the center of her power."

"And why the White House?"

Agata put on a half-apologetic, half-enigmatic smile. "That I can't reveal."

Something was making my fingers and toes tingle. "What's happening?"

"A great being is overshadowing us."

An intensifying force parted the veil of the inner world. The landscape dimmed, and now I could see a Being of Light hovering by the Washington Monument. Blazing blue garments and a crown adorned his form. Beams of white light came off his chest and a sevenfold flame burned on his brow.

My Soul commanded me to kneel. I didn't. I couldn't move.

The Being of Light raised his scepter and a voice rang in my head like the bell of a great cathedral. "Son of Earth, I am sent by your Timeless Self to grant you a just reward. Because you have forgiven your enemy, you have earned my empowerment. Do you accept it?"

"I do," I answered in my mind.

"So be it."

A blue shaft discharged from his scepter the way a solar flare breaks from the surface of the sun. The shaft reached my heart, converted my body to a live energy wire. My consciousness expanded spherically, enfolding all in its path. The boundaries of my identity blurred—the people, the trees, the land, all merging into one.

Pure bliss.

"When faced with grave danger, speak this fiat of power."

I imprinted the fiat in my memory. "Thank you, I will always be grateful."

The Being of Light offered no more words of wisdom and rose high in the atmosphere until he became a distant dot.

I squinted.

"Trance?" Leah asked.

"Give me a sec. I can't think straight. I have to come back to my body." I massaged the sides of my head and tapped my sternum. "No. More real than a trance. More real than conscious reality. I saw a Being of Light."

She perked up. "Did he wear a crown?"

"Think so."

"Did you see the password?"

"What password?"

Her eyes rolled, long eyelashes fluttering. "You need to sit down."

"Not here," Agata said, in a manner that would compel anyone to obey her. "Follow me to that tree."

With each step and fresh air clearing my brain cells, outer awareness rebounded. "I did spot something on the crown, just couldn't make it out."

"If you couldn't see it, I guess you're off the hook."

Her pardon had no strings attached and sounded sincere.

We reached the elm tree and faced the White House, about a half mile to the north.

Agata drew a square in the air. "I'd like you to help me create the pyramid."

"Absolutely."

"I'll keep an eye out for Arashi," Leah said.

"Sure." Agata motioned me to sit by the tree. "Imagine a pyramid over the building, each line of the base two hundred feet wide. Mark the four corners. When you're done, close your eyes and center."

I did as instructed even though my head hadn't completely cleared. The buzz of the tourists and the city faded away.

"Recall the buildings, the trees, the lawns. . . . Locate the corners of the base and see a white sphere over each corner. . . . Wait. . . . "

I pictured the spheres, which slowly began to spin. A stream of blue fire dashed from the northwest corner like an ignited line of gunpowder, reached the northeast corner, and kept charging from sphere to sphere. The line closed the square, and the outline swelled with a sudden motion to a flaming wall.

The yelp of a dog disturbed my concentration. I countered the distraction with deep, rhythmic breaths.

"Now lift your attention to the heavens. . . . Magnify your love. . . . Send it to the Cosmic Ocean of primordial energy that fills the seemingly empty space everywhere. . . . Allow your heart to commune with its holiness, and when you feel ready, draw the energy over the buildings."

In answer to our combined wills, billions of points of energy descended toward the earth. The cataract of glistening white light reached the White House and took the form of an ovoid, swirling clockwise at great speed. The points of primordial energy weren't just majestic to behold. They were sentient. They pulsated with life, obediently waiting for the command of the Masters of Energy who had magnetized them.

Awe swept through me, and for the briefest instant I communed with the infinite mind of the Great Geometer. *The more points of energy you magnetize, the greater your access to the limitless power.*

Agata's steady voice went on. "Now, will the energy to mold into the pyramid."

The ovoid of energy crystallized into a pyramid without a capstone. Its base melded in place with the flaming wall, the capstone floating high above it.

"Almost there."

A headache out of nowhere badgered my temples. Maroon streaks crisscrossed my mental screen and before long it went tomb-dark.

I kept my calm. "Arashi knows we're here, Agata. He's on his way."

"I don't see him," Leah said.

"You wouldn't. He's causing trouble at our end."

"Shhh," Agata said. "You lower the capstone. I'll take care of the interference."

Agata whispered something.

The top of my head vibrated. The mental screen cleared and the pain dissolved.

I visualized the capstone descending until only a yard separated it from the main body of the pyramid. Sparks of lightning flew between them. And then, the bottom of the capstone rested on the top of the pyramid, the two parts joining together in a seamless structure.

I delighted in the inebriating rush of completing the pyramid, my eyes skimming the sky. Something in me half expected the Being of Light to come down and coronate me with a laurel wreath.

*Puh-leeze.*

Agata slapped me on the back. "That's that. Thank you both."

"You're welcome. Working with you is an honor."

"Same here," Leah said, stepping toward me, hands buried in her coat pockets. "What's the plan with Arashi?"

"I have a surprise," I said.

"Like what?"

"You'll see."

"And I have a clue for both of you," Agata said. "The Being of Light you saw steps down the quality of God Power to a point where humanity can receive it. If it is indeed the being you seek, you can invoke him and check the crown for the password. Find the *Sacred Mantras* book at the center."

"Thank you. I wish we could spend more time together."

"Hope we meet again," Leah added.

"We will, soon." She waved goodbye. "Adios. I need to catch my flight to San Diego. My little ones are waiting."

By now, the pounding behind my temples had returned and grew into mallet blows.

Standing under the elm tree, the Washington Monument behind us, I assessed the terrain. The park grounds didn't seem so festive now. The wind picked up, bringing with it a musty odor from the nearby pond. Off in the far distance, storm clouds roiled, but above us the sun still ruled.

Its rays brought me hope.

Leah nodded for me to follow. "Arashi's a no show. Let's go."

"I can't run forever. I have to settle this." *Have to prove myself to you and Master Theo. Have to trust the Light.*

"They took my gun at the library."

"Forget guns, I said I have a surprise."

"I'd rather leave. We have a lot to do."

"We wait here," I said. "Trust me."

Leah squirmed. "Famous last words."

"Look, I'm staying. You can leave if you really want to."

She didn't move.

Minutes later, a surefooted Arashi, clad in his trench coat, strode up the pathway. I willed the adrenaline jostling my neurons to slow down. More self-control, more access to the divine power. That's how a Master of Energy defeats the adversary.

Medusa trailed Arashi in a hot-pink pea coat, fishnet tights, and a black miniskirt that hugged her curves with deliberate obscenity. She had apparently gone from the sophisticated model look to high-end hooker.

"Hide behind me," I said. "And don't talk."

"We should—"

"Do it. Please."

She took cover, breathing harder. Was it Arashi or was it that she hated not calling the shots? Or was it her secret?

Arashi and Medusa closed the distance and stopped at thirty feet. Medusa batted her eyes at me, fingertips fondling her abstract-art necklace. "Well, hello professor, we meet again."

I ignored her, shifted my attention to Arashi. Our gazes collided like two mountain goats locking horns over a female.

"Don't move," he said, lifting up his cleft chin, his I'm-the-alpha-male-here tone trying to beat me into submission.

I spread my feet wide. "What took you so long? You run out of poison?"

"Coward, a girl saved your ass. You brought shame on your order." He spat on the ground. "You're finished."

"I see Medusa took her revenge."

Arashi traced the scratch marks on his face, squared his jaw. Medusa gloated.

He peered behind me, the cold-blooded face now softening, turning tender. Becoming human. I wanted to believe this was the real guy, the real Arashi—the real Brother Arashi—buried beneath the rubble of the Red Scorpion identity.

"Naisis," he said, "don't hide. I won't hurt you."

Leah didn't respond. Smart girl.

"The professor's weak," Medusa said. "It's *her* we should kill."

"Lay off. She's mine. It's your last warning."

Medusa swore at him and put her fists on her hips, the archetype of the jealous woman.

Arashi waited until Medusa shrank under his glare and put out a hand to Leah. "Naisis, come with me. You deserve someone who's your equal. Say 'Yes' and you can have it all. Forbidden knowledge, power, endless passion."

I heard the spritz of Leah's inhaler. "You disgust me. Get away from me." The words came out rushed and slightly slurred and white-hot-steel resolute.

Arashi's mask of hardboiled-coolness shattered. I could feel the long-suppressed anger, festering in his bones, pouring out.

"The Dark Master has foreseen our future together," he said. "You will rule at my side. You will obey my slightest wish. You will give me supreme pleasure."

"Never."

"I'll dispense with this novice right away. Then we take off for Nepal."

My blood smoldered, demanded I wring Arashi's neck. It was a simple matter of Greek honor. No one hurls insults like these at your woman and stays alive. At the very least, you break their kneecaps and rearrange their face.

*You lose it, you fail.*

I forced myself to calm down. "Leave. You can't win this battle."

Arashi tried hard not to laugh. "Who's going to stop me? You?"

"The Light will stop you Arashi. The Light."

"Always naïve."

"*You're* naïve. No, you're a fool. You're the Dark Master's puppet, pretending you're in charge. Get off the left-handed path."

"I possess the deepest secrets of energy manipulation. I impose my will on the universe to get anything I want, when I want it. Men tremble at my command. What has the right-handed path brought *you*? A crappy job and a lonely life. And that was before it put you on a path that's going to kill you. You have some fancy aspiration about serving life. I serve myself."

"Arashi, think. Think of your love for Leah. Are you going to impose your will on *her*? Turn her into your puppet? Will that make you happy?"

Behind me, I felt Leah flinch, but she stayed in place and kept quiet. Perfect.

Arashi took on a distant look, wrestled with himself. "It's too late for me. I've crossed the point of no return."

The far-away honk from a boat cruising the Potomac sounded as grim as a death knell.

"I have it on good authority that it's not too late, Arashi. Turn back to the Light, fan the Timeless Flame. *Before* your name fades from the Book of Life."

I watched Arashi turn away from might-have-beens, replacing them with cold fury. "Enough." He nodded at Medusa. "Move back."

Medusa pulled down the sleeves of her pea coat and took three backward steps.

I kept an eye on her just in case, ready to react if she decided to sink her energy claws into Leah.

Arashi threw back his shoulders and pronounced a guttural curse.

An invisible noose gripped my throat and tightened. The walls of my windpipe clenched shut, obeying Arashi's intent to deliver death by asphyxia.

I sent a quick prayer to my Timeless Self.

My third eye stirred and now I could see both the inner and outer worlds with open eyes. I grabbed the silver noose around my neck with my mind and visualized it unraveling, its threads turning into luminous skeins that could do me no harm. A second later, and I was breathing normally again.

"Not bad," Arashi said, a snicker slithering out of his mouth. "Go ahead. Ask the Light to stop me now." He pointed a thick index finger at me and uttered another curse, pouring into it the full force of his fury.

A stream of red, vapor-like energy erupted before him. Next to it a black one. Seething with smoldering heat, the columns crested and ebbed. Coiling energy lines streaked and sparked. The columns shot to ten feet and lunged at each other, twining like mating snakes.

Dark currents struck my aura.

I recalled my encounter with the Being of Light. I filled the chalice of my consciousness with that cosmic feeling of oneness. And I let go of any notion that I was the doer.

My pulse slowed. Time froze. Left hand on heart, right arm stretched out with palm facing Arashi, I spoke the fiat of power with the resonant voice and the calm certainty of one who serves the Light. One who trusts the Light. One who trusts God.

"In the name *I AM that I AM, Elohim, El Shaddai.* You. Have. No. Power."

My throat chakra burned. My feet shook. High above me, points of energy swarmed.

I steadied myself, humbled before the manifest divine power.

The columns in front of Arashi had merged into a sinuous form with a reptile snout. Two crimson slits glared. A forked tongue lashed out.

With a hellish hiss, the cobra charged, its red-black striped body twisting.

I thought of Medusa's energy grenades and my paralysis when they struck. Arashi had far greater mastery in energy manipulation. If this cobra bit me, I might not survive.

Its jaws flung open. Its fangs dropped.

My legs wanted to run as if they had a mind of their own.

I ordered them to keep still.

Around us, tourists wandered the grounds, oblivious to the conflict.

The cobra locked its hypnotic eyeballs into mine.

A screech smote the air. Great talons dug through the cobra's body. The flaming blue eagle created by the fiat of power I had uttered flapped its wings, ascended with the snake.

The cobra coiled around its legs, squeezing them hard to set itself free.

The eagle slowed down and looked at the cobra with fierce eyes.

The snake unwound a ring of its scaly body and thrust its fangs into the bird's underbelly.

The eagle swayed, let out a pained shriek. Still clutching its adversary, it plunged headfirst.

I ignored a sting of anxiety jabbing my stomach.

The bird fell with the escalating speed of a downed fighter jet.

Arashi adjusted his leather tie, ready to declare victory, ready to gallop over and claim the hard-won female.

The sting of anxiety speared me, pouring its venom of defeat.

Right before impact, the eagle swung up in the air in an elliptical curve. It freed its legs from the clasp of the cobra and pecked it over and over, gouging deep wounds. The cobra fought back but it was no match for the great bird.

The eagle opened its hooks and the snake went into a free fall. On its way down, the snake blew up, transformed into a swirl of flame flowers, the dark energy becoming Light. The ethereal flowers drifted gently to the ground.

*You of little faith.*

The eagle glided toward the earth and floated over Arashi.

"Finish the job. I don't need your mercy."

Something in the timbre of Arashi's voice sent a little, cold spasm down the back of my neck. From Medusa's expression, I could tell her fear had grown as big as her gaping mouth. She kicked off her high heels, whipped around, and sprinted down the trail.

It was the crowning moment of my triumph. The moment I could crush Arashi, make him pay. Yet sadness welled up at the craziness of it all. The bottomless desire to win, no matter what the cost. Arashi, the ancient Brother deceived by the Darkness for so long. Aiming to kill me at every step. Spewing hatred and denying brotherly love. It was just . . . pathetic.

"I'm not a killer. Leave before I change my mi—"

A sudden motion. A gleam. A blade.

"Get down!"

I lunged. Leah followed.

Arashi's dagger ripped through my coat sleeve, scraped my arm.

Arashi hit the ground, barreled down the hill, and ran.

The blue eagle took a victory lap around the Monument, saluted the sun with a drawn-out cry, and went into a dive. Its features dissolved into points of energy until it disappeared into the boundless expanse of the Cosmic Ocean, form returning to formlessness. My third eye stopped pulsing and the vision of the inner world shut down.

I jumped up, blowing out the tension. "Are you okay?"

She cleared strands of dried grass off her coat. "Getting there. Your arm?"

"No biggie. Thanks for trusting me."

"Thank *you*."

I had either entered a dream state, or for the first time ever she had lowered her defenses and permitted a touch of admiration to show.

*Whoa!*

...

We drove to the center without further incident.

The afternoon light pouring through the windows highlighted the mystical paintings on the walls. With the pervasive silence, the empty chairs, and the scent of frankincense, even the cafeteria was a quiet space.

Leah and I huddled over a wooden round table at the back of

the room. She sipped some peppermint tea and lowered the cup. "It feels good to be here."

"It's my favorite spot in Washington." I thumbed through the little book I picked out from the library. "Here's the mantra of the Being of Light. I hope by some synchronicity it's the real deal. If I can't make out the password, you can try."

"You've done pretty well so far," she said, her normal take-charge temperament now relaxed.

"Thanks for the vote of confidence."

"Fortune favors the bold. Remember Hercules?"

"Hercules was my hero. I couldn't wait to grow up and rid the land of the monsters."

"Sure. The land is your subconscious and the monsters, un-transmuted energies you must regenerate. If you dare."

I adored her right then. "I get a kick out of it when you quote my book."

"Hey, thanks again. What you did meant a lot to me."

I needed to change the subject. I downed the last drops of my coffee. "Who was your childhood hero?"

"Wonder Woman."

"Really? Should I be scared?"

"A little." The voice had just enough menace to keep me on my toes. "My new heroine is Maria Montessori, Italy's first woman doctor. You know of her method?"

"Sure, though I haven't read the literature on it. Guess it explains your work with the Winslow Hope Foundation."

"That's right. I went to a Montessori school myself."

"How many schools have you guys built?"

"Forty-four. My goal is three hundred over the next decade."

"Pretty ambitious. Another reason to keep the planet together. I'll talk to some people I know for donations."

"You'd better."

"Deal," I said. "I'm going upstairs now. You?"

"I'll wait here."

I walked to the sanctuary. I lit the two white candles on the altar, settled into a chair, and meditated. I needed to center and be at peace before I invoked the Being of Light.

Moment by moment, breath by breath, I entered into a deep state. The pain from the wounds and bruises lessened, and even the image of Leah vanished from its permanent spot at the back of my mind.

A movement shattered my meditation. Four mental forms, four astral spears, one from each cardinal point, darted in mid-air toward my chest. Empowered by Arashi's endless hatred, the spears had actually penetrated the spiritual shield of the center.

My teeth clamped. He would never forgive me for humiliating him in front of Leah.

I wrested the fragments of my attention into a single point at the root of my nose and willed the spears to turn around.

They slowed without breaking off their advance.

I fueled my awareness with the iron-clad conviction that hatred cannot, *will* not, overpower me.

The spears edged a little closer, then halted.

I could feel Arashi's mind exerting energy, trying to ram the spears through my lungs. I issued a firm mental demand as I exhaled, commanding the sinister mental forms to be transmuted into light, be raised to a higher vibratory frequency.

The spears turned into a flock of feather-like mental forms and meandered away.

Ring upon expanding ring, I stretched my senses, searching for any new sign of danger.

All was clear. I was ready for the mantra.

"In the center of the Sun, I stand,

"In the center of the Earth, I go,

"In the center of the Atom, I blaze,

"In the center of the Heart, I am."

I chanted the mantra three times.

My throat chakra throbbed. An angel materialized on the screen of my mind, a white sphere nesting in his cupped hands. "Place this in your chest."

He didn't have to ask me twice. The sphere exploded with a colossal release of energy, almost splitting my sternum. My ethereal body rocketed straight up, and I found myself floating across from the Being of Light I had seen earlier by the Washington Monument, empty space all around us. His halo radiated like a solar corona, blue cape flapping as if stroked by cosmic winds.

I bowed.

"Son of Earth, you have called and I have answered. Behold the Adept's Password you seek. Reveal it to no man."

The flames over his brow parted in the middle, unveiling four strange characters etched on the golden crown.

At last. I branded the password into the banks of my memory.

"When all seems lost and the typhoon of despair capsizes the ship of your mind, dare to believe in the impossible. Hold tight the hand of your Timeless Self. Call to the Powers of Light in the Name *I AM that I AM* and you *shall* be victorious."

I saluted him with the Sign and silently swore never to forget his instruction. My ethereal body coasted back to the sanctuary, aura dripping with spiritual fire. I knelt before the altar and offered prayers of gratitude.

I returned to the cafeteria. Leah sat at the same spot, ruminating over her second cup of tea. It was as though a cloud of doom enfolded her, smothering her with its dark tidings.

"We're good to go."

"What? Great."

I copied the password on a piece of paper. "Here. Don't look at it unless I don't make it. Then *you* go after the scroll."

Leah's shoulders drooped. She put the paper in her pocket.

"Why the long face?"

"Half a million people died."

I wilted into my chair and labored to breathe.

"Nine on the Richter scale," Leah went on. "It's at—"

"Don't. I don't want to know where. I can't bear it."

Leah straightened her back and sublimated the feeling into steely resolve. "We can't be weak."

"We can't pretend we don't feel, either." I had much more to say but I let it go. It was time for action, not psychological processing.

Leah must have read my thoughts. "Plane's on standby."

"What plane?"

"My dad's Boeing and pilot, courtesy of Master Theo's subtle persuasive powers."

"I can imagine."

"How do you think I got to Washington so fast?"

"Let's roll."

"Here. From Master Theo." She handed me a purple envelope. "I brought it with me and he said to give it to you after you found the password. He assumed we would. Nice of him."

I broke the seal of the envelope.

> Diokles and Leah,
>
> Congratulations on a job well done.
>
> The third ordeal is at hand. Leave for India without delay. The pilot has the coordinates and will refuel at Barcelona.
>
> Mataji is expecting you and will provide everything you need. Trust her with your life.
>
> Locate the cave at Mount Kailash and extract the scroll. I await you at Headquarters for the final ordeal—the victory over Death and the speaking of the Lost Name of God.
>
> Challenge: Brahman is birthless
> Password: The Truth is One
>
> Glory be to the invincible Light of Truth,
>
> Theodore

P.S. Your encounters in Washington were mere practice for the horrors that prowl in India and Tibet. You are walking into Red Scorpion territory. You will face the ancient tests of the cave. No matter what you see, no matter what you feel, never give up. Never turn back. You are a Master of Energy.

# PART III

# THE DESCENT

# CHAPTER 13

**10:25 p.m. India Standard Time, Day 5, Secret Military Airport, 212 Miles Southeast of Varanasi, India**

The phosphorescent blue lights on the military airport runway carved a path in the nighttime darkness. I could feel that soon, too soon, this new world would greet us with gifts of enemies and traps and ordeals.

The journey to India was trouble free, save a minor sparring incident with Leah. We sat on opposing aisle seats to keep a safe distance between us, spoke little, and slept a lot. The burden of the mission had grown, forcing us to conserve our energies for the coming battles.

Leah tugged the collar of her mod turtleneck sweater. "We're here. How are you feeling?"

"Ready to kick some major Red Scorpion butt. You?"

Silence.

Time to use Tony's trademarked, spill-your-female-secrets line. "What's going on?"

"Not sure I should tell you."

"What if I say 'please'?"

She crossed her arms over her chest. "I dreamt of you a while ago."

*Great.* "And?"

"I saw you dying in a wall of fire."

*Shoot.* "Were you with me?"

"You burned alone. Helpless."

"Okay . . . at least you're still alive."

Leah snapped her eyelids shut as though she were making a desperate attempt to erase the vision, find comfort in a private chamber of her mind. The pained expression warping her face betrayed her. She failed on both counts.

"Hey," I said, "sometimes a dream is just a dream. You know, facing imagined fears, processing memories, normal Psych 101 stuff. Stay positive."

"You're not listening. This was no indigestion nightmare. It felt real."

This time, the warning registered on my survival radar. Was the dream a true premonition of my inevitable fate, or the rising up to the surface of Leah's not-so-subconscious fears?

"I can't let a dream stop me from doing my duty."

"I didn't ask you to quit. I just want you to be careful."

"Thanks, warning taken. But remember, we defeated Arashi once. We can do it again."

"It's not Arashi. It's the cave I'm worried about. So many unknowns lurking."

"I'll take care of the problem."

"Men. . . . You're all from *Mars.*"

Her voice may have had a smidgen of emotion. "That's old stuff."

"Yeah, tens of thousands of years. Are you telling me it's changed in the last two decades?"

"Guess not."

"Do I have to spell it out? I need a little reassurance here."

I knew of no better way to provide reassurance than giving her refuge in my arms. But she still hadn't opened up about whatever it was that kept the barriers up. So I forced my hands not to grab her waist and my mouth not to kiss her lips. Good thing the seatbelt provided restraint.

Leah sensed my intention and scooted toward the window, the longing for intimacy still potent.

Then it came to me. When you hear the menacing footsteps of Death give chase from behind, you want to hide in your secret abode with the Beloved. You want to make sure they know at every level of their being you adore them. You want to cling to life. Who knew? Maybe I *did* have some Venusian genes after all.

"Leah, there are no guarantees. But I'll succeed, even if it's just for you. Are you feeling better?"

"Don't worry, I'll be okay."

"I wish you had gone back home when I asked you. Can't believe your father risked your safety."

"He didn't do it without an argument." Leah leaned back on her seat. "We're very close, and I want to make him proud. I just can't be his little girl forever."

For a fleeting moment, I contemplated my own motivations. Saving lives was number one. And coming through for Master Theo would be grand.

The Boeing Business Jet touched ground smoothly. The captain, an all-American, former fighter pilot, was the best money could buy. The airplane taxied to a stop. Leah and I unbuckled our seatbelts and stood up. The captain opened the door and showed us out.

"Don't go anywhere," I said. "We'll come back within forty-eight hours, max."

"Roger that, *sir*."

Leah handed the captain an envelope. "If I don't come back, give this to Dad."

"Yes, *ma'am*."

I wished I were about to receive a love letter too.

Leah pointed at my slate-blue, sub-zero parka. "Don't forget your coat."

"Yes, dear."

She shook her head, sighing in that mischievous, lighthearted way that raised my blood pressure.

I held onto the handrail all the way down lest I tumbled to the earth. Leah followed close behind me, her brown Ralph Lauren ankle boots sending hollow echoes off the metal steps into the endless space surrounding the military base. In the distance, moving beams from guard-post-mounted searchlights combed the perimeter for intruders. The air smelled of damp earth, burned machine oil, and danger. It was as if we didn't land in a friendly country but on a strange planet.

Our feet touched the tarmac. A tall Indian man in a grey business suit, flanked by two soldiers with automatic rifles, welcomed us with sphinxlike silence. I took my time to size him up. Despite the plain clothes, the Intelligence Bureau agent sported a crew cut and had the bearing of a hardened military officer. His square face was complemented with a hawk nose, an aggressive jaw, and the friendliness of an iceberg.

Without warning, the agent shone his flashlight in my face. "Mr. Philaretos, I presume." He over-enunciated each syllable.

"No. The name is Bond, James Bond." I didn't budge, I didn't smile.

He gave me the look. "I'm not laughing."

"That's your choice."

"I hope those who chose you knew what they were doing."

"I've survived so far."

He examined me from head to toe, moving the flashlight along with his gaze. "You don't strike me as the fighter type. And you're a foreigner. You don't know the ways of the East or the ways of the enemy."

"And yet, here I am."

Leah bit her inward lip curl and I could tell she hated the battle of testosterones.

I sent her a mental order to trust me and stay calm. The agent and I were testing each other's mettle. No need for her to interfere, I had the situation under control.

"My opinion on the matter is irrelevant, son," the agent said. "Soon, you will be tried by the fire."

And there was the fire again. "What's your name, agent?"

"My apologies, I'm not authorized to reveal it."

"No worries. I like to make deep connections with my new friends."

He didn't appreciate the irony. "Passport, please. Same for you, madam."

The agent inspected our documents and passed them back. "Our sages say Brahman is birthless."

"They also say that Truth is One."

The fierce gaze softened. "I guess you'll do." The agent pointed with his eyebrows toward a running military Land Rover. "Come. It takes two hours to reach the Temple of the Mother of the World."

One of the soldiers took the wheel and I opened the door for Leah. She didn't seem to be in a mood to talk.

The vehicle crossed the entrance checkpoint of the base and pulled on to a dirt road. I was only too aware that it would take a single rocket-propelled grenade hitting the Land Rover on the way to Varanasi—and *boom*. The vehicle would turn to an inferno.

...

A little over two hours later we reached the outskirts of Varanasi. No explosions so far, but that in itself was curious. Why didn't the Red Scorpions blow us up?

Leah. Arashi wanted her alive. So what was his next move? Up close and personal? A murder/kidnapping, like he had tried in Washington?

I kept quiet. Leah seemed lost in her thoughts and so did the agent. The two soldiers didn't dare speak without permission. It was a silent journey.

We entered the city's maze of streets and alleyways. The Land Rover, horn blaring, plowed through garlanded cows, rickshaws, and cars with their own blaring horns. Life never stopped in Varanasi. Tightly packed buildings simmered and glowed with strong emotions accumulated over the centuries. The lingering smell of smoke from the funeral pyres at the banks of the Ganges reminded everyone that nothing is permanent.

For a moment, I let my guard down and pretended I was a pilgrim to the mystic city. I absorbed the spiritual power emanating from the sacred temples. I meditated, chanted with holy men and women, and gave devotions.

"Over there," the agent said.

His order dispelled my vision of earthly nirvana.

The driver took a right turn on to a narrow back street and pulled up to a door in a massive wall. The tires whipped up a cloud of dust.

"Out, now."

The soldiers and I scrambled through the doors. Leah took her time to fix her hair and apply lipstick. I surmised there was more behind her delay than a need for grooming. On the one hand, she took a moment to collect herself. On the other, she wanted to send a message to the agent and myself—that she preferred to *give*, not take orders.

I waved at her to come out.

The agent knocked.

The door cracked open to reveal a serene old man of average height. He wore saffron robes and a string of rudraksha beads around his neck. His white beard reached below his collarbones, and his forehead displayed the painted white and yellow lines of his order.

The old man's smile, teeth white and intact, didn't just stop the cold seeping into my bones. It probed my Soul, saw the worry vexing it, and assured it I would be safe and sound. We had arrived at friendly territory.

The agent bowed his head over folded hands. "Most Honored Swami, I present the guests Her Holiness is expecting from America. Would you do me the honor and inform her they are here?"

The swami ambled outside, taking charge by his sheer presence, a lion that didn't need to roar. "She knows. I thank you on her behalf for conducting them safely."

"We will stand guard until they are ready to depart."

"Thank you, but we have no need of your protection. You may go back to your base."

"My orders, sir. I must provide security for the Americ—"

*Crack!*

The warning shot pocked the wall above the agent's head.

"Drop your weapons."

There it was, Arashi's next move. My survival instinct kicked in, sharpened my senses, liberated my muscles. Out of the corners of my eyes, I scanned the surroundings.

Leah stiffened, eyes unblinking and calculating. The swami also stood still, though the serene smile never left his face. The soldiers dropped their weapons and raised their hands.

Black-clad men with AK-47s swarmed around us, led by someone who was just over five feet, soiled turban and all. He had a beak of a nose, a graying stubble at least one week old, and a mustache reaching down to his jaw line.

The agent dropped his pistol to the ground.

The chieftain turned his eyes on Leah. His intent was clear.

"Back off," she said. The high pitch sent an SOS signal.

I took a step forward, fists clenched. "Get lost, you scumbag."

The chieftain pointed his AK-47 toward my chest. "Watch it, lover boy. You want to live, no?" He rubbed together the thumb and forefinger of his left hand. "Arashi pays me extra for taking you alive. I wouldn't want to lose my baksheesh." He stared over at Leah. "Tie the slut and the lover boy. Kill the rest."

In a fraction of a second, I went over my options.

Option one, fight. Lunge at the chieftain and go for his throat. Distract the thugs and die from a hundred bullet wounds. Fighting would preserve my honor, give the soldiers a chance to grab their weapons, and maybe by some miracle save Leah. Not viable.

Option two, flee. Make a run for the open door and get inside the compound. In other words, die as a coward or live as a coward. Never.

Option three, freeze. Be a good boy. Let them capture us and take us to Arashi's dungeon. No. Back to option one. I marshaled my strength and tried to leap.

I could not. An unseen power kept me restrained.

"Children, do not disturb the peace of the Mother of the World," the swami said, in the calm guru voice he must use with his devotees. "Leave, lest her wrath awakens and smites you."

The chieftain glared at the swami, decades of obvious upper-caste hatred oozing from his face. "Shut up, old lizard. I'm finished taking orders from Brahmins."

"This is your last warning," the swami said.

"And this is your last breath." The chieftain waved a fleshy finger at the man next to him. "Ramesh, plant a bullet in his skull."

Ramesh, a burly man in his early twenties, put his finger on the trigger and aimed. . . . And nothing.

"I told you to shoot him."

"Can't, I can't. My finger is numb."

"Stupid son of a monkey." The chieftain trained his weapon on the swami. "Go to hell."

The chieftain's howl of agony savaged my ears. His weapon hit the ground. The odor of singed flesh flowed into my nostrils.

The chieftain dropped on his knees and licked his hand. "What in Yama's name did you do to me? Kill him, you fools."

No one moved.

The swami intensified his warm smile. "Children, I forgive you. Let ignorance blind you no more. Go in peace."

I doubted the thugs grasped the meaning of the swami's admonition, except for the "Go" part. They raced toward the street corner, bumping against each other, disappearing into the shadows. The lion had sent the hyenas packing, bruised tails between their legs.

*Yes.*

"I shall make you all pay," the chieftain yelled. "I *swear* by my father's grave."

I found myself able to move again and turned toward Leah.

She did her best to regain her composure and sound brave. "I'm fine. Glad the swami is on our side."

Her assurances failed to disguise the hurt. I stepped closer, determined to shield her with my body's warmth from the cold and the inner pain. Then I backpedaled away from the danger zone. "Thank you for saving our lives, sir."

"I am more than happy to give my assistance."

The soldiers were huddled against the compound wall, looking like they wanted it to swallow them up and hide them. The agent's eyes pled for forgiveness, the last chunks of ice on the frozen face melting. "Honored Swami, please accept my deepest apologies."

My heart went out to him.

"It is not your fault or that of the soldiers. The thugs hid well and lay in waiting. That is why the soldiers missed them. I sensed their presence and waited till they made their move."

The agent and the soldiers prostrated before the swami.

He blessed them and addressed us. "Now that the preliminaries are over, Mataji will receive you."

The swami pushed open the door of the compound. "I hope you made the necessary preparations. You will not be the same after encountering the high priestess. She embodies all aspects of the Divine Feminine."

The door led into a large courtyard with the main structure in the center. The white limestone temple was square and four stories tall. Ornate carvings adorned its outer walls and a multitiered dome crowned its roof. Spindly spires pierced the night sky, silent sentries guarding the manifest presence of the Mother of the World.

I paused and paid homage to the temple with a whispered salutation, felt its beating heart. Leah and the swami walked toward the buildings to the right. I caught up with them, and we climbed up a wooden staircase to reach a solid cedar door. The swami struck the brass door knocker three times.

"Do come in."

He waved goodbye and strode back down the stairs.

I held the door for Leah and tiptoed after her. It's not every day you enter the private quarters of a high priestess.

The hearth at the far left of the high-ceilinged chamber welcomed us with its crackle and blaze. Gold-leafed moldings framed the windows and door, and underfoot, hand-knotted Kashmiri rugs covered the hardwood floor.

A nine-foot marble statue of the Mother of the World sat before the back wall, surrounded by pots of multicolored flowers. Their gentle scent floated in the large room. Beyond sanctity, Mataji's quarters emanated comfort and protection, a safe house behind enemy lines.

Mataji stood before the statue, her petite figure enveloped in a white silk sari, threaded ponytail flowing down to her waist.

Her dark skin seemed translucent, as though her veins carried a crystal clear liquid and not blood. It was hard to gauge her years. I knew she must be in her early seventies, but she appeared much younger, having learned to control the damaging effects of time.

Her brown eyes met mine, and for a moment I mistook her for a divine apparition.

I brought my hands together in salutation and offered her the yellow envelope from Master Theo. "Your Holiness, I'm Diokles, and this is Leah."

"No formalities please. Call me Mataji, or Mother."

Her accent was classic Indian, flavored with touches of Britain. Her voice was delicate, words spoken with a calm yet firm cadence.

"Yes, Your Holiness."

Mataji opened her arms. "Oh, stop that. Come here."

"Pardon me?"

"You had a rough night. You need a hug."

I surrendered to her embrace. Gentle currents of energy coursed through my muscles until tension changed into peace. It was clear Mataji possessed great spiritual attainment.

I nodded my thanks and stepped back.

Her gaze moved to Leah.

Leah ran to her. She tucked her chin on Mataji's shoulder and returned the tight hug. Tears came loose. Tears of grief, loss, and relief. I shed a few myself, recognizing the breakthrough for what it was.

Mataji cradled Leah and stroked her hair, her expression the epitome of maternal tenderness. For that long minute and maybe forever, Leah had found the embodiment of a loving mother she so missed.

Mataji adjusted her sash. "There. Now we can attend to business." She walked toward the back wall and motioned us to follow. We sat across from the statue on plush silk pillows, I to Mataji's right and Leah to her left.

"Do you have the Adept's Password?"

"Yes."

"Splendid. A helicopter will transport you to the cave at dawn. Night travel is too dangerous."

"Master Theo mentioned a map."

She produced a small treasure chest made of carved teak wood, banded with gold. "Here."

I received it with both hands and pulled open the golden clasp. A round-cut emerald, gleaming with the light of the candles, rested on a folded parchment. I drew out the parchment delicately.

Leah stood up and positioned herself right behind me to see the map. The drawing showed a mountain. A gap divided it vertically and pointed to three ovals at its foothill. Below the mountain, a crescent moon was drawn to the left and a sun to the right.

"It's obviously Mount Kailash, but not much of a map."

"The cave is on the south face of the mountain," Leah said.

I arched a thick, amused eyebrow. "How so?"

"I looked up the topography on Google Earth before we left. The sun and the moon stand for two lakes below the mountain on the south."

"Yes, Lake Manasarovar and Lake Rakshasa Tal," Mataji said. "You'll also recall a giant crevice cuts through the south side."

"One of the ovals is the entrance to the cave," Leah said.

"Spot on," Mataji said.

I raised both thumbs.

Leah acknowledged me with a look of longing I hadn't seen on her before, a lady welcoming her knight back to the castle after a long war, eyes saying all that could not be spoken.

*Concentrate on the map.*

"Per the ancient map, each of the three ovals stands for an aperture into the mountain," Mataji continued, seemingly oblivious to the exchange of affection between Leah and myself. "Unless the geology has changed, the entrance to the cave is the aperture on the far left."

"How will I know for sure?"

"You'll see a rough-hewn third eye inside."

"And the emerald?"

"The key to the secret door."

I pressed the little dent between my nose and lips with my index finger, eyelids half-shutting. "I get the picture."

Leah stood up. "I can hardly wait for the morning."

"You, my dear, are staying here," Mataji said.

"Why?" Leah replied, her eyes widening. "Diokles needs me, I can help."

"Only one initiate at a time can face the tests of the cave. Besides, here in the compound you are safe."

Leah dropped back on the pillow.

"What about the Chinese?" I asked, quickly changing the subject. "I don't think they take well to border violations."

Mataji studied a moonbeam coming under the door, highlighting the wool rug. "The helicopter has stealth technology. After you cross the border, you have about four hours before they track you down and arrest you. That's the best estimate of the Intelligence Bureau."

"Only four hours?"

"Yes. Your pilot's name is Kesang. He's a Tibetan spy for the Intelligence Bureau. If he gets caught, we risk an incident between China and India. And he would rather commit suicide than go back to a Chinese prison."

"So I show up on time, or tough luck all around."

"Correct. . . . Why are you staring at the statue?"

"I expected to see a fierce deity with a lot of hands. This mother figure has only two, and a veiled face."

"At this temple, we worship the archetypal Divine Feminine, the Mother before she becomes individualized. Our Sisterhood began in the land we now call India, even before Atlantis sank. Ever since, the Sisterhood has drawn her presence with daily adorations. In an unbroken chain."

A deep desire to know the Mother possessed me. "Tell me more."

"The Mother constantly woos all of her children back Home. She seeks them out to share her unconditional love and bestow her blessings."

A hallowed hush fell in the chamber.

"The Mother is concerned about the loss of so many lives. Therefore, to you, Diokles, she grants an empowerment to help you with a test in the cave. Do you accept it?"

"Absolutely."

"To you, Leah, she brings healing of your innermost wound. Do *you* accept it?"

The last shards of Leah's lawyer facade crumbled. A few more tears trickled out. "Yes, Mother."

"Very good." Mataji brought her feet to a lotus position. "After we sing and chant, I will guide you through the ancient Divine Mother Meditation."

I sang along. My body moved to the rhythm of the sound, the haunting melody of the bhajan awakening memories from bygone days, dissolving the cares of the world.

The chants of Mataji and Leah had become a distant hum when my base chakra stirred. Gentle pinches spread across my spine. Breath emptied from my lungs. A primeval sound vibrated through my brain. The heat in my spine built up. Thread after thread of liquid fire reached my head.

Then, the kundalini erupted.

My neck jerked backwards. My ethereal body took flight. And there in the midst of space, I hovered across from the Mother of the World, boundless and infinite, yet appearing in form. Shafts of blue flame surged all around her. Filigree garments, sparkling with a pink fire, enfolded her holy frame. Long hair streamed down to her waist in free-flowing strands. A crown of stars adorned her head and a veil hid her face, her open arms welcoming the long-lost son back Home.

In the presence of such majesty, I felt no bigger than a speck of dust.

"The Mother of the World will reveal her face," an angel said. "Are you prepared?"

"I am."

With a swift movement of her hands, the Mother lifted her veil.

Rays of shooting white light pierced the darkness, and I beheld the holy face—more radiant than the sun, more beautiful than a thousand dawns, more powerful than lightning.

Millions of points of energy caressed me. A warm, swaddling raiment formed. And out of the core of Existence itself a voice like the whisper of gentle winds spoke.

"My Beloved, out of the Great Deep I have come to draw you nearer to me this day.

"I am your eternal Mother.

"I am the Light of the Feminine Ray.

"I am the Womb of the Cosmos.

"Take refuge in my Divine Embrace.

"Accept my comfort.

"Receive my Love."

Waves of perfect love rippling from her heart flooded the shores of my being, setting my chakras aflame. All sense of separation dissolved and I rested in the center of timelessness, knowing myself as one with the Divine Feminine, one with the stars, one with the galaxies.

"Mother, *at last,* I have come Home.

"The chains of illusion are broken.

"Duality no more holds sway.

"Your presence makes me whole.

"In the vastness of cosmos, I will seek you.

"On your Great White Throne, I will honor you.

"In the fabric of matter, I will adore you."

The stars fashioning her crown sparkled. "The secret I grant through the lips of my priestess awaits. I now depart but I am always near. Remember me when the shadows of fear eclipse the sun of your courage. Remember the Mother of the World."

I descended to the room and entered my body a new man. It was as if the Mother's divine heart had absorbed the garment of my consciousness, cleansed it from its worldly stains with her love, and brought it forth white and pure.

What a gift.

I took a fleeting look at Leah and Mataji. Deep stillness rested on their faces. Leah seemed so saturated with sacred fire, so transformed, I almost didn't recognize her. Mataji came to outer awareness first.

"Could you—"

"Hush my son, absorb the essence of the Mother in silence."

I returned to the valley of bliss. . . .

A gentle "Hello" from Mataji brought me back.

"You had a question," she said.

"What's the empowerment?"

"The Mother confirms what both of you have felt. Only by offering your body to the fire can you reach the scroll."

I kept up the eye contact, the solemnity of her message not disturbing my peace. "I know death isn't real. Even tonight, I experienced the inner worlds."

"True enough. Except you speak from the level of the Adult Self, still suffused with ecstatic bliss. You temporarily forget that the Soul, the synthetic ego, and the Instinct—the other self-states—also live in your energy field. Each with its own set of rules and beliefs. Each having its own agenda. Each responding differently to external stimuli."

"Right. I know."

"When you face the flames, your survival instinct will inundate you with the fear of death. It will command the body to fight, flee, or freeze to save itself from annihilation."

"As it should."

"Indeed, that is its job. Yet you cannot let the fear of death decide for you. You must override it and choose with your *conscious* free will to jump into the flames or turn back."

Leah tensed as she realized her premonition was real.

"It boils down to courage versus self-preservation," Mataji said.

I shifted my weight on the pillow and exchanged a worried look with Leah. "Is this right, Mother? Doable?"

"Observe the Instinct speaking through your mouth this very moment."

"But . . . who . . . what human being offers their body to be burned?"

She reached over and held my shoulder. "What's asked of you is beyond human. Remember, you are working on the second sub-degree of the exalted Seventh. You are on the path to becoming a fully realized Master of Energy."

The reminder didn't bring much comfort. "So is this ordeal the Baptism by Fire?"

"Not per se. It is an accelerated step toward it."

"I see." Actually, I wasn't sure I did.

"The Mother grants you the authority to tame your Instinct. To retrieve a major portion of your subconscious free will. Specifically, those fragments of your free will that are now imprisoned in the clutches of the great primal fear."

"How?"

"You will know when you face the ordeal."

I made no response, latched onto the final drops of bliss dissipating from my aura.

"Up," Mataji said, leaping to her feet with great ease, an obvious benefit from years of hatha yoga.

We also stood.

"One more thing before I send you to your rooms. You thought I didn't notice your displays of affection. You forgot all mothers have eyes on the back of their heads."

Leah's fair cheeks grew pink with a mom-caught-me blush. I suspected mine were doing the same.

Mataji laughed. The amused musical sound dispersed the tension. "I rejoice in your endearment."

I felt like Romeo seeing the candlelight in Juliet's bedroom window in the balcony scene.

"Thank you, Mother," Leah said, "we're so grateful." She turned to me and mouthed something.

I made it out that she asked me to say thank you. "Thank you, Mother."

"I'm not finished yet. I must share something with Leah."

I rubbed my hands. "Let's hear it."

Mataji smiled. "My message is for Leah's ears alone."

Leah walked over and Mataji whispered to her the forbidden secret.

The pink ripened to red and invaded the rest of her face and neck.

"The helicopter arrives at 6:30 a.m. sharp," Mataji said, unmoved. "Do not be late."

# CHAPTER 14

**6:16 a.m., Day 6, Guest Room, Temple of the Mother of the World**

The aroma of coffee seeped under the guest room door. I inhaled deeply. Not that I needed any. The coming ordeal had left me oversupplied with adrenaline.

Hidden behind the tall buildings of Varanasi, the courtyard and my room were still in shadow. I sat on the futon couch for a last-minute meditation on the Timeless Self when boots crunching on gravel announced a visitor.

"Are you up?" Leah asked.

"It's open."

Leah marched in. The green fatigues did a poor job camouflaging her hourglass figure. "Morning."

I hauled my gaze from her frame and anchored it into her pupils. "Why the military outfit?"

"To match yours."

Something inside my head clicked. "No."

"I'm coming," she said with the determination of a drill sergeant.

"Mataji doesn't take well to disobedience."

"I'll talk her into it."

"You may have to talk the universe into it. Only one initiate at a time can take the trials. That sounded like a cosmic rule."

"We'll find a way around it."

I made the timeout sign. "There is no 'we' here. You haven't talked me into it. I said no. Negotiation over."

"I insist."

"Leah, I'm trying to talk some sense into you. I won't let you take any more risks. Period."

Leah's lower lip stuck out in a cute, exaggerated pout. She took off her baseball cap with the Boston Celtics logo and threw it at me.

The cap hit the wooden wall behind the couch.

"You missed."

"I want to come with you, help you," she said. "I can't handle the stress here alone."

"It should be easy compared to what I'm facing."

Silence.

"Please, Leah, I need to focus on what I'm doing, not worry about you. Promise me you won't do anything crazy, like following me or leaving the compound. I need to know you're safe."

"Fine." Leah walked toward me in timid steps. "May I join you?"

Something in her tone made my legs go weak. I showed her the couch. "Please."

She sat by me, our knees touching. She had evidently conquered the phobia about being touched. I struggled to make my anxious smile look normal.

She dug something out of her purse, a small ruby heart, and edged closer. Her perfume, mixed with her natural, womanly essence and body heat, made me dizzy. Her leg brushed against mine again. She opened the left pocket of my fatigue shirt and slipped in the little heart. "I want you to have this. I've kept it in my purse since we met."

"I'll treasure it as long as I live."

Leah freed her ponytail from its silver clasp. The strawberry-blond curls cascaded down her cheeks and shoulders. Her face drew near.

She closed her eyes.

The room held its breath.

I had never felt so giddy, so entranced, so elated. If this was a dream, I wanted to never wake up.

*Hear, O Heaven and Earth, I have traversed time and space to find my Beloved. To keep my ancient vow. To fuse the halves into one. Behold, I now taste her lips, in the name of Timeless Love.*

I drew a bit closer.

*Whump-whump, whump-whump.* The sound of rotors trespassed through the window.

Leah pulled back. "Helicopter's here. It's time, Diokles." The switch to take-charge mode was instant, but I could still hear the longing and the letdown in her voice. She scooted to the end of the couch.

My euphoria vanished. "Lady, by yonder blessed moon, I swear, I'll come back to you."

She blew me the unfulfilled kiss. When it landed, I sensed her fears, her hopes, and her love.

"I'll wait on my balcony, Romeo."

I staggered to my feet, sublimating the energy of the tryst, storing it in my reserves. Wrong time and place for twin-soul romance. I got my bearings and sprinted through the door.

"Be careful," she said.

I could feel her gaze on my back enfolding me with the softness of angel wings, bidding me to come back safe.

Out of the sun's glaring backdrop, a granite-gray helicopter sped in the direction of the courtyard. Head held high, Mataji stood in front of the main temple doors, watching it approach.

I went to her.

"You are late," she said.

"I apologize."

"Any questions?"

"Is the pilot a Brother? How much does he know?"

"He is my disciple, I trust him with my life. Anything else?"

I thought a moment. "No."

"I go with the swami to Agra within the hour. We will place the energy pyramid of India over the Taj Mahal. Leah stays here. Not even the Dark Master himself would dare cross into the Divine Mother's force field and enter the compound."

"Good."

"One last thing. The cave is a strange, magical realm tucked between the physical and inner worlds. It will amplify your fears tenfold and try to take over your mind. Stay centered when you think you are going mad."

"I'll do my best."

She held me close.

The beat of the rotors overhead sent a cloud of dust and bits of rock spiraling upward. Mataji gathered the flapping folds of her sari. The pilot righted the helicopter and brought the skids down to the ground.

The large transport craft had no visible weapons. Black paint covered the insignia of the Indian Air Force. External fuel tanks mounted on its sides told me we would go straight to Mount Kailash and back without any stops.

I beelined toward the chopper and climbed in.

Kesang acknowledged me with a raised hand. With a Stetson hat and a bandanna around his neck, he could have been the Tibetan version of the Marlboro Man. Sans the baby blues and the cigarette hanging out of the mouth. He was the color of dark amber, with a flat-bellied body, and a string of stitch marks below the right ear. He wore a foliage-green flight suit, a headset, and an alert expression. He was taller than I expected and older, late thirties at the most. Overall, Kesang seemed as reliable as a cowboy's well-oiled Colt.

I buckled my harness and settled on the seat. Kesang reached over and handed me a headset. He examined the controls and pulled the navigation stick.

My stomach climbed up faster than the rest of my body parts. I peered through the side window down at a swiftly disappearing Mataji, and spotted Leah next to her waving at me.

I groaned inwardly, pressed my heart down to block it from flying to her, and waved back. *Keep your lips warm, Juliet. I'm taking a rain check on that kiss.*

The helicopter soared northwest.

I tapped the microphone. "You hearing me okay?"

"Positive."

"I'm told you're cozy with the Chinese Army." Smooth ice-breakers have always been one of my strong suits.

"Like Frodo with the Black Riders."

So he had spent some time in Western culture. "Got you."

Kesang spoke in a clipped military cadence. His rugged low voice, resonating in the back of his throat, showed no bitterness and no anger. Impressive.

"You have family?" I asked.

"A wife and three little girls."

"Good for you, man. Hope to have some of my own some day."

"Who's the lucky woman?"

"Her name's Leah. She was the one waving."

"Very pretty. If I wasn't married, you'd have some serious competition."

I smacked him on the shoulder and laughed along. If Leah were a fly on the cockpit wall, she would roll her eyes just about now. Feistiness. Another of the thousand reasons I loved her.

The helicopter reached cruising altitude. The city buildings below looked like stacked matchboxes, and the Ganges, a giant liquid artery, nurturing Varanasi with its glistening light.

"You know about Arashi, right?"

"I've been briefed," he said.

"You have any weapons?"

"An M4 Carbine."

"We're flying into the mouth of the red dragon with just a rifle?"

"Not to worry. You saw that box in the belly of the chopper?"

"No."

"That, my friend, is a Directional Infrared Countermeasures system. Gets heat-seeking missiles drunk."

"Huh?"

"It detects missiles and jams their navigation instruments with an infrared beam. Automatically."

"Cool."

"So what's bothering you?"

I put my fisted hands in my lap. "It's not like Arashi to lay low. There's a trap here somewhere."

"Like?"

"Don't know," I said. "The chieftain said Arashi wanted me alive. Why?"

He didn't respond.

"I'm going to catch a few winks, okay?"

"Say what?"

"I'm taking a nap."

"Okay."

I closed my eyes and lost myself in soothing visions of Leah. My fingers squeezed the little heart in my pocket and soon I slipped into a light sleep.

...

My headset crackled. "Hey, wake up. We're almost there."

I dug myself out of my stupor and glided back to consciousness. The din of the helicopter blades filled the cockpit. My shoulders felt numb and my lips tasted like salt.

"There's Mount Kailash," Kesang said. "Tibetans call it Kang Rinpoche, precious jewel of the snows."

Soaring thousands of feet high, the mountain did resemble a rough jewel made of granite and ice. A pilgrim route circled its outer slopes. Morning light, reflecting off crystal peaks, made it hard to see. Fog-shrouded ridges and darkened ravines added to the desolation of the terrain. Coupled with the brooding clouds charging from behind it, Mount Kailash didn't inspire much hope.

"Kesang, why did you accept the mission . . . with your history and all?"

"I want to play a part in this coming era," he said. "It's all about giving people opportunity."

"Thanks, man, appreciate it."

"Don't thank me yet. We've killed forty-seven minutes since we crossed the border. And the Chinese choppers will find us sooner or later. You have a little over three hours to surface."

"So I show up on time or you split."

"You ever heard of the water-dungeon torture?"

"Nope, just water boarding."

"How about snake bite?"

"Unless you're talking about literal snakes, negative."

He replaced the Stetson with a black sock hat. "I thought not. If you did, you wouldn't ask."

It wasn't hard to detect the bitterness now tightening his face.

"One last favor," I said.

"Shoot."

"If I change my permanent address to the cave, inform the Post Office."

"I'm recording your lame jokes for posterity."

"Hey, the ladies love my jokes."

"Really? I'm soo impressed.

"And tell Leah this. She ever marries another man, I'm coming back from the Other Side to haunt them both."

"Done. Listen, when I radioed in, Mataji mentioned some fire ordeal."

"Yep. Can't wait."

"Here, spare your precious face."

"A ski mask?"

"A Special Forces ski mask," he said, "with Kevlar fibers. Every Greek goddess would bawl if you lost any of your magnificence."

"You got *that* right." I had always prized humor as the universal antidote to stuffiness and stress. I ran my fingertips over the synthetic cloth. It might be a bad idea to cut corners. "Am I allowed to use the mask?"

"You are now. I asked Mataji. Same with these heavy-duty goggles."

Had to give it to Kesang. He knew the ropes.

The helicopter reached the foothills below the tip of the giant crevice and hovered fifty feet above ground. The noise sent a pair of reddish-brown mountain goats with spiraling horns bolting down a trail.

"Good sign," Kesang said.

"How so?"

"Elementary, my dear Watson. No one's lurking there or the goats wouldn't stay."

A Sherlock Holmes reference? Kesang kept growing on me. "Which is it? Europe or the States?"

"Six years in Austin, Texas. I have degrees in Asian History and International Affairs."

I surveyed the treeless mountainside through my binoculars until I located the three apertures. And something else.

I stomped my boot on the cockpit floor, hands strangling the binoculars. There were several sets of footprints in the snow leading to the left cave.

"What?"

I pointed. "Look there. Arashi beat us to the scroll."

Kesang took the binoculars with one hand and checked the footprints. If he was worried, he didn't show it. "Could be. They're not fresh."

Sure enough, when we were hovering over them, I could see that snow powder half-filled the tracks.

I debated between punching the cockpit wall or myself. "That's why Arashi disappeared. I wonder if he's still in the cave."

"I'd say, whoever came here is long gone. They didn't walk here, and I haven't seen any signs of a craft. Maybe he left empty-handed."

"Or maybe someone dropped him off like you're about to do for me. I'll know soon."

Kesang guided the helicopter toward the opening and brought it straight down. The skids pushed through the snow and hit the uneven surface. A jolt rebounded through my soles, all the way up to my scalp.

"Don't dawdle," Kesang said.

We shook tight hands and gave a fist bump. I zipped my goose down coat, pulled the hood over my head, and jumped out. The snow buried my legs up to the knees. The idling rotors kicked up whirling crystals that stung my face. My nose hairs and eyelids froze. My lungs fought to suck down the high-altitude air. Any time, any day, I would trade the mountain for the ocean.

Kesang shut the engine off.

Nothing moved, nothing made a sound, save the screeches of two vultures overhead, mixing with the flapping of their wings and the whistling of the wind. No welcoming committee and hopefully no trap.

My legs plowed forward, each step an act of hard labor. A few minutes later, I came to a stop before the foothill and stared at the cave's open jaws.

Goose bumps laced my arms. The cave summoned me.

# CHAPTER 15

**8:58 a.m., Day 6, Passageway to the Secret Cave, Mount Kailash, Tibet**

I fed my body to the jaws of the cave, holding firm in my resolve to come out of its belly alive.

Wide enough to accommodate a car, the natural passage cut deep into the mountainside. Slanting sunrays and the beam of my flashlight showed the way. Bayonets of ice, dangling from the domed roof, gave silent warning of a terrible fate to would-be trespassers.

I advanced slowly, my hearing on hyper-alert. Twenty feet inward, I made a right turn, expecting nothing worse than sleeping bats.

The frozen bodies of two men and a woman lay by the dead end of the passage, eyes bulging, mouths locked in a scream. They were wearing khaki fatigues and had no visible wounds. Round medallions, engraved with red scorpions, hung around their necks. Two Uzis, a ceremonial dagger, and a black sphere added mystery to the scene of carnage.

I leaned on the wall and fought the urge to vomit. This explained the footprints. Slowly, the queasiness eased, leaving me hoping I would avoid whatever creature had turned Mount Kailash into the Red Scorpions' icy grave.

I offered a prayer on the Red Scorpions' behalf, even as I thanked God their mission was a failure. But where was Arashi?

The flashlight discovered the upright third eye that marked the correct cave. Ten inches tall and hewn in the rock below the apex of the dead end, it was hard to miss. I extracted the emerald from my pocket, Mataji's words humming in my ears. *The emerald is the key to the secret door.*

Only one feature qualified for the lock—the socket within the pupil of the third eye. I pressed the emerald into it. A perfect fit.

I ducked to the ground to avoid any descending axes.

Nothing happened.

Thirty seconds passed and no passages opened, no hidden doorways appeared.

I blew out a frustrated breath that converted to a puff of steam. "Come on. Go, go."

A section of the rock wall parted with a shriek of rusty gears.

I jumped up, brushed off the dust that had landed on my face, and crossed in.

A sourceless light permeated the large circular cavern. Strange occult symbols were etched on the basalt walls. The roof was lost in darkness. Jagged shadows rose up like specters ready to swoop and drink my blood.

I saw no tunnels and no passageways. I came to a stop. Another dead end. I sniffed as though the smell of the ages would solve my problem. My mouth watered and I spat the rank saliva.

I probed with my inner senses for a sign, a clue, a hidden door. The only thing I found was a feeling of imminent doom.

I fended that off and continued my search when a rumble shattered my concentration. A gust blew the parka hood off my head, chilled the back of my thighs, hiked up the hairs of my neck into spikes.

A column of misty vapors descended at the back of the cave. The outline of a figure appeared.

Tendrils of fear wrung my chest. My quaking legs took a backward step. My palms shielded my ears. Then I ordered the part of myself wanting to flee to stand its ground.

The seven-foot figure clutched a sword with both hands. His fierce features seemed sculpted out of cool white fire, an elongated blue flame burning in the middle of his brow. His wings rose above his head and his blue robes touched the ground. A warrior angel. I started breathing again. He was on my side.

"Who enters the holy cave?"

Booming and haunting as a divine trumpet heralding Judgment Day, the challenge ricocheted off the walls, vibrated through my bones.

I bowed my head and brought my hands together in salutation. "An initiate in the service of life."

His unmoving eyes gave no encouragement.

I edged closer.

"Cease your advance at once. Have you not seen the corpses of your fellow mortals?"

My hands lifted, palms up, facing him. "I hear and obey."

"How did you find the cave? *Give answer.*"

"By the assistance of the Inner Order that ever serves the Light."

He placed the sword back into the scabbard. "It is well."

I lowered my hands.

"From whence do you come?"

"I come from America, the land of the New Atlantis."

"What do you seek?"

"The Scroll of the Lost Name."

He glowered at me as if he caught me violating a sacred tomb. "Foolish man. Know you not certain death awaits those who dare take the tests of the elements? None who crosses the threshold can retreat. Away."

"I persist."

"Depart at once."

"I took an oath."

"Son of Earth, I have duly performed my duty and delivered the warning. You have chosen to heed me not. Your life is in your hands. Do you possess the Adept's Password?"

"I do."

"How did you secure it?"

"By my labors and by the Grace of God."

"How many letters does it have?"

"Four."

"Come hither and speak the password."

The command knocked me off guard. I didn't speak Atlantean.

I tapped my coat pockets for paper and pen. "I can draw it."

"That is not acceptable."

All right, maybe he wasn't on my side. "There must be another way."

"Indeed."

"What is it? Do I need to lie prostrate and beg?"

No answer, no reaction. It was hard to read what he thought.

"How 'bout sacrificing a goat?" I couldn't believe the words coming out of my mouth. The cave was beginning to take over my mind.

"Your persistence, irreverent as it is, obliges my cooperation."

"I'm sorry about that. I'm under some pressure here."

He whipped his arm around, the motion so intense it compelled my gaze to follow. His finger pointed to a rectangular slab, cut within the rock. "Draw close to the tablet."

How did I miss that? I rushed over to the tablet. Three-inch square buttons covered the tablet's surface, each button displaying a carved character. It was an ancient stone keyboard of the Atlantean tongue.

"Press the letters in the correct order and you succeed. Mistake them and you plunge into the chasm. The fourth letter will herald your demise or your victory."

I examined the semi-concealed trapdoor I was standing on.

"Does your courage betray you? You can still withdraw."

"No, I really can't."

His countenance remained stern.

*Timeless Self, be with me.*

I clipped my gloves to my belt and recalled the Adept's Password. I scrutinized the tablet and spied the first letter. It was the third square from the right on the top row.

But a fraction of a second before I pressed it, a realization hit me. How the heck was Atlantean read? From left to right like English? Or from right to left like Hebrew?

My hand remained suspended in midair.

I had to think. I was an Atlantean at one time, after all. Atlantean was an ancient tongue, most likely read like Hebrew rather than English. I would go from right to left.

I pressed the first letter.

The button slid in by a half inch and stopped.

Second letter, fifth row. Done.

Third letter, fourth row. Done.

Fourth letter, seventh row. I traced the inscribed character with my fingertip, felt its age, absorbed its essence into my Soul. Anything but press the last button.

"One. Two. Three." Done.

A rolling sound blistered my ears. A dust cloud filled the cave, blocked the view.

The dust thinned out and I caught sight of the angel, the secret entrance behind him, open and unwelcoming.

"Son of Earth, you have proven worthy." Though he didn't smile, a smidgen of satisfaction softened his eternal sternness. "Proceed to the next cavern to commence your tests."

I ran my fingers through dust-powdered hair. *Can't wait.*

...

I darted through the opening. The small square cavern stank with the same ancient musty smell. A vaulted ceiling capped its walls. Veins of gold shimmered in white light that pervaded the space.

The entryway thundered shut behind me, closed me in.

Four neatly aligned square holes appeared on the north side of the cavern, right below the ceiling.

I stepped around a boulder and reached the wall. Four geometric patterns, chiseled on the rock at eye level, lined up symmetrically under each hole. First from the left, a triangle. Easy. It stood for fire. Next to it, a circle—air. A crescent moon—water. A square—earth.

I held my chin and puzzled over the intentions of the ancient builder who had devised this obstacle. If the test were to decipher the patterns, he hadn't worked very hard. Or back then, their meaning was hidden. Or they were purposely easy to figure out because they led to a snare.

I peered at the ground around me. No trapdoor.

Okay, the four patterns were a map that showed the order of the tests. There was no fire here, so I was in the cave of the Earth Element. The Fire Element was last. Which meant, I needed to go through the hole of the crescent to reach the cave of the Water Element.

The groan of my survival instinct came through. What if I took the wrong tunnel and ended up falling into a pit of snakes?

I listened for sounds of hissing. Instead, my ears captured the faint burble of falling water.

My fingers explored the carved crescent. The stone was cold to the touch. I gave it a push. No movement.

I placed my left foot and right hand in two cracks of the basalt mass towering before me. I squeezed, tensing all muscles . . . and dropped back onto my boots. The wall had no other footholds or handholds I could see. I needed something to step on, something big.

The boulder weighed at least a ton. Scrap *that* plan.

I could gather rocks and build a platform, but it'd take too long and wouldn't hold.

My body drooped under its weight, under the weight of defeat. Some Master of Energy. Couldn't even pass the first test.

I held back a swear word. "Tell me what to do."

The rock wall kept silent, as inanimate objects so often do.

A memory of my father sitting alone at the kitchen table of the seventh-floor apartment coursed through my head. He downed yet another shot of Jack Daniels to numb his grief over losing everything after the war. For wasting away and not making the grade.

I punched the crescent, packing all my might into each hit. "No, no. I don't want to end up like him. I don't want to fail." My fist struck the crescent again and again.

Pain bore through my hand like a dull drill, raced up my arm. I welcomed it, letting it consume my anger and rising guilt.

The crescent caved in. Something above me creaked. A gangly creature landed on the small of my back, rolled to the ground.

My body jerked. "Agghhhhhhh! Snake!" I lunged to the left to avoid the attacking snout.

Then I noticed that the snake hung from a rusty hook protruding below the tunnel. It was a rope.

I sent forgiveness to my dad and asked for his in return for escaping to America and leaving him behind. I held no grudge anymore. He did the best he could.

The next question was, could you trust a twelve-thousand-year-old rope?

It was frayed at the edges but when I tested it, it held. It was probably magical, like everything else in this strange place. I took off the binoculars and the parka and threw them to the side, then pulled myself up. My head poked through the cobwebs and I climbed inside the tunnel. I dropped to all fours and crawled forward. Gravel tore my fatigues and scraped my kneecaps and forearms. The gurgle grew louder, wooed me to hurry on. The narrow walls seemed to constrict and fall on me.

After maybe forty feet, the tunnel emptied into a grotto. I climbed out and stretched my limbs. Lazy muscles, rarely forced to work, protested with dull aches.

I checked my watch. A little over two hours before the Chinese hunted down the helicopter. And me. I tried to cling to that sense of urgency, but the untamed beauty of the grotto momentarily bewitched me into forgetting my predicament.

At the far end, a stream cascaded from a cleft overhead. Its clear water poured into a pool. Stalactites, hanging from the low ceiling like giant, wet fingers, pointed the way I should go. The walls, coated with tiny refracting crystals, whispered of a potent magic.

I tasted the smell of wet earth and closed my eyes. In my daydream, the rain had just stopped and I was standing in a park. I took in the fresh air, felt the dewdrops on my face, watched the double rainbow with Leah beneath it.

I blinked and my attention came back to the cave. It seemed that swimming under the lake was the only way ahead. But what if it were a trap?

My inner faculties opened up, probed the lake for any danger. No signal circled back. I took a deep breath and prepared to plunge when a girlish laugh made me jump.

I turned in the direction of the rightmost stalactite. "Who's there?"

"A water nymph, silly."

"Sure, and I'm Poseidon."

"I speak truth."

The velvety, I'm-a-maiden-in-love voice cast a potent spell.

"Come out and show yourself."

"No man can see my face."

"Why? You sound pretty." I scolded myself for flirting, giving in to the enchantment.

The water nymph rewarded me with a seductive giggle.

"You real or some cute hallucination?"

"*You* decide."

"I'm in a hurry? What do you need?"

"I come with a warning."

"Take a number."

"I have watched your journey thus far. You are very brave."

The flattery set off alarm bells. "You must have watched someone else."

"Hear me and know my words are true. A water monster guards the pool. No mortal-born can escape its jaws."

The solemn proclamation made my shoulders go up. "Glad you told me. I'm *definitely* no match for the Kraken." I checked out the surface of the pool for good measure, wondered what was generating those air bubbles.

"Beware, you handsome, fearless fool. You deserve to live, enjoy life."

Her dart hit bull's-eye, flung my mind to Leah. I brought my mind back and tried to move. But I couldn't. "We done here?"

"I promise you, you *will* see the monster and it *will* attack."

"Well, I hope it finds my flesh to its taste."

"Five seconds. That is the time you have to flee when its eyes lock onto you."

"Why should I believe you?"

"Ignore my counsel at your peril."

The invisible glue loosened up and my legs joggled free.

"I beseech you. Turn back now."

Her pleading was so heart-rending, it surely would have compelled the Kraken to weep, spare Andromeda.

I waved goodbye to the thin air. "See you later, water nymph. Thanks anyway."

I kept my clothes on and dived.

The pool sucked me down, clinched every inch of my skin with a thousand frigid fingers. I propelled myself forward with scissor kicks and long strokes, and spotted the passageway ahead, an opening cutting across the width of the pool.

But it was occupied.

The monster resembled a green dragon that half-morphed into a shark. Scales covered its body, a row of fins running down its tail. Its webbed feet dug into the grey sand. Froth crept out of its flared nostrils. Its hell-hot eyes gobbled me up from afar.

If the nymph could be believed, the five-second clock had started.

My head throbbed with a rushing sound crushing between my ears. Strain, building behind my ribcage from lack of oxygen, grew to a stab. But shock at the sight of the beast drowned my survival instinct, overrode its aim to take over and reverse the path.

With a wobble of its trunk, the water monster lurched. Its jaws, lined with rows of teeth, snapped open to feast on the stupid prey.

I braced myself for the inevitable. What else could I do? I didn't have the snake-haired head of the Gorgon to turn the monster into stone. And the five seconds had passed. It was too late to swim back.

I ignored the cries of my Instinct to retreat and swam forward. I wanted to travel to the Great Beyond a brave man.

The jaws snapped shut.

The monster's teeth sank into my flesh.

Except . . . I felt no bones cracking, I saw no sprays of blood mixing with the water. My clothed cadaver kept moving through the lake, through the intestines of the monster. I felt I should be watching it from above.

Then it dawned on me. The monster was an illusion. And I was still dwelling in my mortal form.

My eardrums pounded, about to rupture. My lungs burned, seconds away from asphyxiation.

I used the body's anguish as fuel and pushed, pushed, pushed.

My head popped through the pool's surface. How sweet was air.

"Diokles, at laaast. I've been expecting you."

The smooth, accentless voice fogged my mind. It was the voice of a sophisticated dark power seeking to disarm and possess— the voice of an arch-deceiver. Apparently, the ordeal of the Air Element had started.

I paddled to stay afloat and peeked through wet strands of hair at the apparition. He stood ten feet away in front of bronze doors that sealed up a vaulted corridor. He had aloof, aristocratic features, deep-set grey eyes that made no effort to hide their contempt, and wore all-black garments. This was someone or something that had millennia of experience in the battle of Light versus Darkness.

I clambered out of the pool and struggled to stand up, face the new threat. Instead, lungs panting, I collapsed on my back.

The holographic figure pointed a slender finger at me. "I am your deliverer."

I rolled on my side, still panting, to take a better look. "Deliver my . . . uhm. . . ."

"You're afraid to say, ass?"

"Fine . . . deliver my ass."

"Tsk, tsk, tsk. I didn't think you so vulgar."

"I entreat you, Your Majesty . . . *do* accept . . . my apologies."

"I have no time for jests. I came here to discuss an offer."

"Don't bother."

"You can't survive the flames without my help."

My breathing was steadying. "I would fail my test just by accepting your help."

"Arrogance will get you killed."

"You think I'm such a fool to bargain with you?"

"Au contraire, I believe you are brilliant. I believe you will accept my proposition when I reveal the facts your mentors withheld."

"Oh?"

"The doors open to a corridor of flames. Unless you are the purest among mankind—and we both know you are not—your odds of surviving the trial are fifty-fifty, maybe less."

A muted, crackling sound seeped through the bronze doors as if to confirm the revelation.

I perused the aging face. "Why should I trust you?"

"Because you *know* I'm speaking the truth."

I relived Leah's dream, felt the flames melt my skin. Then, I fought down the suffocating, primal urge to get up and run. He wasn't lying.

"The Fire Element obeys my command. My power will conduct you safely through the corridor and back." His voice lowered to a hypnotic hiss. "No taking chances, no scorching, no death."

"What . . . what did you say?"

"No taking chances, no scorching, no death."

"No death. I get the scroll. The earth is saved."

"Indeed."

"I'm sold. You want me to kiss the royal rings?"

The Deliverer aimed holographic hands at me.

I scooted backwards, thinking bolts of energy would shoot out to punish my insolence.

"Not so brave, I see."

The taunt stung.

"Enough. I guard your pitiful life, you snatch the scroll. You speak the Lost Name, you save Earth. Then you return the scroll to its rightful owner."

"And who might that be?"

"Me. The supreme talisman belongs to meee." The glint in his eyes proclaimed madness, dangerous madness. "I become the scroll's keeper and *you*, the world's greatest hero."

Empowered by his dark emotions, the proclamation swelled to a potent curse that thickened the fog in my mind and strengthened the Deliverer's hold over me.

How dare he tempt me with such a devious choice? I hated him. And I hated myself even more for considering the offer. For being so weak.

A part of me rebelled outright, wanted to tell the Deliverer to go to hell, where he belonged. Yet some prodding I couldn't resist shut my mouth, told me to act now, told me to wise up and accept his offer.

I rolled toward the lake, away from the menacing stare. My arms rose heavenward in a desperate plea for help.

Should we steal to feed our family? Should we lie, like politicians, to cling to power, even power we can use for good? Should we torture terrorists to get secrets that would save a million others?

So what if I broke the Cosmic Law just this one time? Doing my duty is what counted, saving the planet from destruction, giving all those people a break. An opportunity to live their precious lives to their allotted cycle, work out their karma. Learn, advance, serve. Was it not worth it to lose my honor for their sake?

I turned around to give my answer to the Deliverer. Upon seeing his wicked presence again, my fogged-out mind discerned a simple truth. Accepting the offer was more than a one-time bargain with the devil. It was an utter betrayal of the Light. It was bowing to the evil will of the Deliverer. It was turning to the Darkness.

This truth cleared my head, resurrected the crucified Master of Energy in me from the tomb of sophistry. I would not let the ends justify my means.

The Deliverer wore an expression of smugness. It was time to change that. It was time to slam-dunk my rebuke down his holographic throat. I pushed up on my elbows and rose to full height. "Mr. Deliverer?"

"Yes."

"Go to hell."

He dismissed my reply with the back-and-forth gesture you use to clear away someone's bad breath. "My old friend Theodore brainwashed you well."

"Don't stain his name with your foul tongue."

"You prove my point."

"Get lost."

"Poor, ignorant lad. You cleave to false ideals like utopian ages of enlightenment. You believe in the inherent superiority of the virtues. You espouse compassion for the so-called suffering of weaklings, forgetting they are nothing more than bugs to step over on your path to domination."

"Save the lecture for your peons and—" *Click.* The slain Red Scorpions in the passageway to the cave. "I see. You can't defeat the warrior angel, and you want *me* to do your dirty work. I'm not buying into your scheme."

"I have another reward. A very special reward."

"Like what?"

"The woman of your dreams. Besides, unless you accept my offer, I can't guarantee Leah's safety. She's in our hands even as we speak."

"You're a liar."

"Be intelligent. Save the planet *and* the girl."

I wanted to run over and erase the mocking grin from his grey lips. For good. But I didn't. "You vouch for this deal?"

"Goes without saying."

"And my vow of celibacy?"

"You renounce it, of course. Who will dare oppose you?"

"Where do I sign?"

"No paperwork needed. Just swear by the Lost Name."

I placed my palm over my heart. "I swear by. . . ."

"Go on."

"I swear. By the Lost Name. Of God." The words slogged out, each one a jagged stone scraping my palate. No matter. I was going through with my decision and I was prepared to pay the price.

"Get on with it before I change my mind."

"I swear by the Lost Name of God, I will *never* do evil that good may come."

The spikes of controlled anger issuing from the Deliverer threatened to nail me to the rocky floor. "So you choose annihilation. For yourself and the woman you love."

"I'm sorry. Someone recently told me the odds are fifty-fifty. That's a pretty good gamble."

"I will punish your stupidity. You have the word of the Dark Master."

The apparition dissipated, leaving no trace.

The familiar rumble and gust announced the coming of the warrior angel. Before I even enjoyed the kick I got out of sticking it to the Dark Master, the warrior angel appeared.

"Son of Earth, the test of the Air Element, the test of the mind, is crowned with victory."

"Is he right about my chances?"

"Yes."

I made no attempt to hide my frustration. "How come I found out from *him*?"

"The Dark Master sprang his trap to undermine your confidence in the Powers of Light. Only after you rebuked him could you learn the truth from me."

The old "Need to Earn your Own Way" rule. "What now?"

"The last ordeal is upon you, and the inner battle begins. The battle of courage against fear."

I nodded, though I was suddenly tired of fighting.

The angel made a circular gesture with his forefinger. The bronze doors swung open and pounded the external walls of the corridor. The flames leapt and shrank, burning with no visible source of fuel. Heat, drying my hands and cheeks, banished any notion the flames were illusory. They were alive all right, and they dared me to take them on, to run into the red-hot corridor, into the inferno.

I clamped my jaw and steadied my buckling knees, embarrassed to look scared in front of the angel.

"I take my leave. May you prove worthy and win."

The warrior angel disappeared and I was left alone. Alone with the swelter and the course of my destiny.

I bulldozed the fear out of the way, and put on the gloves and Kevlar ski mask. The goggles were gone and I had no time to look for them.

I took a tentative step forward.

*No you won't.* In a dizzying nanosecond, my survival instinct staked its claim to the body's preservation, took absolute control. My heartbeat charged, my pulse shaking my veins. My muscles throbbed with fresh energy, tightened, and contracted. A metallic tang deluged my mouth.

I pivoted on the balls of my feet.

Right before I retreated for the lake, I rallied the last fragments of my conscious will and hit the brakes. I turned toward the fire.

The Instinct unleashed the full force of its outrage, for yet again trying to shove it down. For yet again refusing to obey it.

My feet inched forward toward the lake.

I made them stop.

In response, a spasm rocked my body. All energy pulled away from my extremities, rushed to the solar plexus. My arms and legs gave up and I dropped to the ground.

I was paralyzed, couldn't even wiggle my toes. The Instinct had changed tactics. It compelled me to play dead so I didn't end up dead.

"Stop it. Let me go. I have a mission."

*I have my own mission. To save your hide.*

"There's a higher purpose, a higher law."

*Only one law counts, the law of self-preservation.*

I stared at the basalt ceiling with petrified eyes.

Isn't survival at the root of everything? Who was I to question countless years of primitive wisdom? Why should I reverse the laws of nature?

I felt the Instinct's approval but it didn't let up. It didn't trust.

A fleeting image out of nowhere showed up in my head.

I waved the image of Mataji away.

The image returned.

"Go away, you liar. Where's that bloody empowerment I'm supposed to have?"

The image didn't respond with words. Instead, a clear awareness emerged within my mind. Remembering the Mother of the World was exactly the empowerment I needed.

Resolve rose from the ruins of my mind, and then a whisper. "I take refuge in the Divine Embrace."

No progress. The Instinct's grip remained strong as ever.

I repeated the affirmation.

Nothing. I was still lying on my back, immobilized.

I recalled the vision of the Mother of the World and cried out the affirmation. "I take refuge in the Divine Embrace."

My fingertips and toes tingled. The grip of the Instinct slipped a notch.

I gasped, half-bending at the waist. I could move. I loaded the affirmation with the weight of my hopes, empowering it with my adoration for the Divine Feminine. "I take refuge in the Divine Embrace."

The return current of the Mother's perfect love transformed the energies of fear, retrieving my imprisoned free will, fragment by fragment.

I repeated the affirmation over and over.

The freeze response subsided and the Instinct, now tamed, submitted. More blood flowed to my stiff limbs, zinged nerve endings to activity. A measure of calmness returned.

Now I had to decide, consciously, that I would go through with the ordeal.

My muscles begged for a respite before the encounter. The emotional roller coaster had taken a heavy toll.

Precious minutes passed and I had little strength left.

I took whatever rest a few seconds could give and stumbled to my feet. I was a Master of Energy. I believed in the impossible. I could rise to the challenge. It was time to stop philosophizing and act.

My fingers fished out the ruby heart from my left chest pocket. I cradled it tightly in my palm, giving my full attention to Leah. I saw every detail of her face and figure, inhaled the scent of her perfume. I traced the periphery of her lips with longing fingertips, and felt her breath misting my chin. More than anything, I wanted to hold her in my arms, fly away from this cremation chamber.

I set aside the chimera and prepared to run.

*Flash.*

Leah, dressed in a white garment, stands outside a Grecian house. She is Cleomene, Spartan mother and wife. The terrible bidding every woman must give her husband before sending him off to war brings tears to her eyes. But she holds onto her proud composure.

She steps close to a man in armor and points to his shield. "A coward has no place in my bed, no abode in my home. Return with this shield or on it."

The man lays down his helmet, pulls her close, and kisses her hard on the mouth. Cleaving to each other's bodies, they exchange loving murmurs, taste for one last time the nectar of twin-soul bliss.

*Flash.*

A narrow stretch of land between a foothill and the sea. Bloodied bodies decompose under the midday sun. Her husband lies among them, skin cold and ashen, arrows through neck and thighs. The expression on his face defies death, shows the satisfaction that the loss of family and life was a worthy sacrifice.

Hard for me to believe. Yet that was the way of the Spartan warrior. I remembered now. I had done this before. I could do it again.

The heat in the cramped space wrenched me back to the present. Energy pulsations discharged from my crown with a rhythmic beat. A rising tide of fearlessness brought back much of my stamina.

I kissed the little heart, surrendering it to what must be.

It was a moment of single-minded clarity, miles above human reason. A moment when you transcend the limited sense of self. A moment when you banish all fear and doubt. A moment when you willingly offer all that you are to the greater cause.

"Go."

Still soaked, I harnessed the momentum of a short sprint and bolted head down into the furnace with the force of a battering ram.

The flames engulfed me, licked with scalding tongues, laughing at the dope who took on their dare.

I buried my face in the bend of my left arm, racing in a straight line, eyes closed.

Burning coffins, skeletons, and scythes streaked in succession within my head, deepening the cloying blindness, doing their best to sabotage my will.

I wiped them clean with a mental stroke, replaced them with a radiating, white-fire sun. I thought of the sun, high up on the sky of my mind, as the light at the end of the proverbial tunnel. The light that would soon greet me at the other side of the corridor.

Water and sweat drenching my clothes evaporated with a fizz, added steam to the conflagration. Heat discovered my skin.

I suppressed a howl and ran faster, hoping the corridor was short, designed by the ancient builder to test my courage, not guarantee my death.

*Whooosh.* The flames ignited my fatigues in a single burst.

Scorching sensations spread on my flesh. Pain rolled up and down in searing waves. A scream dashed through my lungs, mixed with the crackling cacophony of the fire. My eyes watered, my fingers splayed. The little heart went flying.

Panic attacked me with a sharp sword.

I dueled with it and won. I still had it in me to keep running, to resist.

A roar came from above. Through the skin of my eyelids, I saw a blaze flashing in my path. The flames grew thicker, formed blisters, feasted on my tissues, slowed my advance.

My lungs clumped, implored for air. My head spun. The power propelling my muscles dwindled.

I ignored the SOS signals, forced myself to pick up speed.

Pressure slammed my chest with such intensity, I was afraid it would crack my ribs. Smoke from the consumed clothes battered my nostrils, battled to break in. A ringing sound gyrated within my brain.

*Have to hold on till I get out of the corridor.*

A second later, I succumbed to the need for air, sucked in an involuntary breath. The inhale brought with it smoke, flaming shreds, the stench of charred meat. My nose hairs singed. The smoke and heat snaked down, suffocating me, boiling my insides as though I had drunk molten lead. I coughed, which made things worse. The white sun in my mind was sinking fast.

The lack of oxygen turned my legs to liquid and I tripped on my feet. My left shoulder collided with the rough wall. I lost my balance and plunged to the ground. My knees and palms broke the fall, held at first, then gave way. My chin smashed to the earth. Sharp pain dashed up my jawbones, reverberated through my skull.

The flames took advantage of the checkmate and went for the kill.

I had no grievance against the flames. They were doing their appointed job. Weeding out the unworthy, the weaklings, the fools. I just wanted them to make an exception. For me.

Petition denied.

*Have to push. Have to crawl on.*

My limbs felt beyond numb. I was flatlining.

I caught a glimpse of the vision of hope. The sun was missing, set behind a sea of blood.

A fresh spurt of adrenaline rushed out of a deep place. The survival instinct, which had tried to keep me out of here, was now on my side.

I dug into the hot, rocky floor. Muscles that still worked carried my body one foot forward.

Nails broke. Fingertips bled. The last trickles of my life force fled.

And another foot.

And another.

And then, I was out.

My heart clenched. My throat rattled. The top of my head buzzed. Time slowed as in suspended animation. The pain receded and the flames vanished.

I didn't know if the damage was illusory and the illusion was lifting, or if the damage was real and somehow I was being healed as a reward for surviving. It didn't matter.

After a moment, I leapt up. The cave was unevenly shaped and the largest of them all. Patches of mineral formations encrusted the rippled ceiling. Rock debris covered the floor. I saw no openings on the coarse walls.

A three-foot-tall gold chest rested against the back wall. On the side facing me, intricate symbols in bas-relief blended symmetrically with a knot-design motif. A miniature circular temple sat on the covering slab.

*The scroll.*

A surge of elation coursed through me. For the first time in twelve thousand years, human eyes, *my eyes*, would behold the Lost Name of God.

I glided effortlessly toward the chest and pushed the thin, dusty slab covering the chest.

My hands went right through.

*What the—*

I flew to the other side of the chest and pressed again. The cover didn't budge.

*This must be a mistake.*

I examined my translucent hands and my disbelief shifted closer to acceptance. No wonder the pain faded. I was having an out-of-body experience.

A quiver pulled my attention to a white energy field above me. The field shaped into a cylindrical tunnel extending upwards, right through the mass of the rocks. The white tunnel was sentient and it beckoned me to enter its mouth.

I willed my ethereal form to drift to the entrance of the cave. A naked body with deep burns lay prostrate on the ground. It was deserted and hollowed out, a car without a driver abandoned by the roadside.

I was dead. I had failed.

Whoever said death wasn't real must have been on drugs. I needed my body and I needed it *now*. I put everything on the line, fought the bad guys, passed the tests set before me. And right when I was ready to taste the fruits of my labor, I had to die.

I took another peek at the empty shell. "Blessed body, handiwork of God, incarnate temple of Divinity. How I wish I could animate your lifeless limbs."

With nothing to hold onto, I gave in to the grief dragging me away from the Light and into the great abyss. There was no escaping it this time. I was dead and my beloved was lost to me.

You think you know how much you love someone but you don't. Not until you can't talk to them or hear their voice. Not until your body feels rigid and cold to their touch.

"You are loved. You are worthy. You are powerful."

"Who said that?" I swept the cave for the source of the insult. Even as I discovered no one, I perceived the words came to me via telepathy by a benevolent being, waiting for me at the end of the white tunnel.

"Death is not real."

"It seems real enough to me."

"It is just the next step on—"

"*Please,* stop."

"It is just the next step on the timeless journey to eternity."

"Yes, yes, I know that. That's not my problem."

"Come."

"No. I want to see her, say goodbye."

Without waiting for permission, I thought of Leah and flooded her image with love. What's the worst he would do to me for disobeying? Kill me?

My ethereal body blasted through the rock walls and the intervening space, and in no time I floated behind Leah. She stood by a window of the sparsely furnished room at the temple compound. Her arms were crossed, fingertips clutching the sleeves of her beige pullover, teeth digging into her upper lip.

I could read her thoughts, experience her feelings. It was way too early for the helicopter to return and she knew it. Still, she surveyed the horizon, listening for the sound of the rotors.

A dog's wail ripped the agitated silence.

"Leah, I'm here."

No response, not even a tiny, intuitive nod.

I lowered myself right behind her and stroked her hair with my airy hand. "Leah, look at me."

She wheeled around, teetering as though the wooden floor had shifted under her legs.

"I'm here."

She stared right through me with dazed eyes. Her body heaved. Unshackled sobs broke out.

She knew.

"Goodbye, my darling love, I failed you again. Forgive me."

Dark feelings surrounded me, lashed me with steel whips, carving soul wounds so deep no time could ever heal. "Leah, I'll come back. I'll find you in the next life. Nothing will stop me, I swear. I'll hold you, kiss you, love you. We'll watch the sunset every day. We'll raise our red-haired boy and dark-haired girl. We'll grow old together."

Leah wiped her tears away.

I chose to believe she heard me and understood. To accept she was unaware was unbearable. Worse than death.

I brushed her cheek with the back of my hand, pretended I could feel the texture of her skin. I savored the imagined sensation. I wanted to never forget it, take it with me to the Other Side.

"I have to go now. . . . I love you. Forever."

Something in Leah shifted. She straightened her back and raised her chin high. She was the Spartan wife again, and this time around she wouldn't surrender to the Fates. She wouldn't give up her man without a fight.

I rolled my unearthly eyes. That stubbornness was one of the many reasons I loved her.

Her knees sank to the floor. Hands rose in supplication. Her aura flared, spread in the room, a wildfire in a field of dry wheat.

"*God Almighty, Elohim Savaoth, El Elyon, rescue* him." Her voice was soft. Yet no cannonade could have drowned it out. No thunder. No tumult out of hell. Nothing. Nothing could overcome the voice of a twin soul charged with the invincible power of Timeless Love.

A column of pink light erupted over Leah and surged through the ceiling toward the sky, sucking me with it.

And I hurt!

All my limbs regained feeling, lungs drawing in stale air faster than panting dogs. I was lying face down, nose and cheeks pressing on rock shards. Every inch of my body screamed in pain. The walls of my throat were dry-caked shut. But I would cut my tongue before I complained, before I let anything dam up the swelling river of gratitude and all-consuming victory.

I was alive.

It didn't matter if Leah's prayer rescued me. It didn't matter if the benevolent being would send me back after we chatted in some celestial palace. It didn't matter if I had just witnessed a miracle. I cared only that I was alive and I could still make a difference. Spend *this* life with Leah. Honor my Master.

Life Supreme, I would exalt you.

Cherish each grain of time in the hourglass of your dreams.

Grow gentle flowers from the seeds of your sorrows.

Eat to the last morsel the manna of your joys.

I will love, I will serve, I will Be.

I slowly, painfully pulled off the Kevlar ski mask, hoping my skin wouldn't peel off with it. It didn't. I rolled on my back to take inventory of the damage. Thank God, I had no broken bones. My body still felt like a toe hit by an anvil, but I could function.

"Son of Earth, you have done well," the warrior angel said. "I salute you and your beloved, in the name of Timeless Love."

The happiness of seeing the stern face again soothed the pain a bit. And that was when I realized I didn't even have a leaf to cover my nakedness. Except for the boots and the mask, every piece of clothing had burned away.

"Thank you, thank you. You don't happen to have any burn cream?"

"I will grant something better."

The angel drew the sword from the scabbard with his right hand, pointed it at me, and touched his heart with the left. An emerald-green ray shot from the tip of the sword and grew into a spinning spiral that wrapped my body from head to toe. With every round, the healing energy restored the flesh and alleviated the pain.

The spiral completed its perfect work and I witnessed my regeneration from the ashes of suffering, a phoenix at the moment of rebirth.

I climbed to my feet, brought my hands together, and bowed low.

The angel acknowledged my reverence with a slight bow of his own. "All glory belongs to God."

"Amen."

He stepped closer. "Son of Earth, you have passed the tests of the four elements. The feat bestows upon you the privilege of harnessing their power, as long as your purpose is unselfish and your heart pure." He fastened his fierce gaze into my eyes, read my Soul. "Listen well. I now impart to you the seed syllables of the four elements and the invocation."

The secret knowledge was imprinted in my consciousness with a branding iron.

"Wait," I said. "Did I defeat Death?"

"You have mastered the *fear* of death, a great step forward. Much work remains before you conquer the Son of Night."

"Whatever it takes."

"Time is short. The scroll awaits, as do your adversaries."

I watched the warrior angel fade away. Who was he talking about? Arashi? The Dark Master? The Chinese? Something I hadn't seen yet?

Well, I'd worry about these threats later.

I crossed the space to the golden chest and placed my hands, my beautiful hands, my hands of flesh and blood, on the slab. *One. Two. Three. Push.*

It didn't dislodge. Weight was not the issue. It was locked.

My fingers latched onto the short edge of the rectangular slab and pressed again. "C'mon, I'm on the side of the angels."

I was missing something.

I took a deep breath. Less adrenaline, more self-control. I paced around the chest, tapping my temples. The number four.

Four letters in the password. Four elements to master. Four symbols of the elements carved in the first cave—triangle, circle, crescent moon, and square, from left to right. Four main tests in four caves. And, four seed syllables, one for each element.

I intoned the four syllables in the order of the symbols in the first cave. The sound boomeranged and mixed with the slab's quaver.

I pressed again. Nothing.

The cover shook, though, so I was on the right track. Just doing something wrong, something was out of order.

The tablet with the Atlantean characters. I had pushed down the letters of the password from right to left.

I spoke the seed syllables, beginning with that of the Earth Element.

The clanking sound of the unlocking slab serenaded my ears. It was a sound of triumph. With a scrape of gold on gold, I lowered the cover to the ground.

Shining yellow light escaped, flooding the space with brilliance. It was as though a miniature sun had risen in the midst of the cave.

A leather tube with a carrying strap lay at the bottom of the chest. I snatched it and planted a kiss.

Energy shot through my fingers and lips, caused my body to resonate like a tuning fork. I slung the tube over my shoulder, not letting the shaking stop me from breaking into a run. This wasn't the time for a victory lap.

Of course, I had no idea if I was late for my helicopter rendezvous with Kesang. The flames had ruined my watch, and my body clock had shut down for an undetermined time. One-third of the way into the empty corridor, I picked up the ruby heart from the ground. I sent my love to the purifying Fire. I entered the next cavern through the open bronze doors and sent my love to the life-giving Air. Into the lake and under the passageway to the grotto. I sent my love to the rejuvenating Water.

"Hey, cute hallucination, you still here?"

Nope. Onward through the narrow tunnel, down the snake rope and into the square cavern. I grabbed my coat and threw it over my dripping birthday suit. I sent my love to the grounding Earth.

I crossed through the open entryway into the last cave, newly forged phoenix wings fluttering, ready to soar to freedom.

I was about to sprint all the way out when a vision of horror in the distance froze me in my tracks. The slain Red Scorpions in their khaki fatigues, now upright and halfway alive, had just barged into the cave. Mouths still frozen open, sepulchral grunts spewing out of their throats, they moved with clumsy motions, life-size marionettes being pulled by strings.

I clutched the tube and prepared for evasive maneuvers.

The zombified Red Scorpions spread out and continued their robotic march.

I gave myself kudos for keeping a cool head, and for almost effortlessly fighting back the chills.

Rumbles from the bowels of the cave, mixing with a distant mechanical sound, vibrated through the ground and across the walls. I didn't need a degree in geology to know the cave was collapsing.

The Red Scorpions closed in.

I charged to their left to steer clear.

Acting as one body, they blocked my path.

I swiveled just in time to avoid them and kept running toward the square cavern. My plan was to climb back up to the tunnel and pull the rope. I'd rather get buried alive than get captured.

The familiar sound from behind me brought with it a surge of hope.

Without stopping, I craned my neck. "What took you so long?"

The warrior angel lifted his blazing sword and swung it from left to right, pointing above their heads. The Red Scorpions toppled to the ground. The sword had cut the invisible strings that gave them dark life.

I turned around, humbled at such display of the power of Light. "I love you, blessed angel, I owe you so much."

"Farewell, Son of Earth."

"Don't you worry. As soon as I reach Varanasi, I'll sacrifice a nice fat goat for you."

Finally, *finally*, he cracked a tiny smile that somehow fanned the elongated, blue flame on his brow.

The stench of sulfur suffocated me. I held my breath and raced to the entryway of the cave, sidestepping the infernal remains.

I sensed the wrath of the Dark Master rising, clawing at me. I gave him the two-fingered victory sign, just to rub it in.

The din of helicopter rotors grew louder.

This had better be Kesang. I wasn't in the mood to learn the details of the water-dungeon torture.

# Chapter 16

**12:11 p.m., Day 6, Outside the Secret Cave**

The beat of rotors flooded the entryway of the cave. I flattened my back against the rock wall and examined the helicopter hovering right above ground, forty feet away.

It was familiar. Kesang.

I didn't allow relief to slow my revved-up muscles and darted through the snow toward the open door. The wind had stopped, and the midday sun reigned over the mountain range.

I squinted against the glare and gulped the fresh air, not minding that it burned my throat. I climbed into the helicopter, slammed the door shut, and secured the harness. Kesang pulled up quickly enough to press me into my seat and then turned southwest toward the Indian border.

I set the tube down and rubbed my hands to get warm. Exhaustion sank my body down. I would have given anything for a dry, double shot cappuccino.

A sound drew my attention back to the hillside. A cloud of dust coming out of the entrance of the cave rose skyward. The cave's jaws had snapped shut forever.

I couldn't wait to return to Leah and to America. I would miss neither the cave nor the lunar terrain, but I would never forget the warrior angel.

Kesang passed me the headset and I slipped it on. "What happened to you? You're butt naked."

"Water."

He handed me a plastic bottle of water and a blanket. "Looks like you had some fun in there. Tell me everything."

I wrapped the wool blanket around my legs, chugged the entire bottle, and gave Kesang the cell-phone-texting version of events.

"*Man,*" Kesang said. "Better than watching the Dallas Cowboys play in Super Bowl. Can't wait to tell the story to my kids."

"You waited, Kesang. . . . You're a Brother."

Kesang reached into a green duffel bag, dug out a piece of flat bread, and broke it in half. "Here. Let's celebrate your survival and the return of the scroll over balep."

I took a bite. "Mmmm. What is it?"

"Tibetan barley bread with a touch of cinnamon. Baked by the tender hands of my long-suffering wife."

"Really? What's her name?"

"Nima."

"I bet she's your twin soul."

"Who knows?"

"You really love her, don't you?" I asked.

"I adore her."

"Me too."

"My wife?"

I didn't have enough strength to reach over and whack the back of his neck. "*You* know who."

"Good thing you clarified. I almost challenged you to a duel."

"I'd never fight you without my pants on. It'd be too intimidating."

Kesang's booming laughter could have easily caused an avalanche. "You win."

I watched the snowy peaks and shadowed ravines racing below, imagining how happy Leah would be to see me alive. How she'd blush when I touched her hand. How it would feel when I collected on that kiss. . . .

"You waiting for a parade?" Kesang asked. "Check out the scroll."

I reached for the leather tube when a pop of gunshots made itself known over the din of the propellers.

The image of a dead soldier from the war I lived through as a child, stomach riddled with bullets, crisscrossed through my head. But I brought that memory under control. I was done with fearing my past.

Kesang let out a guttural sound that must have been a Tibetan expletive.

I searched for the attacking chopper behind us. "We hit?"

"Warning shots," Kesang answered through clenched teeth. "They want us to land, but that's not going to happen." He pulled the stick and the helicopter, already moving fast, slapped me back into my seat.

"I know their patrol choppers," Kesang said. "This baby is *way* faster."

Another round of rattling gunshots.

By some miracle, we weren't hit and kept pulling ahead of our pursuers. Then something flared on the faraway, Chinese chopper. A coiling trail of smoke zoomed through the sky.

"Damn," Kesang said, "incoming."

"Enemy projectile within range," a male electronic voice said. "Enemy projectile within range." *Taa. Taa. Taa.*

The head of the smoke trail grew to a missile. Ten seconds, at best, before it hit our helicopter. Newfound courage and all, my heart was running faster than the throttled-up engine.

Kesang kept tight hands on the stick, eyes unblinking. The bulging veins on his temples had turned purple.

A red beam shot out from below our helicopter.

The missile jerked, veered off to the right in short, erratic movements.

"*Yes.*" Kesang threw his head back. "Wish I could see their faces."

My heartbeat slowed down. "We good?"

"Almost out of range. They'll never catch up with us."

"Nicely done," I said.

"Thanks. Now about that scroll?"

"Roger that."

I grabbed the tube, pulled the cap off, and reached in. As soon as I touched the ancient parchment, a jolt of electric energy went up my arm. My spine tingled. My crown chakra swirled.

I took deep breaths. When I sensed my energy field had adjusted to the currents of the scroll, I drew it out. I traced the ivory parchment with my index finger, absorbing its holiness, longing to recover its ancient secret, preparing to behold the Lost Name of God.

Excitement mixed with awe welled up inside me, as I unrolled the scroll.

It was blank.

I dropped the scroll onto my lap. "No. Bloody. Way."

"What's wrong?"

I ran my hands over my head, each breath now a struggle. "It's blank. No words. No name. No nothing."

Kesang didn't respond.

Mounting unease licked the small of my neck with a cold tongue. Had the Lost Name faded over time? Was Master Theo off the mark? Did the scroll conceal yet a deeper mystery? Was Earth doomed if I couldn't figure it out?

I put the scroll back and placed the tube on the floor, the possibilities weighing down my Soul.

*Don't give up. Take control of your mind.*

I forced myself to get a grip, function as a Master of Energy.

"There's always something we can do," Kesang said. "Maybe Mataji will—*hold on.*"

The helicopter nose-dived.

"Evacuate craft," the electronic voice said. "Evacuate craft."

*Taa. Taa. Taa.*

My body lunged forward. Were it not for my harness, I'd now be going through the windshield, heading for the rocky slopes of Tibet.

The engine sputtered, and it suddenly got a lot quieter than I liked. The altimeter spiraled down.

I clutched the handhold to my right with both hands, pressed my boots to the floor.

Kesang wrestled with the controls on the dashboard, hands moving in all directions as though they battled invisible foes.

It did us no good. The helicopter plummeted with the accelerating velocity of a falling bird that was shot dead.

*Taa. Taa. Taa.*

Pity the last earthly sound I'd take with me to the Other Side was the red alert.

"Bullet in the tank," Kesang said. "I'm hoping I can tilt it enough to—"

Just before we hit the ground, or so it seemed, Kesang hit a switch. The engine growled, then roared. The rotors came alive. The helicopter rose with an elliptical maneuver forward, and leveled off.

"We've got a couple of minutes flying time," Kesang said, wiping the sweat off his forehead with the back of his hand, gaze locked straight ahead. "We land now or we die."

"You know my choice."

Kesang pointed to the nearby hillside. "There. That tiny village. The locals will protect us, I'm sure. I'll blend in and you hide. Your face would stick out like a white bull among the yak."

"Whatever you say. I'm the foreigner here."

The helicopter swerved to the right, plunged toward the earth. The cluster of small houses perched on the hillside drew closer. Thick snow pressed down on their flat roofs. Strings of prayer flags fluttered in the wind. The village was quaint, but it was no Shangri-La.

Kesang brought the helicopter down three hundred feet away from the edge of the village. The skids landed hard against the frozen ground. Seconds later, the engine died again.

"Keep the wireless," Kesang said, handing me a sealed metal box. "We'll radio for help when we're safe."

I reached for the box and slung its strap across my shoulder next to the tube with the scroll. Kesang walked to the back of the cockpit, flipped a square suitcase open, and turned on a switch.

*Tick. Tick. Tick. Tick.* The red numbers on a screen inside the box dropped in step with the hair-raising sound. Fifty-nine. Fifty-eight. Fifty-seven. Fifty-six.

I kicked the door open and jumped out.

The snow reached up to my knees. A chilly headwind blasted my cheeks and bare legs. A daze almost took over my brain. But thanks to my survival instinct, adrenaline gave my boots wings.

I charged toward the village, holding onto my blanket. Kesang followed right behind me.

*Boooom.*

The explosion shoved me to the ground, burying my face in the snow. A stabbing pain tore through my eardrums. My hands flew up to cover my head from the flying debris.

After the rock chips stopped pelting my body, Kesang scuttled over and helped me up. The stench of burned diesel and oil filled the mountainside. Billowing black plumes of smoke mixed with the steam of the melting snow. The helicopter had turned to a pile of metal rubble and fire.

Kesang and I struggled on until we reached the village. A small crowd of men had gathered on the road, staring at me with the curiosity of children examining an exotic animal. I was apparently the first half-naked white man to visit their village.

A wiry man, slouching under the load of his long life, motioned us to stop. The old man wore an animal-skin coat and a fur hat that reached over his ears. His blotchy skin showed through his thin white beard. Deep wrinkles carved his face.

Kesang shook the ice off his hair, bowed his head, and brought his hands together in salutation.

Nostrils flaring, the old man returned the greeting, then proceeded to chew up Kesang.

Kesang tried to speak, but the old man wouldn't let him. I followed the old man's wagging finger and understood. Our arrival explosion had broken most of the windows in the village.

No matter how many times Kesang bowed his head, I could tell from the old man's tone he wouldn't budge. I didn't dare interrupt lest I violated some local protocol, even though I knew the choppers that had been following us would catch up fairly soon.

The minutes ticked on and I was about to start screaming at both of them myself when I realized that I knew about the windows because I could hear the old man's thoughts in my head. I focused my gaze on the old man's third eye and his scrambled thoughts became clear. Coming back from the dead in the cave must have changed my brain wiring so that I could now read minds.

"Give him cash," I whispered to Kesang, "for the windows. He wants to look good in front of his people."

"I don't want to offend him."

"Just offer it. Trust me. He'll never admit he wants money, but that's what he wants."

Kesang produced a stack of American dollars secured with a rubber band and offered it to the old man with a deep bow.

I was right. The old man's fierce eyes softened. Still. He didn't back down.

"Keep handing it to him. He's playing hard to get."

The old man checked me out.

*Come on. Take it. It's only fair, after the damage we did.*

His smile revealed tobacco-stained teeth and his acceptance of the peace offering. He stuffed the money in his coat pocket and bent over until his forehead touched Kesang's.

Kesang rattled something off.

The old man nodded and barked what seemed to be his orders to the other men.

I grabbed Kesang's shoulder. "What's the plan?"

"We hide. The Chinese will show up any minute."

We ran to the back of the village stable.

Kesang pointed to a round lid on the ground under a wooden canopy. "Quick. Hide in the well."

"You sure?"

"If you run, they'll follow your footprints."

"How 'bout our footprints to the village?"

"See those guys? They're walking to the helicopter and back. They'll say they looked for survivors and found none. Pray the soldiers believe we died in the blast."

The soldiers would see no footprints coming to the well. The villagers had shoveled the snow off the path.

Kesang lifted the wooden lid and I handed him my blanket.

"Go down," he said. "I still have to get this flight suit off."

I lowered myself into the rock-built well, my feet reaching for the dug-out steps of its wall. Past cobwebs and mustiness wafting up my nostrils, I descended into the earth. Kesang shut the lid over me and all went dark.

I kept my feet in the footholds of the wall in front of me, and with the tube and wireless on my back, pushed against the wall behind me. My lips had dried up and the hairs of my legs had turned to tiny icicles. Stinging sensations blanketed my skin, as though needles poked through the flesh down to the bone. With every passing second, my tissues constricted. I recognized the symptoms. I was freezing to death.

*Thermoplasis. Try thermoplasis.*

I visualized my body transform into a balloon of white light with a yellow flame burning at its base. My breath locked into a rhythmic pattern.

*In. I am magnetizing the sacred fire.*
*Hold. I am absorbing the sacred fire.*
*Out. I am magnifying the sacred fire.*
*Hold. I am radiating the sacred fire.*

Nothing. The cold gained ground.

I fueled the flame with my desire to live and saw it expand until it filled the mental balloon. Heat embraced my feet, travelled to all my extremities. The quivering of my legs stopped and now I could feel my toes. A strange peace came over me and for a moment I forgot where I was.

The distant sound of helicopter blades reminded me.

I yanked the shreds of my attention back to my third eye and rebuilt the image of the yellow fire and the balloon. The heat returned and I lost all sense of time, each passing minute an eternity being lived in a parallel universe. . . .

A pandemonium of muffled sounds now reached my ears. Yelling. Banging doors. Bleating animals.

Heavy footsteps approached.

I climbed further down the well until I sank under water, mind clear and calm as if I had the situation under control. The morning ordeals had trained me well.

Just in time. Someone lifted the lid.

I kept still.

A beam of light shone down.

I imagined myself invisible.

The beam moved around.

My lungs burned, demanded air.

I ordered them to wait.

The lid dropped back in place. Footsteps marched away.

*Phew.* I went up to the surface, mouth pulling in the musty air in deep gulps. The cold struck again, sent shivers through my body. I countered it with another round of thermoplasis. . . .

Daylight came through the open lid.

"Hey, you alive?" Kesang asked.

"For the most part. What's going on?"

"They left. We're clear."

I climbed out, water dripping down my legs. It wouldn't be long before it turned to ice. "Anyone get hurt?"

"No. Give me the wireless."

"It's wet."

"No worries, it's waterproof."

I passed over the metal box.

"I'll call up the cavalry," Kesang said. "They should come for us within an hour."

# Chapter 17

Kesang's message to the Intelligence Bureau had taken care of everything. They sent a helicopter that carried us back to Varanasi without incident. They even brought me new fatigues and boots. Within minutes, I would be meeting Mataji. And Leah. And we could figure out what to do with the scroll.

The helicopter touched down in the center of the temple compound, sending gales of dust through the yard. I reached for Kesang's shoulder. "I owe you big time."

His rough hand capped my own. "Save the world, and we'll be even."

I stepped out, eyes scanning for Leah. Strange she didn't come in the yard to greet me. Maybe she felt shy after our failed attempt to kiss. Or she was resting. Or she planned a surprise. I couldn't wait to find out.

The helicopter took off. A nun, unfazed by the flying dust and the noise, signaled me to come. I ran toward the main door of the temple.

The nun bowed. "Her Holiness is expecting you in her private quarters."

"Thank you." I made my way to the left and up the wooden staircase to the second floor. I struck the brass door knocker once and waited.

"Come in."

I threw the door open and rushed in. "Your Holiness, I have the—"

Everything looked the same as the night before—the oriental furniture, the marble statue of the Mother of the World, and Mataji in her silk white sari. Except for one thing.

I tightened my lips, strove for control. "Where is she?"

"Arashi kidnapped her," Mataji said, her tone slow and grave. "He wants to exchange her for the scroll."

The words passed through my ears into the center of my brain, and exploded one by one. My blood boiled, threatening to singe my veins. "Must be a mistake. Has to be. I saw her in the guest room when I was out of my body. She was waiting for me."

Mataji held out a hand to me.

I didn't take it. "What happened?"

"They played on her benevolence and she was tricked. She left the compound to visit an orphanage a block away. Just before I came back from Agra."

I took a heavy step closer to Mataji. "She promised me she wouldn't leave the compound."

"It was one of the nuns," Mataji said, her gaze holding me. "She told Leah I had given my permission for a short visit and—"

"And that it'd be great to visit with the children and bring a little joy to their lives . . . I can't believe she was so stupid."

"We all have weaknesses," Mataji said, "no matter how spiritually advanced we think we are."

"Even you?"

"Even me. . . . Observe yourself now, for example. Surely you can sense the primal anger coming off your protective instinct."

"You're right, Your Holiness. Forgive me."

"The nun was instructed well. She tempted Leah using the softest spot in her heart—her love for disadvantaged children. And Leah could not resist."

"There's another reason she let her guard down. She was all too happy for saving me." I pulled the collar of my shirt as though it had become an assassin's garrote. "How did you find out?"

"The nun confessed everything. They told her they would kill her father if she failed to cooperate, and that they would not hurt Leah."

"I can't believe it. Who are 'they'?"

"Arashi's thugs."

"The chieftain. He'll pay too."

"Arashi demands that you go to the old Surya fort at 6:00 p.m. Just you or he will kill her."

I took the tube off my shoulder and placed it on the table to my right. "You keep the scroll, Your Holiness. I'm going after her right now. Take it to America if I don't come back. Master Theo will figure out a way to discover the Name."

"What do you mean?"

How could I have forgotten to mention this? "The scroll is blank."

Mataji walked over, picked up the tube, and closed her eyes. After a moment, she said, "It is no use giving it to me or any-one else. Only the rightful owner of the scroll can unveil its secret."

"And that would be me," I said through shallow gulps of air. "Great."

"It takes half an hour to reach the Surya fort from here. You have forty-five minutes to make your choice."

"What should I do? I can't betray her."

"I love her like my child, but I cannot decide for you, Diokles."

"Mother, *please*."

"There is a divine solution to every human problem. Whatever your choice, you have my unconditional support. If you decide to face Arashi, I will provide a Land Rover. If you decide to return to America, a helicopter will take you back to your plane at the military base." Mataji pulled the hanging folds of her sari and headed for the door. "The Light has accomplished great things through you already. I know you will do the right thing now."

"Thank you."

She shut the door, leaving me alone. Alone with the empty room and a choking sense of despair.

I scanned the surroundings once again. The room now felt like a cage. Except for a chorus of humming crickets, the compound had somehow fallen silent. I dragged my body to the nearby couch.

Sacrifice the woman I loved for the sake of duty? Or try to rescue her and risk losing the scroll and causing the death of untold lives?

I hid my face behind my palms, as if taking cover in the darkness would spare me from making a choice. No help came my way. Instead, a primal fire burning inside gathered force and my protective instinct took over the reins of my consciousness. My lips twitched, my muscles tensed. I wanted to bite something off. Break bones. Destroy anyone who stood in my path.

Then my Instinct spoke. *I will find her. Save her. She's mine. The most prized member of my clan. I don't give a damn about the world. Only a coward deserts his woman.*

I jumped to my feet.

And as quickly sat back down.

*Whoa!* I couldn't let the Instinct possess me. Bringing the scroll to America as soon as possible was the only option available to me. I had a job to do. I had taken a vow. As much as it pained me, as much as it tortured me, as much as it caused me to hate myself, I had to give her up. For the sake of humanity.

*What? You traitor. No. No. No.*

My Instinct was right. I couldn't abandon her. She had saved my life. And I loved her. I loved her. I loved her. I *should* try to rescue her from Arashi's claws.

But what if Arashi took me out? He wouldn't take any chances this time. Maybe that's why he had disappeared—he was plotting and building up his dark powers. Making sure he would be ready for me. I didn't care if I died. Except, he'd keep Leah *and* the scroll. And the Dark Master would win.

What did I love most? What *should* I love most? My woman or my duty?

The dilemma tore me apart. A stupor settled over me. My limbs became numb.

The minutes kept ticking by. I had to think clearly. I had to act. I cradled my temples and willed the mental fog away. I would take the scroll to America. Save the planet.

My Instinct rebelled. With a groan and a new adrenaline rush, it demanded I get off my butt and charge through the door to find Leah. Now.

I pictured her captive, locked up in a cold cell at the lair of the Red Scorpions in Nepal. How would I ever get her out of there? Arashi would never bring her to the Surya fort. He'd never keep his end of the bargain. But if I didn't show up, I'd be signing her death warrant.

But maybe Arashi wouldn't harm Leah after all. In his own twisted way, he loved her too. Maybe as much as I did. Or more. If *he* had to choose between Leah and anything else, he wouldn't hesitate for one second. No. I wasn't worried about *him*. The grave danger came from the Dark Master. He would strangle her with his own hands just to punish my insolence. To keep his evil promise. To laugh at my expense.

I was a fool to have listened to her. I should have made her go back to Master Theo while I could. It was all my fault.

I took the ruby heart out my pocket and as I squeezed it in my palm, I remembered what she had said in Washington, just two days ago. *I'll never forgive you if you compromise the mission for my sake. You have to sacrifice everything to get the scroll.*

Leah. Everything was coming together so perfectly for us. Why did you have to be so dumb? So stubborn? Why didn't you listen to me? You rich, spoiled brat. You—

I stood up and hurled the little gemstone against the wall. It broke in two and so did my heart.

I searched the floor like a maniac until I located one of the pieces. I picked it up with trembling fingers and kissed it. Where the hell was the other one? I kept looking. Was my failure to find it a sign of losing her forever, no matter which choice I made?

Come on. Since when did I believe in superstition?

I sat back on the couch, locked my hands behind my neck. I needed to get my act together. Make my decision. I was a Master of Energy, trained to put service to life above my personal interest. To sacrifice. To give my all for mankind.

It was no use. The usual platitudes weren't working. I couldn't imagine life without her. And I couldn't shake off the burden of my terrible responsibility. I was stuck.

I looked at the statue of the Mother of the World, hoping some of its holiness would permeate my Soul, illumine me, tell me what to do.

No such luck.

Then, out of the distant blue, visions of terror blinded me, visions of a post-apocalyptic world—sinking continents, mountains of bodies, throngs of screaming children.

I was being selfish. I would do my duty and take the scroll to America. Defeat Death, speak the Name, and come for Leah afterward.

The Instinct pounded the walls of my gut. I shoved it down into a dark cave of my subconscious and ordered it to quiet down.

I stood, pushing back the oncoming tears. The matter was settled and I no longer had the luxury of indulging in human weakness. Didn't I know better than most that we are more than flesh and blood? Had I not been taught the Light is invincible and always prevails?

I had barely found my balance when a tingling sensation raced around my head, activated my crown. A force, far greater than any conscious control I could exert, pushed me back to the couch, straightened my spine. My breath accelerated. My eyelids shut.

With my inner sight, I now saw an energy disc form around my waist, parallel to the floor, a sort of spinning blue-white Tai Chi. The force flowing through me intensified, compelling the disc to whirl clockwise at an incredible speed.

A sudden energy jolt pushed me further into the cushions and my ethereal body soared toward the stars. I saw the golden staircase and floated to its base. Clad in my glowing purple cape, I walked up the steps until I beheld my Timeless Self standing on the celestial platform in the fullness of his splendor.

A translucent five-pointed star rested behind him. A soft yellow glow came off his long garment, and the white halo behind his head emitted needle-like rays in all directions. A jewel-studded golden grail, liquid fire showing above the rim, flashed in his right hand.

I knelt before the Timeless Self and clasped my hands in supplication.

"The time has come for a union with me far greater than before," he said, his voice of thunder rippling through the heavenly firmament. "Do you accept?"

"I do."

"So be it. The sacred fire shall regenerate your being."

He tipped the grail, and a torrent of liquid white fire reached the top of my head.

Surging spirals of energy stormed up and down my ethereal form, transmuting foci of negativity, raising my vibrational frequency, restoring divine perfection.

An angel reached for the empty grail and took it away. The Timeless Self opened his arms. "Arise and come to me."

I stood up and stepped near him.

"Rejoice, O Universe, I and my son are one this day. His presence is my Presence. His word is my Word. His power is my Power."

His arms closed around me. The Light in his heart burst. A blazing white sphere engulfed us, all form dissolving in the fervent heat of the Divine Embrace.

The veil of the Great Forgetfulness was torn asunder forever. All sorrow and sense of struggle melted away in a molten sea of ecstatic bliss. At last, Spirit and matter had fused, and neither would be the same ever again. . . .

"Go to her, Beloved," the Timeless Self said. "Go, rescue the one you love. I now clear the way for your perfect victory." The elongated yellow flame in the center of his brow flared. "Henceforth, look to me for all your needs. And remember always—you are Fire out of Fire, you are Life out of Life, you *are* Myself."

Still burning from head to toe with his sacred essence, I beamed my consciousness down to Earth and back into my body in Mataji's quarters. An exhilarating familiarity with the ecstatic state I had just experienced possessed me, as if I were not experiencing something new but finally noticing something that had been there all along. It was as if I had returned from a long exile to the court of my father, the king, who restored my birthright as a servant son. Gave me command of his armies of Light. Sent me out to his kingdom to relieve suffering in his Name.

The statue of the Mother of the World seemed to smile at me, and I knew she too wanted to rejoice in my victory, congratulate me for passing my test and receiving the Baptism by Fire—the second of the Deeper Mysteries.

I leapt off the couch to search for Mataji and prepare for the coming encounter.

# CHAPTER 18

**6:03 p.m., Day 6, Ruins of Surya Fort, Thirty Miles NW of Varanasi**

I brought the Land Rover to a stop right in front of the massive stone archway of the Surya fort, scanning for the slightest movement around me, listening for the faintest sound, ready to leap to action.

I got out, the leather tube with the scroll on my back. A black Hummer was parked nearby. Mostly intact red-sandstone walls enclosed the deserted Surya fort on all sides, a perfect setting for a trap. I paused to check for any signs of life. All was sepulcher-still.

"Timeless Self, take command, get me out of here alive," I whispered.

My crown chakra throbbed.

*Thank you.*

I crossed through the archway, the echo of my boots on the winding cobblestone path the only sound. Crumbling structures and broken pillars littered the vast courtyard. Monuments of the distant past, they had surrendered their glory to weeds and ruin.

I advanced in short, resolute strides until I spotted a man clad in black standing before the north wall. The setting sun, bathing the grounds in dusk shadows, cast an eerie glow on his handsome face. A woman sat on the ground next to him, tied up and gagged.

Leah. Only forty feet now separated us.

A part of me wanted to run over and beat Arashi unconscious with my fists. But reason prevailed and I forced myself to remain reasonably composed. Self-control always worked out better in the end.

"You're late," Arashi said, spreading his feet wide, his voice a whip lashing a lazy servant.

"You brought her."

"How else would she witness your defeat?"

Leah was trying to say something through the gag. I could hear some of her thoughts within my head but couldn't make out what they were. It would have been unwise to take my eyes off Arashi and concentrate on her third eye.

"Pray you didn't harm her."

Arashi's lipless mouth warped to an ironic smile. "What if I did?"

"Arashi, do the right thing. Let her go."

"Put down the scroll and I'll let you leave unharmed."

I took a step forward. "Stop denying who you really are. *Just stop.* Don't send billions of people to their deaths so you can get what you want like a stubborn two-year-old. You can still turn to the Light."

He didn't blink, he didn't look away. Yet a shade of melancholy behind his eyes betrayed the inner struggle.

The cry of a monkey pierced the air, mournful and desolate as the lament of a mother watching the last dirt clods fall over her child's coffin.

"I'm not about to quit at the moment of my triumph," Arashi said.

"It won't be a triumph. It won't make you happy. I'm begging you. Do the right thing."

"For the last time, put down the scroll."

"Molon labe."

"What?"

"Come and take it."

"Your puny powers won't save you this time. I have the crystal red scorpion from the high altar of the Dark Master."

I leveled my chin and straightened my back. I was ready for battle.

Leah kept trying to break free to no avail.

Arashi dug out a dagger from the brown leather satchel hanging at his side and sliced his left palm with a swift cut. He threw the dagger away, stretched his palm forward, and spun counterclockwise in measured movements. Blood gushed to the ground, making a red circle around him. He then pulled a statuette of an attacking scorpion from the satchel, centered it in his hand, and let more blood drip on it. Harsh, throaty words spewed out of his mouth.

I raised a portion of my consciousness to the celestial plane and allowed myself to feel safe and secure in the arms of the Timeless Self. My third eye stirred and now I could see two red beams shoot forward from the crystal scorpion's eyes. The beams converged into one and struck the ground halfway between Arashi and me, a spherical energy mist forming out of its tip. The outline of a figure took shape in the center of the swirling mist. Absorbing the energy surrounding it, the figure swelled and turned into a giant silver-and-red scorpion. Vertical slivers of fire burned within the hollow, infernal pits that were its eyes. Its scaly frame writhed. Its pincers clicked open and shut.

The evil energy creature examined me. Dark riptides pummeled my body.

The scorpion raised its tail and snapped it back and forth. A swarm of red globules spilled out of its stinger. The swarm soared toward me, each globule turning into a little red scorpion as it approached.

"Sorry to see you go," Arashi said. "You were beginning to grow on me."

I couldn't tell if he was genuinely regretful or just sarcastic, though I was hoping for the former. Then I had to concentrate all my efforts on keeping my emotions under control, providing a suitable vessel for the power from above.

The flying scorpions grew bigger and were seconds away from stinging my body when a river of white light cascaded over me. The white light instantly turned into a cylinder, extending five feet all around. One by one, the scorpions collided with the scintillating energy cylinder, exploding like tiny fireworks.

I released a breath I hadn't realized I was holding and sent up a quick prayer of gratitude.

The giant scorpion charged, pincers open.

Five words flared before my line of vision—*I AM that I AM.* I seized them with my mind and saw them expand to a height of one foot. Then, I quickly exhaled and visualized the words gliding with the air current toward the scorpion.

The flaming Holy Name struck the energy creature.

It stumbled, fell on its legs.

The Holy Name grew, engulfed it.

The slivers in the scorpion's hollow eye sockets vanished. Its frame collapsed upon itself and dissolved. Energy spirals fluttered away like rainbow-hued whirlwinds, once again perfection transforming imperfection.

"I underestimated you," Arashi said. "Again."

"Let her go, Arashi."

He wiped his forehead, jaw muscles bulging below the skin. "Not quite yet."

I risked a quick look at Leah, nodding that everything would be okay. I connected with her third eye, and the message she had been trying to give me now became clear. *Watch out! Behind you.*

I swiveled. Another black-clad man that seemingly appeared out of nowhere was releasing the string of a bow.

I dropped. The arrow passed over me before my body hit the ground.

Footsteps pounded the cobblestone path.

I rolled, crouched, searched for cover. No need. The steps were going the other way. Why didn't the shooter come to finish me off? Unless. . . . I spun towards Arashi.

The red smudge on his shirt right below the sternum gave me the answer. Face twisting, hand clutching the arrow, Arashi swayed from side to side. Unable to keep his balance, he plunged face down, body sprawling out. The crystal scorpion statuette shattered.

I scrambled to my feet, sprinted toward Leah and Arashi. Leah nodded at me to attend to him first. I rolled him onto his back. He was still breathing heavily through his open mouth while blood continued to ooze from his wound. Its copper tang struck my nostrils. The arrow had broken off from the fall, the arrowhead still in his gut.

Arashi stared at me with half-open, glazed eyes. "Run," he managed to whisper.

"No. I'm taking you to a hospital."

"Always naïve." Arashi coughed. Red foam spilled out of his lips. "The arrow's poisoned."

I could feel his life force draining away. There was no point trying to give him any false hope. We both knew he wouldn't survive.

A car engine roared. Arashi's accomplice had escaped.

I didn't care.

"The Dark Master set up a trap," Arashi said. "They're waiting to ambush you in case you survived. Ten miles from here. When you reach the crossroad, turn to the right instead." A spasm shook his torso. He coughed again. "Hurry."

"Arashi, renounce the Dark Master. You can do this. You can still turn to the Light."

"I'm not worthy."

"You are the emanation of the Timeless Self no matter what. You are made of divine fire. Your self-worth is unconditional. And you didn't have to warn me. You're a Brother."

"You're crazy."

"Maybe. Ask for forgiveness and swear by the Lost Name you will serve the Light."

"Too many lives, too many crimes."

"You know Cosmic Law. You can demolish any mountain of karma no matter how high. You'll have to come back and pay your debt to life, serve every single man and woman you hurt, do whatever it takes. You'll have to do good works, and yes, suffer. But then you will be free, and eternity is a long time."

Arashi didn't respond and turned his head away, his cheeks puffing up.

The descending power from above crested in my heart and seized me. "O Arashi, Arashi, let go of your stubbornness and pride. The arms of your Timeless Self are always open. You *are* welcome back Home. Forgive yourself and choose Life—not Death."

A sudden guttural sound rumbled in his throat. I feared it was his final death rattle and that I had lost him.

I knelt by his side, grabbed his hand.

He squeezed mine back with the strength of a little child. Tears running down his face mixed with thick drops of blood dripping out of his nose. "I swear by the Lost Name. . . ."

I propped him up, helped him hold his head high.

"To serve the Light. . . . May God have mercy."

"May the angels record your vow in the Book of Life," I said.

With a labored motion, Arashi looked at Leah and then back at me. "Take care of . . . her."

"I will."

His head fell back. His hand went limp. His chest stopped moving.

I closed his eyes and gently laid him down. I would ask Mataji to come for him.

I grabbed Arashi's knife from the ground, cut the ropes binding Leah's hands and feet, and untied the gag. She clasped my extended hand and rose to her feet. I kept a tight grip and we bolted through the castle ruins to the Land Rover without exchanging a word. I'd never let go. Never again.

I started the car and pulled on to the dirt road. The tires kicked up dust.

"Thank God you came," Leah said, pressing her palms to her upper eyelids, letting out a droning, tired sigh.

"That's who to thank, all right. Are you okay?"

"You could say that."

"Did he hurt you?"

"Except for tying me up, he didn't touch me."

I floored the accelerator. "Mataji told me what happened."

"I'm *so* sorry. I almost ruined the mission. . . . I still can't believe a sister betrayed me."

I glanced at her, eyes telegraphing that I understood and harbored no condemnation. "I have *you*, I have the scroll. Everything's good."

"I hope so."

"I like the disheveled look."

"Why, thank you."

My fingers tightened on the steering wheel. "Did I ever tell you I love you?

"I don't think so."

"I love you. Like the flame loves the torch. Like the zephyr loves the trees. Like the sea foam loves the shore. Like the mountain loves the snow. I love you."

She reached over and touched my hair. "I love *you*, forever and always."

That singular, gentle touch began the fusion of our beings, opening the portals of our past, present, and future together.

All the while we were talking, I had been sending my consciousness ahead, keeping my spiritual sight open. I had been through the fire, literally, and faced down my worst fears. I didn't think the Dark Master's trap would be anything as simple as land mines in the road.

On the other hand, maybe he was counting on arrogance on my part. I kept an eye out for land mines as well.

When I reached the crossroad—little more than a place where two sets of ruts met—I made a right. All my instincts were telling me that Arashi could be trusted, and I would find a road back to Varanasi eventually.

Then I heard something that surprised me. It was a distant, screeching lament.

"Ravens," I said.

Within minutes, the black cloud was zooming over the car. The Dark Master's trap was apparently mobile and had caught up with us. The flapping of hundreds of wings added to the pandemonium.

"This is giving me the creeps," Leah said.

"Yeah, me too." Ravens, although intelligent birds, had never been a good omen. I accelerated. Even on this old country road full of potholes, the SUV should be able to outrun the ravens.

But they were able to keep up with us. And more ravens seemed to be flowing in from the surrounding countryside. The skies darkened, as if we were in the middle of an eclipse.

Then, without any warning, the flock surged ahead, and drove itself into the road ahead of us. The ravens disappeared, and a wall of orange-brown flames sprang up and spread across.

I cut the wheel left, pulling off the road and into the surrounding brush, trying to outflank the flames. It had never been much of a road anyway.

The fiery barricade wavered a moment, then spread out in front of us.

I slammed on the brakes, slapped the car into reverse, and thanks to my newly found hypersensitivity and a lot of soft sand, executed a neat bootlegger's turn. I glanced over at Leah, and she was right there with me. She even seemed to be enjoying herself.

The flames receded into the background as we retraced our steps. By the time we reached the crossroad again, they—and the ravens—were nowhere to be seen.

I looked down the main road as far as my third eye could see. It seemed clear.

"What do you think?" I said.

"It's possible he just uprooted the trap and sent it ahead of us," Leah said after a moment.

"Yeah. But it wasn't much of a trap, was it? An immobile wall of fire?"

"Maybe it was more impressive where it was originally. We might have seen the makeshift version. . . . What other choice do we have?"

"We could head out cross-country," I said.

"And risk getting stuck in the sand until the world ends? I say, stick to the road."

So I drove back on to the main road, and worked to put distance between us and the fire as quickly as possible.

We were no more than two miles down the road when a wall of flames burst from the ground ahead of us.

Again, I slammed on the brakes and turned back to make another turn. And that's when I saw the second wall, racing down the road toward us.

The two walls spread, rose to over twenty feet high, and closed all around us like a noose.

But why fire? The Dark Master had to know I had conquered fire. But perhaps he knew what that battle had cost me and was hoping to stir fears of a second engagement.

With one mind, the titanic tongues of flame leapt toward the sky. Then they bent forward. Then they lunged. Toward us. Every tree and bush was instantly consumed in their path. The earth turned black. Bulging clouds of grey smoke billowed up. The Dark Master knew Arashi had died and more importantly that he had turned back to the Light. Now more than ever, the Dark Master was hell-bent on exacting punishment.

But we weren't going to let that happen.

I kicked the door open and sprinted in front of the Land Rover. Arms opened up, palms parallel to the ground, I uttered the seed syllable of the Fire Element the warrior angel had revealed to me in the cave, followed by the invocation *"Recall to mind your pure estate."*

Leah joined me, her cry blending with mine. "Recall to mind your pure estate."

Nothing. The colossal fire ring kept closing in on us.

The crackling sound clawed at my ears and I struggled to breathe. My skin stung. A few more seconds and the flames would engulf and scorch us.

"Louder," I said.

We both poured our whole hearts into the invocation.

Suddenly, the roaring wall of fire stopped, close enough that I could smell my hair beginning to singe.

"Back down," I said, *"back down."*

The flames receded about thirty feet all around. A booming sound followed, and the flames parted on the east side like a set-alight Red Sea.

"Jump in the car," I said.

We pulled through the gap, and I again pushed the Land Rover as hard as I could.

Eventually, the road improved some, and I managed a steady eighty-five miles per hour, keeping an eye for any cars coming from behind. We reached the temple of the Mother of the World without any further challenges.

I parked in front of the gate. "We made it."

Leah slumped on her seat as if she wanted to shrink. She probably felt embarrassed to meet Mataji.

I took the opportunity to get out of the car first and open the door for her. She stepped out. "I need to apologize to Mataji and—"

I crushed her in my arms, just to make sure I wasn't dreaming, just to make sure she knew how much I had missed her.

She buried her head in my chest, wrapping her arms around me as though the world would end the next minute, and I took in her intoxicating scent. Then I searched for her lips and kissed her, soul-to-soul. It was one of those magical moments when you are enfolded in the pain and bliss of Timeless Love. When you experience eternity in one cosmic flash. When you implore for no end to the ecstasy.

The kiss ended and a new one began. And a new one. . . .

For a moment, I thought about proposing we elope. Escape to a secret hideaway and spend the rest of our lives alone, away from everything.

The fantasy evaporated instantly. It was time to return to America. Time to do battle with Death.

# PART IV

# THE ASCENT

# CHAPTER 19

**11:15 a.m., Day 7, Master Theo's Study, Headquarters of the Inner Order, Jackson, Wyoming**

During the entire flight back to America, my heart overflowed with the sheer joy of having Leah sit next to me, safe. The flight took us directly to Wyoming. There, terrible news greeted us—close to three quarters of a million people had died from a tsunami in the Indian Ocean. Ranjit drove us to the mansion and we gathered in Master Theo's study to plan our next move.

"We don't have much time," Master Theo said, from behind his rosewood desk, his baritone voice grim. "Our destination is the Half Dome Mountain in Yosemite National Park, where you will enter another secret cave. It's a death-rebirth chamber, the equivalent of the Great Pyramid for the Western Hemisphere. It has been rendering its mystic service to initiates for thousands of years."

"I'm done with fire corridors, right?"

"No outer fire this time. Your experiences will mostly be inner."

I took note of the word "mostly." "What about the cave, will it mess with my mind again?"

"Some, yes. . . . Now, I would offer you the customary opportunity to withdraw, but under the circumstances it's not possible. Mataji is right. Only *you* can unveil the scroll's secret. And again, congratulations for passing the tests."

"Thank you. I have no intention of quitting now. And I sense I'll discover the Name when I'm there. I have to."

"Very well then."

Zara, resting in front of the fireplace in a sphinx position, let out a soft bark as if to encourage me. I appreciated the vote of confidence. I needed every single one I could get.

Leah pressed her arms on the handles of her Queen Anne chair and looked away. I could feel the sorrow coming off her entire being. No doubt she was anguishing over the news, experiencing in her heart the pain of those who were gone, and the grief of those who had lost their loved ones. She understood loss.

I silently swore I would prevail over any inner or outer obstacle and liberate the great power of the Lost Name. "What now?"

"Your instructions," Master Theo said.

Leah and I pulled our chairs closer to the desk.

"The final aim of the Mysteries and of life itself is immortality. Immortality through the Soul's permanent union with the Timeless Self. Becoming a permanent cell in the universal body of God. It has been called by many names—theosis, ascension, liberation. At the Inner Order, we know it as the Grand Regeneration, the fifth sub-degree of the exalted Seventh."

Master Theo examined a sunbeam that managed to come through the closed curtains and draw a luminous line on the wool carpet. "Over many lifetimes you have fulfilled a number of the requirements on the journey toward immortality. You balanced much of the karma of your past misdeeds. You practiced the virtues. You put on portions of the *I AM* Mind. In short, you practiced right use of energy. And this very week, you have attained the first and second sub-degrees. The third and fourth ones await. If you undergo the Deep Purification without caving in, and if you succeed in crystallizing the Light Body, you will have defeated Death."

"I will not fail . . . by the Grace of God."

"Having defeated Death, you will speak the Name without bringing upon you instant annihilation. You will have become a fully realized Master of Energy. And at a time and place known only by your Timeless Self, you will go through the glorious ritual of the Grand Regeneration, no longer to return to Earth in a body of flesh."

A hallowed stillness filled the room, an overwhelming peace taking hold of me. I looked at Leah. The sadness seemed to have lifted, and she too paid close attention to the words of Master Theo.

"Leah, you've been quiet," Master Theo said, right on cue. In the familiar setting, it was easy to forget that he read minds. "You know I value your input. Do you have any questions? Anything you want to add?"

"Only that I want to go with Diokles into the cave, be there for him." She held up a hand. "Which I know I can't do."

Some things never changed.

"All right. You can travel with us to Half Dome to see Diokles off. Then we'll return here to make invocations on his behalf and visualize his victory while he spends the next three days in the cave."

Leah nodded.

"Why that long?" I asked.

Master Theo touched the tube with the scroll on his desk. "The price of immortality is high."

His manner told me question time was over.

"And now to the warning. Like your mythical ancestor Hercules, you will stand at the center point of the "Y" on the path of life. You will be offered the option of taking the wide and

easy road of selfishness, or the narrow, thorn-strewn road of self-
*lessness*. You will be given a genuine opportunity to turn to the
Darkness and use all the energy and power you have garnered for
egotistical purposes."

A reckless resolve welled up within. "I will never turn to the
Darkness."

"Underestimate the synthetic ego, and you will surely fail. I
trust you will not be arrogant."

"I'll be extra careful."

"There is no middle ground. There is no grey area. Once you
cross the threshold, you will come out of that cave a servant of
the Darkness or an adept of the Light. A slave or a free man."

Master Theo reached into a small chest on the chair beside
him. "A few things you'll need." One by one, he placed on his
desk a lapis lazuli star, a small glass vial, a pouch, and a wooden
red cube. "This seven-pointed star will open a hidden passageway into the secret cave. The bottle contains an elixir I prepared
for you. It will sustain your body for three days without any need
for food or water." He went on explaining how I should use the
pouch and the cube.

"I understand."

"Two more things." He passed over a parchment. "You will
need this to commence the Deep Purification. And here is the
ceremonial purple cape."

"It's beautiful."

"You recall how the high priests of Israel wore elaborate robes
and jewels when they communed with the Presence of God re-
siding in the Ark of the Covenant. Likewise, you must be properly attired when you speak the Name in the Flame Room."

Ranjit peeked through the door. "The car is ready."

Master Theo called Zara to him and scratched her ears. "I'll
finish my instructions on the way."

Zara wagged her tail, the dog equivalent of a farewell. Even though he was an adept, maybe Master Theo needed some comfort too.

Master Theo stood. "It's time."

# CHAPTER 20

Ranjit had driven us to our waiting plane. From there we flew to Modesto City-County Airport near Yosemite Park and into a waiting Bell helicopter. The silence that settled over us for most of the journey grew thicker. It wasn't only that noise from the rotors made it hard to hear. It was that the time for talking had long passed.

I contemplated the coming ordeal. When I thought back to my greater union with the Timeless Self, I found it hard to imagine how I could ever choose to serve the Darkness. The Dark Master simply seemed . . . well, what I had told Arashi was the best description. He seemed a child, throwing a cosmic tantrum at not getting his way. Turning to the Darkness now wouldn't simply be evil. It would be ridiculous.

But I had to remember that Arashi had chosen to serve him. Was I an inherently better person than Arashi? I had to be careful to avoid pride.

Rising from the depths of an equally massive canyon, Half Dome Mountain ascended thousands of feet above the valley floor. The giant granite monolith resembled a rough cathedral cupola cut in two. Nothing grew on its sheer walls. Nothing gave any sign of encouragement. With its top wrapped in dark clouds, and the heavy rain pounding on the helicopter, Half Dome Mountain issued a conquer-me-if-you-dare challenge.

I accepted.

The pilot steered the helicopter over the canyon and toward the southwest side of the mountain. He aimed for a tiny clearing surrounded by lodgepole pine trees and began to bring the helicopter down. I unbuckled the harness and put the backpack and tube on my shoulders. The skids of the craft almost touched the rocky ground when Master Theo, sitting next to the pilot, issued a terse order.

"Pull up now."

The pilot yanked the control stick.

Glass debris flew.

Leah screamed. Her body jerked, kept from falling only by the harness. Blood spurted.

A second bullet blasted into the helicopter, ricocheted off the cockpit wall to the floor.

Raw adrenaline bubbled through my veins. I managed to kneel by Leah without falling, hands holding the edges of her seat. The blood stain between her shoulder blade and heart soaked her white blouse. Her head had dropped over her chest. Her breathing had turned to labored shallow gulps.

"She's hurt, she's hurt! Leah *talk* to me."

She responded with a groan.

A third bullet came through, grazed my head. It hurt, but it was just a scratch. I held onto Leah's seat.

"Diokles, I need you to stay calm," Master Theo said, as he opened the first aid kit, his voice only loud enough to be heard above the noise. "Press down on the wound with this."

I held the wound shut with a white cloth.

"Circle out that way," Master Theo said.

The helicopter swerved. I turned to face him but I held back from speaking. Master Theo now sat motionless, eyes closed, face rigid. His hands had come together in a strange clasp I had not seen before. No, I had seen it once before, when the swami had immobilized the thugs who tried to shoot him. Master Theo was obviously doing the same with the sniper.

By now, Leah's face had become pale. My nerve endings pulsed with alarm. If she didn't make it, I wouldn't want to live either.

The helicopter scraped the tops of a tree line and descended in front of the foothill. Below us, I spotted a small waterfall, the signpost and natural camouflage of the hollow that led to the secret cave. Thick shrubs grew on both sides of its base. Water splashed into what seemed a shallow pool. A pair of marmots scampered away.

Hands still locked in that unusual hand clasp, Master Theo blinked his eyes open. "Medusa is immobilized. You should be able to enter unharmed."

Bloody Medusa. She obviously held me responsible for Arashi's death. Her plan must have been to wait for me to exit the helicopter, take me out, and get the scroll. When she saw the helicopter reversing course, she had to act. She must have been tempted to take an easy shot at the engine and kill us all, but I realized she didn't do that because she didn't dare disobey the Dark Master. He wanted revenge and punishment too, but he wanted the scroll more. If the helicopter crashed, the scroll would have been destroyed.

"What about Leah? I can't just leave her."

"Yes, you can, Diokles. We'll fly her straight to the nearest hospital."

"Master Theo, please. I want *you* to help her. Now."

"I promise you, I will do everything I can. You have to stay focused on the task at hand. And above all, control your anger when you're in the cave, or all will be lost."

The helicopter now hovered a few feet above ground.

"You'll have to jump out. We can't land here."

I squeezed Leah's hands and whispered in her ear. "Leah, I love you. You *will* live." I threw the door open and leapt. My feet didn't hold me and I rolled on my side, bruising a few muscles on the way. Rain whipped my face. The wind numbed my hands. The atmosphere was thick with the smell of wet earth.

I sat on my haunches and scanned the terrain. Good thing Medusa was well hidden or I might have been unable to stop myself from going after her first.

I broke into a run and reached the edge of the pool. Testing each step, I passed through the cascading waterfall and stood before the hollow on the foothill. My teeth clattered from the biting cold. I wiped strands of hair off my forehead and searched the rock wall. Only the protruding wedge one foot above me qualified for what I was looking for. I reached up and felt around with my hand until I discovered the carved slot. I pulled the seven-pointed star out of my pocket, pushed it level in the slot, and gripped the wedge to keep my balance.

Nothing happened at first. Then, with a slow sound of stone grinding against stone, a section of the wall swiveled, and I found myself standing in a puddle inside the mountain, inside another new world that would once again test my mettle.

I took no time to marvel at this feat of ancient engineering and climbed the rough-hewn steps. I paused at the top of the narrow corridor, water dripping from my head and fatigues.

By the familiar crystalline light spreading everywhere, I could see a large circular cave. The vaulted ceiling crowned bare, grey rock walls. An enormous quartz crystal in its center threw off white sparks as if to welcome me. A giant star was cut into the rocky floor. Each of its seven tips pointed to a passageway that led deeper into the mountain. Thick pulsations of high-frequency energy crisscrossed the space, and even the very walls seemed to emanate sanctity.

All seemed peaceful, but I wasn't about to let my guard down. I closed the distance to the first passageway on my left in ten steps. It opened into a small, square cavern with a low ceiling. At the end of the cavern opposite the passageway, an ankh cross, symbol of eternal life, was etched on the wall. A simple mandala was drawn in the center of the cavern.

I walked over to the mandala, the clap of my boots on the strangely smooth floor piercing the haunting silence. I took a moment to send my healing love to Leah and tried without success to get her out of my mind. Then, I unzipped my backpack and pulled out the little pouch. I slowly poured the powder around me to form an equilateral triangle that enclosed the mandala.

The triangle effervesced, sending a wall of blue flame two feet into the air, pale light reflecting off the floor surface. The protecting line of force was in place. I dug into the backpack for a second time to get the parchment, and held it open.

"O Great Geometer, Light Supreme whose Presence fills the Universe, hear me,

"By the power of the Lost Name,

"I challenge the hold of the synthetic ego over me this day,

"I command—and I am—the freedom from all untruth and mental manipulation,

"I command—and I am—the breaking of the chains of all human limitation,

"I command—and I am—the fullness of my divine inheritance,

"It is done. And I accept it as done at all levels of my being.

"Receive and multiply my invocation.

"Purify and amend it by the flawless geometry of the Divine Intent."

Crackling energy descended through the top of my head. My chakras quaked, my body swayed.

I steadied myself and reached into the backpack again. I stretched my right hand toward the wall with the ankh cross and held the red cube with my thumb and index finger.

A tongue of flame soared from the triangle, struck the front of the cube, and set it alight. I tossed it before it burned my fingers. It stopped right below the wall with the ankh cross.

A seething spiral of dark energy shot out of the cube, rose to a height of six feet, and began to revolve. Tendrils of vapor, surging and ebbing, materialized around it. Complex energy patterns writhed within. The spiral picked up speed, the energy patterns and vapors melding into a singular figure.

Rumbles reverberated through the granite surfaces. Moving shadows dimmed the radiance of the crystalline light. An odor of decay saturated the air.

The whirling stopped, the three-dimensional figure of a man now distinct. He was about five feet eleven inches tall and wore casual, unpretentious clothes. His brown eyes were fierce and detached at the same time—the eyes of a sophisticated predator. And his face was contorted but familiar . . . really familiar.

It was *my* face.

Despite Master Theo's forewarning, nothing could have prepared me for looking at this unredeemed part of myself "in the flesh," as it were, the conglomerate energy field of my negative thoughts and feelings, the central consciousness of my false beliefs—the synthetic ego.

I called upon every fragment of self-mastery I possessed and held my ground.

The ego's gaze met my own.

I held it.

"You insolent child," the ego said, "how dare you summon me? Have you forgotten I am your master?"

The slithering words swathed my chest like a boa, ripped the air out of my lungs.

I fought back the suffocating embrace, and spoke the same answer as every initiate before me who had faced their ego in this death-rebirth chamber. "O ancient one, you whom I have birthed and nurtured with my life's blood for eons untold. You whom, like Narcissus, I worshiped in my ignorance as my true self. You to whom I have surrendered my free will without a battle. The time has come for you to depart from the house of my consciousness. The time has come for you to be regenerated into Light. By the power of the Lost Name, I command you. Do not resist."

The ego's drawn out, mocking laughter echoed off the cavern walls. "By whose authority do you command thus?"

"By the authority of the *I AM that I AM*."

"Ungrateful bastard. Have you forgotten how many times I rescued you from disaster? It was I who deceived your enemies and destroyed them. I helped you win when losing was unimaginable. I'm the one who consoled you and soothed your pain when everyone else had abandoned you. I filled your loneliness with myself. You need my help. Without me, you can't survive."

"The power of the Timeless Self, the divine Ego, is my refuge and my defense."

"Fine. *Prove* it."

The moving shadows spread, streaks of forked light flashed, the cavern metamorphosing into a deserted graveyard with a small clearing in its center. Still surrounded by the burning triangle, I found myself standing at the edge of the clearing, the ego at the opposite side. Tombstones overlaid with moss glinted with the moon's silvery shafts. Crawling fog made it hard to see, and cold wind penetrated down to the marrow of my bones.

The ego's solar plexus roiled. An energy figure stepped out of it and onto the dead grass of the clearing, a cord connecting him to the ego. I knew this emanation of the ego was my battle adversary, the concentrated death energy that would challenge my right to Be, the personified force of Thanatos.

The adversary wore black robes that reached down to his feet and a conical hood that covered his entire face. A fiendish fire burned in his chartreuse eyes, and he held a long sword with both gloved hands.

All senses alert, and yet with a strange calmness, I concentrated on my crown chakra and let go. My pulse slowed, my body became rigid, my eyelids narrowed. Within seconds, an energetic replica of myself walked out of the triangle, joined to my body with an energy cord of its own. Though I remained faintly aware of my semi-frozen body behind me, my consciousness had transferred to the energetic replica, and I held the sword of Life the Secret Master had given me a few days ago.

The adversary and I circled each other at the middle of the clearing, neither of us making the first move. I glided with the practiced motions of someone who had fought a thousand sword battles, which was probably true. I've had many past lives.

I brought down my sword on what seemed to be an opening to his shoulder. The adversary blocked my hit with precision, clearly anticipating it. The ringing energy blades flared at the point of contact, sending shafts of light flying. I disengaged and went for his throat. He parried with ease. I came at him from another angle and again he countered. It didn't matter that I controlled the flow of the battle. No matter what maneuver I tried, high, low, or sideways, I couldn't gain an advantage. He foresaw my every move as if he intimately knew my every thought and weakness—which he did.

I pushed away the temptation to worry and went back to circling him.

The adversary must have sensed my doubt because he suddenly swiveled and whipped at my gut with an arc cut. I lunged back, evaded the strike. The adversary charged with a tumult of blows coming at me from all sides. Every time, I managed to thwart his blade and even came close to cutting off his arm . . . every time except for the last. The tip of his sword had pierced my right shoulder.

An electric tremor rattled through my arm, and my fingers turned numb, almost dropping the sword. The adversary raised his arms over his head, ready to bring the sword down for the kill.

Time seemed to stop. Images from special moments of my inner life marched before my eyes, bringing with them a bursting realization at a new, deeper level. A realization that dispelled the shadows in the graveyard and in my head. Life divine is invincible. Life cannot be marred by any human concepts or acts. Life will always swallow up Death. If only we tore the veil of the Great Forgetfulness and remembered. If only we allowed ourselves to become Life's instrument. If only we raised our chalice and let Life flow.

The adversary's sword had come down half way.

I kept my gaze fixed into those widening bloodshot eyes when a stream of white fire from my heart coursed up through my chest and down my right arm.

My fingers tightened around the diamond-studded hilt of my sword.

The adversary's blade shimmered, a few inches away from chopping off my head.

I raised the sword of Life straight up, white fire dripping from its edges.

The sword of the adversary shattered.

The sword of Life drew all the fragments like a magnet, and after converting them into pure energy, it absorbed them into itself. My hand shook and I knew the sword's power and mine had increased.

The adversary took two steps back.

I hesitated for a very long second, then lifted my sword and brought it down on his neck.

His body crashed to the ground. The hood dropped off, revealing a skull that rolled away. A new stream of fire shot out of the tip of the sword in the form of a figure-eight, the lower circle of the figure-eight centering on the adversary's chest. The stream flowed back to the sword, redeeming the energies of the lifeless adversary as it moved. Until the adversary was no more.

I put the sword in the scabbard and walked back into the burning triangle. My energy replica merged with my body, sensation returning to my frozen limbs. Life had triumphed over Death, over Thanatos.

For now.

The sound of clapping hands drew my attention to the ego. The graveyard had vanished, with the ego and I standing opposite each other in the cavern as before.

"Bravo," the ego said, "I'm proud of you. Though it wasn't hard to guess that you'd defeat this puny energy figure. But this was just for fun. Now comes the serious business."

With newly grown gray hair and wrinkles on the forehead, the ego looked depleted, as though he had aged twenty years in the span of thirty minutes.

"I'm done with your lies," I said.

"Oh, really? And is it a lie that Leah is dying?"

In the heat of the battle, I had momentarily set aside my anxiety about Leah's survival. Now it roared back with a vengeance.

"God has abandoned you once again. And you still keep going on, blind to the truth."

"You don't even know what truth is."

"And what about the old man? What kind of Master *is* he? You did so much for him and he couldn't even protect Leah. *Our* Leah. And he's using you. You're just a pawn, and too naïve to figure it out. He sent you to your death how many times? And here's what you get for reward. You can't trust him. Me, on the other hand, you can always trust. I am you, after all."

"Shut your bloody mouth."

"Oh, that's right, Master Theo is pure and unselfish. Or is he? You're getting burned up and frozen and facing death at every turn. And what does *he* do? He's sitting in his study, drinking tea in front of the fire with his dog."

"I said shut up."

"*Finally*, you're waking up. Let anger surge through your chakras. It will make you mightier than you ever dreamed of. Forever."

I wanted to pull out the sword of Light, run over, and slice the ego into a thousand pieces. Teach him a lesson he would never forget. Try to eliminate him for good. But then he would win. I could indeed feel a thrilling dark power flowing though my nerves. If I let it, it would surely possess me. And then all would be lost, as Master Theo had warned.

I exerted my will until the flames of anger were sublimated into a delicate peace.

"You're missing the point," the ego said in a tone that traced my spine with an icy, bloodless finger. "Leah is about to give up the ghost, and you're dillydallying. *Look*."

The mists shifted, and the ego gave way to an image of Leah in the helicopter. She sat on the same seat, hands limp by her side, face drooping on her chest. I couldn't even tell if she was breathing. Master Theo, sitting next to the pilot, looked straight ahead.

I threw my head back, hands pressing down on my cranium.

"He doesn't even care if she lives or dies," the ego said, coming back. "He has no more use for her. I'm warning you, she only has minutes to live. If you don't act now, she *will* die and her blood will be on your head."

"Just what are you asking me to do?"

"Swear allegiance to me. Swear to be my willing servant in all things and I promise you—I *will* save her."

"Why should I trust you?"

"Because you have no other choice. And because I care for Leah much more than that Theo character."

I gritted my teeth. "How would you save her?"

"Oh, come on. You're asking me to reveal my deepest secrets?"

"You're lying again. How could you possibly stop her from dying?"

"Swear first by the Lost Name to serve me and then I'll tell you. The power of shadow I wield extends a lot farther than you could ever imagine."

No way Master Theo would desert Leah. No way Master Theo wouldn't do everything in his power, both human and divine, to rescue her. I had my bearings back. "No."

"Look, I'd like to see you consummate your relationship with Leah," the ego said unfazed, "raise those two kids together."

The ego faded away and the scene changed to Leah and I in an upscale mansion. She stood in front of our bedroom door with her hair wet and thrown back, having just come out of the shower. She wore only an oversized white shirt over her fair body, and beckoned me to come.

The ravishing music of a thousand harps stormed my ears. With every rising and falling melody, a tide of bewitching emotions swamped my brain. The music grew louder by the second, slamming my eardrums at a fever pitch.

Leah loosened the shirt one button at a time. It fell to the floor in a little puddle of satin. Then she ran a hand though her hair, her crystal-blue eyes glistening with promise.

I struggled to look away but my eyes refused to obey. Leah's naked body had cast an irresistible spell, awakened a forbidden longing in my gut.

"Take her hand," the ego said, "you have so much to live for."
I didn't, *couldn't* respond.

"Don't throw away such happiness. She's literally the only woman you'll ever love."

I dropped to my knees, pressed my hands against my ears to shut out the Siren songs taking over my mind.

"Don't be a fool. You owe nothing to the old man. Serve me, and you can have Leah to do with her whatever you please."

The rocky ground at my knees felt soft, as if it were beginning to turn into quicksand. Confusion reigned and my strength flailed. Until. . . .

*To do with her whatever you please.* That was Arashi's vision of love. Possession. Ownership. The kind of love that turned other people into objects to be manipulated for your own gratification. Your ego's gratification. His gratification.

I caught sight of the top of the carved ankh cross on the rock wall, peeking right above the mists around the ego. I may have imagined it but it seemed to shine. It seemed to speak to me, encourage me to resist.

I rose slowly to my feet and made an effort to square my shoulders. "No. I will *never* turn to the Darkness."

The music stopped, the pressure within my head easing.

The ego held its cool. "Oh, don't get all superior just because you resisted one temptation. Remember, I know all the skeletons in your closet. I put them there. You are a filthy mortal, a lost cause. You can never become the manifestation of Divinity."

I shielded my face from the sickening glare. For a second. "I know who I am and I know who *you* are."

"Diokles, you have won the battle with the great ego," he said with an air of resignation. "You have defeated me and I concede. I'm at your mercy. I beg you, don't hurt me. Please . . . I'm yourself, your *real* self. Let me live and I'll serve your every whim forever. I'll swiftly answer your every call. I'll impart to you the forbidden secrets you would never discover by yourself. Be compassionate, I beg—"

"Oh, spare me the crocodile tears. It's over."

Dagger-like claws came out of the ego's fingers. Froth sloshed through its teeth. Its brown eyes smoldered. "I tried to talk sense into you, but you wouldn't listen. Now pay the price."

My pulse galloped, my lungs swelled. Now that the ego had exhausted its opportunity to test me through coercion, seduction, and sophistry, I had permission to strike it.

I centered my attention in my heart, and allowing the divine feeling of the peace-commanding presence above to pour through me, I spoke the fearsome fiat of power. The fiat that can only be uttered once in a lifetime.

"Nooooo." The ego's howling scream rebounded across the cavern walls. A spiraling arc of light lobbing out of the center of the ankh cross engulfed him until only a small amount of ash remained on the ground. The stench of decay disappeared, replaced by the fragrance of lilies.

A tide of unfathomable peace flooded every corner of my being, my skin simmering with a gentle warmth. It was as if I were Theseus suddenly seeing the light of day after the journey out of the labyrinth, the slain Minotaur left behind.

# Chapter 21

**9:46 p.m., Day 7, Death-Rebirth Chamber**

The triangle of fire surrounding me had died out. I pulled the little vial from my backpack and downed the bitter elixir that would sustain me for the next three days. The ankh cross now shone with a greater luster and kept growing until it reached the full height of the cavern wall. Master Theo hadn't described this part of the Mystery of Deep Purification, saying I should just let events take their natural course. Not knowing what he meant, I half-expected the cross to turn into some vision of beauty to join me in celebrating the victory over the ego.

Instead, beams of white light blasted out of the center of the cross and hammered my body.

My torso arced backward and I hit the rocky floor, my limbs shaking as if I had a seizure. I crumpled into a ball to ease the mind-numbing pain. The peace I had felt moments ago had morphed into an unfathomable grief.

I tightened my muscles and struggled to get up and escape from the smothering emotion that dragged me down to a dark, bottomless chasm. I failed.

I crawled on my elbows and knees. I didn't go far.

"Get me out of here. Let me go, let me gooo."

Out of the depths of my Soul, a still small voice rose in response. *If we don't cry the salt tears of the world's suffering, who will? If we don't help bear the burden of humanity's karma until they are able, who will? If we don't sacrifice, who will?*

I turned on my back, dripping eyes fixed on the ankh cross, each tear a drop of lava searing my face. Images of people across the planet I had never met—suffering people, hurting people—streamed before me, etching themselves into my heart.

I saw a mother in Kansas clutching a flag, mourning her twenty-year-old son just killed at war.

I saw a young prostitute in Ukraine selling her body to feed the little girl the father had abandoned.

I saw a middle-aged farmer in Bangladesh hanging himself after his crop failed and he couldn't provide for his family.

Fresh pain rippled through me, intensifying with every wave, turning each breath to agony. I screamed, thinking for a moment I would die again . . . until I surrendered to the river of tears and allowed it to wash me clean, allowed it to water the Tree of Life. I cried for the mother and as the mother. I cried for the young woman and as the young woman. I cried for the farmer and as the farmer. I cried for Leah.

Then, presently, I dried my tears and rose to my knees, hands on my breast, one on top of the other. "I pledge my life and all that I am to relieving the suffering of all sentient beings, so help me God."

The cross and the rays disappeared. Time ceased and the pain became bliss. . . .

A scraping noise jerked me out of my ecstatic state, brought me back to the present. A plume of dust puffed out from an opening in the wall in front of me. I blinked my eyes half-open and placed my hands over them. The dust settled and I caught sight of a closed granite chest in the small rectangular grotto. I got to my feet, walked to the entrance of the grotto, and paused. The chest was about seven feet long and four feet tall with Egyptian hieroglyphs inscribed on it and small, lotus-shaped cutouts on its sides.

The massive slab covering the chest stirred. Inch by inch, the slab ascended until it settled right below the narrow ceiling. I stared deep into the sarcophagus, the flesh eater, the gloomy doorway to my immortality.

A strong impulse to enter it pressed upon me. Almost in a trance, I took off my boots and climbed over the edge. I placed the leather tube and the backpack by my feet and settled on my back. The inner surface of the sarcophagus was smooth and felt cold to the touch. The lid descended, sealed me in.

Swept by a power far beyond my human control, my ethereal body blasted right through the sarcophagus and the mountain.

Less than a heartbeat later, I found myself standing in the center of a square celestial temple. Evenly spaced, Egyptian lotus columns lined its glimmering walls, soft light flowing in through arched windows. A polished marble floor spread throughout. Huge hanging torches, bulging with plumes of liquid white fire, filled the space with a mystical glow.

Across from me, an imposing figure sat on an ornate throne. He wore a white robe that reached down to his feet and a turban with a diamond in its center, his hair tucked inside. His heart chakra radiated golden-pink rays and his right hand held the Scales of Justice.

His piercing but compassionate eyes fell upon me and I knelt, giving homage to the one I knew by my inner voice as a great Hierophant of the Mysteries. Behind me, twelve priests and priestesses, clad in ancient Egyptian garments, formed a semicircle and began intoning a sacred mantra.

The Hierophant stepped down from the throne and walked toward me. The priests and priestesses bowed their heads and, moving in rhythmic steps, closed the circle around us. The low-pitched mantra ended, the Hierophant now standing in front of me. A white sphere rested within the right bowl of the Scales of Justice and a murky lump within the left. The right bowl hung all the way down. Apparently, my good karma outweighed the bad.

The scales disappeared and gave way to a scepter crowned with a jewel.

The Hierophant struck the scepter on the floor once. "Candidate for the fourth of the Deeper Mysteries, arise."

I obeyed.

"From time immemorial the Powers of Light have served humanity behind the scenes and guided men and women of goodwill to the Higher Way. Today, you have proved worthy to pursue the Crystallization of the Light Body. Do you accept this honor?"

"I do."

"An ancient initiate of the Light you are. The Timeless Flame on the altar of your heart burns brightly. Lifetime after lifetime of your journey on earth, you have pursued the Mysteries and strived to help your fellow man. Welcome Home."

"Brother, welcome Home," a chorus of voices repeated.

I drank in every one of those magical words like precious nectar. "At last, I have returned."

"While your mortal body rests in the Womb of Rebirth for three days, your Soul shall cross the portals of the higher and the lower worlds. You shall know the secrets of life and death, and your Light Body shall be crystallized and be made permanent."

The Hierophant raised his scepter. "Son of Earth, you have known yourself as the emanation of the Timeless Self in matter. To complete your knowledge, you must attain the final vision of the One—the Universal Timeless Self that has no form, yet inhabits all beings and all creation."

"I hear and obey."

"You have been duly prepared for the journey ahead," he said. "You are now ready to receive the mystic pendant."

One of the priests walked over to the left of the Hierophant, a golden ankh cross on a chain in his cupped hands. Another moved to his right and received the scepter. "By the power vested in me, I now entrust you with the ankh cross," the Hierophant said, as he placed it over my head.

The cross touched my chest, discharging a jolting current of energy. An egg-shaped ovoid formed around me, turning at great speed. My ethereal body united with the ovoid and became a bright white sphere that blasted through the celestial temple's dome. The sphere continued its journey toward the stars. The solar system passed by, became a collection of dots, and vanished. Faster and faster, the sphere zoomed until it reached a white diaphanous cube suspended in the midst of cosmic clouds.

The sphere stopped rotating, slowed its forward movement, and stopped across from the cube. With a sudden burst, the sphere turned back into my ethereal body.

I glided through the heavens, as though I had invisible wings. I had never known such absolute freedom before, and if it were my choice alone, I would never return.

"Son of Earth, the end of your journey draws near," said a large white seraph hovering before me. "Enter the cube and with a one-pointed mind, know the fullness of the One. The One who is Nothing and Everything. The One who has neither beginning nor end. The One who is birthless, deathless, and boundless."

The seraph paused and I took the opportunity to absorb the fires of purity emanating from his holy presence. Then he said, "Forget not Earth, forget not your duty. Nirvana will await your return."

"Thank you." I flew into the cube and sat in a meditative posture. It was small, yet endless. It made no sound, yet it vibrated with life. It existed in time, yet it was timeless.

Ring upon ring, my consciousness expanded, and I was alone, all one, harvesting kernels of experiential wisdom from the vast fields of cosmos.

I saw the Creation as spirals within spirals, unending.

I heard the melody of the Music of the Spheres.

I felt the cool heat of the White Fire Core.

I traversed the cosmic pathways with the seraphim.

I contracted and expanded with the supernova.

I knew the Unmanifest and the Manifest as One Being, One Self.

All sense of time, space, self, and identity dissolved, and I rested in the Great Silence.

# Chapter 22

**Day 9, White Celestial Temple**

After bathing in the fires of the Absolute, I returned to the celestial temple and once again stood before the Hierophant.

"Son of Earth," he said, "for long ages your weary feet have bled on the jagged paths of suffering, and your Soul has struggled onward in the dark cave of birth and rebirth. Now at last, you have completed the anavasis and have seen the Light of the One, which dispels all illusion and ignorance." The diamond on the Hierophant's turban shone, highlighting his austere face. "The time of the katavasis to the lower octaves is upon you. You must now listen for the sounds of sorrow and render comfort and wisdom to those in need. May the sun of Truth shine upon all."

"May the sun of Truth shine upon all," the priests and priestesses affirmed in unison.

The Hierophant returned to his throne.

I concentrated on my third eye and opened my inner senses to the fullest, listening.

I heard the cries of the mother who had lost her son. In no time, my ethereal body shot out of the temple and I stood beside her in the living room of her modest home at Kansas City. I beamed love heart-to-heart and embraced her with my airy arms. I whispered in her ear that God would comfort her and take care of her son. That the child she bore in her womb and raised with so much care and sacrifice would come to earth again in another body. That he would have a new opportunity to live, laugh, and be happy. The darkness blanketing her aura lifted and she stopped crying. In time, she would heal from the terrible loss.

I heard the helpless sobs of the young Ukrainian woman right after a customer, many decades her senior, had closed the door of her dim room. I sped to her place in Kiev and sat on the bed by her side. I focalized the flame of hope and saw it enfold her from head to toe. I told her I didn't judge her for what she did and that I understood she had to survive. That she was loved, worthy, and powerful. That she could now lift her eyes to the Timeless Self, liberate its power, and all would be well. The young woman stood up, a newfound courage now tightening her lips, and I knew this was the last time she would sell her body.

I heard the howls of the Bangladeshi man who thought suicide would deliver him from responsibility, and I found myself next to his crouched inner body in a desolate field. A viscous substance bore down on us. Multilayered, mirror-like walls were scattered asymmetrically all about, psychedelic formations in bold colors moving around and through them like clouds.

I filled my chakras with the energy of faith until it pushed away the gloom weighing him down. I told him that I knew a thing or two about fear and that I almost took my own life when I was a teenager. That the karma of suicide is grave, and that he would find he had bound himself with stronger shackles than before. That whatever Higher Power he believed in would surely forgive him if only he asked.

He clutched my hand and tried to kiss it to thank me. I refused and lifted him up, reminding him to whom all the gratitude and glory belong.

Now I heard the groans of Leah and I was transported to her bedside in the emergency unit of a hospital.

Master Theo immediately sensed my presence and, moments later, his ethereal body was standing next to me. "Her condition is critical. The doctor said she only has a few hours to live. Her father is on his way."

"There must be something we can do."

"The doctors have tried everything. I've been doing what I can, as well, but it doesn't seem to be having any effect."

"I can't go anywhere until I know for sure she won't die."

Master Theo didn't feel the need to remind me what was at stake. And he was right.

I walked over and placed my hands over hers. "Leah, I'm here, can you hear me?"

No response.

I visualized my life force flowing through my hands, up her arms and into the wound, seeing her at the same time getting off the bed vibrant and alive.

Thirty minutes passed. Leah showed no sign of recovery.

I continued my work, intensifying my desire to see her survive.

I lost track of time, still not seeing any progress.

The voice of the Hierophant within my head called me back to the celestial temple. I had to continue listening to the sounds of sorrow across the world and rendering whatever service I could.

I called upon the Law of Timeless Love and kissed her lips.

# CHAPTER 23

**Last Day, White Celestial Temple**

The light of the stars streamed through the transparent golden dome right above me. The white columns seemed to waver in the shimmer from the hanging torches as the Hierophant walked by them and stood before me.

"Rejoice, O Heavens. Rejoice, Ye Earth," the Hierophant said. "The time of the great blessing has come."

"Rejoice, rejoice," the priests and priestesses responded.

"The time when that which is impermanent becomes permanent, that which is mortal becomes immortal, and the victory of Life over Death is made manifest."

A large square of phosphorescent fire now appeared in the Hierophant's hands. He lifted the square and moved it up and down over me. With every pass, my chakras turned faster and the energy matrices of my ethereal body loosened up. My range of vision expanded and became spherical so that now I could see myself from above, from below, and from all around.

"Son of Earth," the Hierophant said. "You are ready for the Crystallization of the Light Body. Speak the invocation I have impressed in your mind. Then center in your heart and magnify the Timeless Flame."

"In the Name *I AM that I AM*, I invoke the full power of Life Eternal.

"I call for the mighty hand of the Great Geometer to sculpt the perfect form out of the stone of my consciousness.

"I call for the combined momentum of all who have defeated Death in times past to be added to my own.

"I call for every erg of energy in my energy field to be raised and regenerated now.

"And I claim my victory. I claim my victory. I claim my victory.

"It is done. And I accept it as done at all levels of my being.

"Receive and multiply my invocation.

"Purify and amend it by the flawless geometry of the Divine Intent."

I visualized the Timeless Flame in the Secret Temple of my Heart spinning—its blue, yellow, and pink plumes melding into a mother-of-pearl hue.

The Flame grew larger and larger until it enveloped my ethereal body in its fiery magnificence. Its radiance eclipsed the light of the torches and seemed to scorch the temple walls. Fractal waves darted away from its periphery, gathered primordial points of energy from the empty space around the temple and brought them back. Pulsing energy currents rose and fell. Threads of light condensed and fused. Then with a blaze and the sound of a thousand whispering winds, the Flame stopped turning and contracted back to its original size in the Secret Temple of my Heart.

In its place now stood a bearded priest. A priest of the sacred fire. His lavender eyes glowed like crystals. Silken robes dripping with liquid light covered his form, a ruby rose embroidered on his chest. A gold-trimmed purple cape covered his shoulders, and a blazing Maltese cross hovered over his head.

An exhilarating sensation of wholeness came upon me. It was as though I were reintegrated, all the pieces of my selfhood taken apart and then put back together correctly at last.

The Hierophant struck his scepter on the floor. "Hear, O Universe, this living Soul has vanquished Death. This living Soul has become the Twice Born."

"We witness," the priests and priestesses said, their voices solemn.

"Son of Heaven, behold your Light Body," the Hierophant said.

"Praise be to the One," I replied.

"Indeed."

"I . . . look like the Secret Master."

"It is because you love him so much." The Hierophant passed the scepter to a priest, then brought his hands over his chest. "Farewell. We shall meet again."

I made the Sign and willed my Light Body back to the sarcophagus. After a brief sense of sinking, as in a vivid dream, my consciousness returned to my sleeping body. The slab rested to one side, and the soft light permeating the cave had brightened.

I gulped in the stale air, craving water. Feeling was returning very slowly to my heavy limbs, making it impossible to move. After several minutes, I made an effort to rotate my wrists and ankles. I couldn't. Despite a crushing awareness that time was running out, waiting was my only choice.

More time passed and I began to have some movement in my arms and legs but still couldn't get up. As soon as I knew my strength would support me, I rolled over and climbed out of the sarcophagus. My muscles ached, and my shoulders and knees felt disjointed.

Without any warning, my vision blurred and the grotto spun. I leaned on the wall and fought the oncoming fainting spell.

When my head cleared, I checked my watch. It was 11:37 p.m. Only twenty-three minutes before the descent of the hammer of woe.

I put on my boots, grabbed my backpack and the tube with the scroll, and shambled out of the death-rebirth chamber into the circular cave, still gaining strength. I located the third passageway from the left and—by then—sprinted into a natural corridor that curved away into the mountainside, my pounding footfalls echoing. Much longer than I had hoped, the corridor finally dead-ended into a towering bronze door, an enormous gong standing to its left. I seized the mallet and struck the gong.

A deafening roar tore through me, making my veins throb with the vibration, stirring my third eye open. I managed not to fall to the ground. The doors swung inward, revealing another cavern. I looked at my watch. Only ten minutes were left.

The large cave was unremarkable, except for one thing—an ethereal sanctuary I could perceive with my inner vision pulsated within the empty space. Everything about it seemed strikingly familiar, the intricate columns crowned with arches, the golden altar with the three steps rising against the back wall, a Timeless Flame burning upon it. Then it struck me. The ethereal sanctuary was a near-exact replica of the Secret Temple of the Heart.

I bowed my head and rushed to the altar. I unzipped the backpack, donned the velvet purple cape, and reached within the leather tube for the Scroll of the Lost Name. An electric current coursed through my fingers and up my arms. Using two small rocks as paperweights, I secured the blank scroll open at the base of the ethereal altar.

"O Great Geometer, reveal to me your mighty Name."

Seven minutes.

The Flame oscillated as if a gust of air passed by. White energy globules formed around it and instantly multiplied, swaddling the entire altar in a crystal mist.

I checked the scroll. Nothing.

*"Please, I implore you."*

I looked at the Flame, trying to ignore my rising heartbeat and constricting chest. The scroll remained as blank as ever.

*We're almost there. Don't let it end this way.*

Suddenly, a lacy grid became visible at the top of the scroll. Within it, characters took shape and crystallized into golden letters. Then, row by row, the grid poured downward, new letters appearing as it moved. Soon, text covered the scroll.

But it didn't form a name.

"Where's the Name? Where's the Name?"

The haunting stillness was my only response. I wrapped my hands around my neck, prostrated before the Flame, and addressed the Timeless Self. "I let go to the flow of Life, I surrender. I the nothing, and you the All."

My ears caught a whooshing sound. I lifted my head. A flaming golden letter had positioned itself over the tip of the Flame to the right and floated there.

A second letter stirred on the scroll. The letter ignited, detached itself from the scroll, and flew to the left of the first one. More letters repeated the sequence and I didn't dare make the slightest move until the precipitation of the Name came to an end.

At last.

I jumped to my feet and there it was—the Lost Name of God in seven letters of living golden fire. I opened my arms, hoping for a last-minute miracle that would empower me to read the Name in its native Atlantean tongue and pronounce it properly.

Ninety seconds.

A gentle sound high above caught my attention. It was a descending blue orb. The orb continued its journey and stopped one foot over me. Two elongated tongues of flame, a yellow and a pink, came out of the orb and struck the top of my head.

Forty seconds.

I did nothing. It was as if my brain were being rewired and I needed time to process the new knowledge.

Fifteen seconds.

I catapulted my gaze toward the blazing Name. I could read it. "God Almighty, strengthen my weakness," I said and uttered the letters one by one.

Chunks of rock broke off the ceiling and crashed to the quaking ground. The bronze doors slammed shut. A rumbling sound saturated the cave. An irresistible force shoved my body down, a cloud of dust rolling over me. I shook uncontrollably, as though every electron wanted to storm away from its orbit and fly solo to a safer place.

The seven burning letters above the Flame doubled in size and rocketed through the ceiling and the mountain.

I blasted out in my Light Body, following them. Higher and higher we went, the letters growing to planet size as they picked up speed.

Below me, I heard Earth's keynote, its unique sound. I saw it turning in the blackness of space. It was a panorama of deep blue, interwoven with dashes of green and grey and tinted with innumerable multicolored specks—so beautiful, so delicate.

Above me, I saw the outline of a colossal head of awesome majesty hovering among the stars—the head of the Great Geometer. Massive shafts of white light discharged all around his face. Two swirling suns made up his eyes. The outline grew more concrete by degrees, a perfect manifestation of formlessness taking form.

So immense was the power coming from the presence of the Great Geometer, I thought I would be annihilated. Instead, my vision expanded to include the deep recesses of cosmos and I watched meteor showers fall, spiral nebulae spin, star systems being born.

The seven massive letters had settled below the divine face, and a holy silence permeated the heavens, as if all the angels of cosmos held their breath. Then, out of the very center of the

Void and coming from everywhere at the same time, the voice of the Great Geometer thundered.

"Son of Heaven, you have spoken my Name, and I AM my Name. I AM the Lord Thy God. I AM the Lord of the Universe. I AM that I AM. Behold Earth, now spared. . . . Fire. Fire. Fire. Light. Light. Light."

The sound of the sacred words resounded throughout the Milky Way. Trillions of points of primordial energy from every corner of the Cosmic Ocean raced in obedience to the almighty command. A herculean white cloud coalesced high in the upper atmosphere over the earth. With every passing moment, the cloud became larger, denser, brighter. Tsunamis of liquid fire crested and ebbed from side to side. Countless particles in all colors of the rainbow broke off its outer edges.

The coruscating cloud reached critical mass and erupted, inundating the infinite emptiness. Smoldering spheres flew off. Showers of crystalline cinders arced away. Giant bolts of lightning streaking with electric threads sprang out from the fiery core of what remained and cascaded toward Earth.

I could see the entire rotating planet in detail. Around the globe, the ethereal pyramids in each country came to life, their edges set alight with a blue-white flare, their capstones signaling like lighthouse beacons. The bolts of lightning encompassed the earth in a fiery embrace.

The first bolt struck the tip of the Great Pyramid of Giza. The second, the tip of the pyramid over the Taj Mahal. The third, the tip of the pyramid over the White House. Within seconds, all bolts reached their targets. The great cathedrals of Europe, Stonehenge in Great Britain, the temple of Apollo at Delphi in Greece, the Trinity Lavra of St. Sergius monastery in Russia, the Shaolin Temple in China, the Basilica of Our Lady of Guadalupe in Mexico, the ruins at Machu Picchu in Peru, and every other energy pyramid the Masters of Energy had erected.

The pyramids absorbed the blazing streams until they exhausted themselves. Then, ripples of light radiated from the capstones in concentric circles, expanding outward until they met. Sparks filled the atmosphere, and a tight web of light enveloped Earth, transforming on contact the energies of the descending hammer of woe.

The outline of the Great Geometer began to dissolve. "Return to Earth now. You have served well. . . . And tell all my children I love them."

# CHAPTER 24

**12:00 p.m., One Week Later, Private Room, Headquarters of the Inner Order, Jackson, Wyoming**

The helicopter that picked me up from Half Dome Mountain took me directly to the hospital where Leah was recovering. The doctors were stunned at her unexpected turnaround and swift progress. Master Theo said it was my kiss that turned things around. Of course, neither I nor Master Theo gave them any clues about the healing power of Timeless Love.

Four days later, we both went to Headquarters as the guests of Master Theo. Leah was weak and her wound hadn't healed completely. But she was alive and we were together.

Medusa was taken into custody without bail by the FBI, awaiting trial for murder. It was she, not Arashi, who had killed Dwayne. I had forgiven her, but she remained unrepentant to the bitter end. As for the Scroll of the Lost Name, it would remain in the possession of Master Theo and his successors in the Inner Order, safe and protected from the claws of the Dark Master.

I laughed when I learned that Mr. Sharpstone's report to the Dean at George Washington University had gotten me in trouble for teaching "superstition." Somehow, being forced to take an unpaid leave of absence, while the Dean's Office investigated the charges against me, didn't bother me that much. Maybe the fact that Mr. Winslow offered me a job as the co-director of the Winslow Hope Foundation with Leah and doubled my professor salary had something to do with it. I would miss my students, but I suspected one or two of the best were ready to join the Inner Order.

Leah revealed that she had been inappropriately touched as a child by a trusted caretaker. It seemed that that soul wound had completely healed and now she felt free to talk about it.

I pressed the little ruby heart between my forefinger and thumb. After escaping from the Dark Master's trap in India, I found the missing half in my room at the compound and had it repaired after I returned to America.

A knock on the door interrupted my thoughts.

"Hurry," Leah said. "Everyone's waiting for us."

"Coming." I glanced at my watch—12:15 p.m. Leah and I were the guests of honor at today's celebration, which was about to start.

I opened the door, offered her my arm, and we walked together toward the grand ballroom. She wore an azure gown that matched her eyes, her curls falling to her shoulders, and I, a dark-blue suit with a white shirt and ruby bowtie.

"You never shared what the Lost Name is," Leah said.

"You know I'm not allowed to tell you. One day, you'll discover it for yourself."

The soaring music of Beethoven's "Ode to Joy" played by a string quintet filled the ballroom. At least one hundred formally attired guests chatted happily. A delicate fragrance of freshly cut roses wafted out of crystal vases sitting on tall tripods. Shafts of sunlight pouring through the large windows affirmed the promise of a better tomorrow.

"Welcome," Mr. Winslow said, showing us the way in. He patted my shoulder and kissed Leah on the cheek.

I realized he had been waiting at the entrance to make sure he would be the first one to greet us. "Thank you, Mr. Winslow."

I looked around and spotted three familiar faces coming my way. "Agata, so good to see you again. Mataji, so glad you could come." I shook hands with both of them and gave Kesang a tight hug. After what we had been through together in Tibet, words weren't enough.

The music stopped. Master Theo stepped on the platform at the farthest end of the ballroom. "Your attention, please."

A hush fell over the assembled guests and they all turned toward Master Theo. He placed his left hand on his heart and made the Sign with the right, bringing it straight down and then forward at a ninety-degree angle. Everyone followed suit.

"Brothers and Sisters of the Light," he said, "we have gathered here today to celebrate Earth's victory, and honor the young man and woman who made it possible."

Master Theo motioned us to approach, and we walked up the center aisle to the platform.

"Ladies and gentlemen," he said, "I present to you Leah Winslow and Diokles Philaretos."

A rolling applause, mixed with shouts of "hear, hear" and "bravo," went up. Leah and I smiled at one another and the guests, and bowed.

Master Theo placed a round medallion over Leah's neck and another over mine. The medallions seemed to be made of platinum and depicted a helmeted head in profile. It was the grey-eyed goddess of Homer, the Spear Shaker of Francis Bacon—Pallas Athena.

"At the beginning of each new spiritual cycle, the Mysteries are renewed and reborn in many forms," Master Theo said. "And so it is now with the coming Era of Universal Enlightenment. Thus, a new mission awaits you both. First, to complete your studies in the secret precepts of the Timeless Self. Then, to infuse them with the elixir of spiritual wisdom *you* have distilled in your quest for the scroll. And finally, to share them with the world.

"You will show seekers how to liberate the power of their Timeless Self so they can become inspired, empowered, and free, and render *their* appointed service to life. And you will remind them that wielding this limitless spiritual power is a call to courage, a call to duty, a call to nobility.

"Above all, you will be the servant of their Timeless Self.

"And you will always keep in mind that we never teach anything per se. We simply help the Soul bring to awareness that which it already knows deep within. We help the Soul tear away the veil of the Great Forgetfulness and remember eternal Truth. We help the Soul attain gnosis."

Master Theo pointed at me with an open hand. "Diokles, do you accept your new duties?"

"I do."

"Leah, do you accept your new duties?"

"I do."

"Very well. The archives of the Inner Order will reveal all their secrets to you, and all of our resources, both tangible and intangible, will be at your disposal. Together with other organizations dedicated to the Light and spiritual people from all nations, races, and creeds, and by the Grace of God, we will bring to earth the Era of Universal Enlightenment." Master Theo clasped his hands in prayer. "Hear, O Heaven and Earth, for this and every opportunity to serve, we are grateful."

"We are grateful," a multitude of voices repeated after him.

My heart throbbed. A white light flashed at the back of my mind and the ballroom dimmed, a spiral staircase rising through the ceiling now forming before me. My consciousness stepped out in my Light Body and I saw Leah go out of her physical body as well. She was now dressed in a white, silken gown that touched the floor, a gossamer veil covering her face. I held her hand and we walked up the staircase, soon finding ourselves at the Secret Master's celestial temple.

He wore his gold-trimmed purple uniform and cape, and stood before the golden altar with the enormous amethyst. The marble-like walls sparkled with pastel colors as if they too wanted to contribute to the festive atmosphere.

"You have done well," the Secret Master said.

"Thank you," we said with one voice.

His hands arose. "O Powers of Light, invest these ones, about to embark on their new mission, with the Scepter of Power."

A gold scepter appeared in his right hand. "You shall receive this scepter when we conclude the ceremony." He looked past us. "My Lady, please step forward."

I turned around. A Being of Light whom I knew to be the twin soul of the Secret Master stood a few feet behind us. An elegant indigo garment adorned her form, her hair pulled back in the chignon style. Her heart chakra radiated fine pink rays, her deep eyes revealing great wisdom.

"Let the sacred ceremony commence," the Secret Master said.

A heavenly melody sounded and the Lady took her place next to him. Two angels approached, each holding a pink cape in their hands. They stood behind Leah and me, put the capes over our shoulders, and clasped them in front. A crown appeared over me and a tiara over Leah. We accepted them and lowered them onto our heads.

The Secret Master touched each of my shoulders with the tip of his sword, sending ripples of energy through my aura. He walked in front of Leah and repeated the rite. "Over the next week, invoke the power of this transfer of Light for the protection of your love, for the bonding of yourselves as twin souls, and for the perfect union of the divine polarity."

The Secret Master gave each of us a gold ring. I anchored my eyes into Leah's and she, into my own. I placed the ring on Leah's finger and she, on mine.

"I desire that you return to the land of your birth before you commence your mission," the Secret Master said addressing me, "and perform the marriage ceremony there." He took our hands, brought them together, and placed his on top. "I bless you, and if you so agree, I now release you both from your vows of celibacy."

"I agree," I said, already planning the greatest big, fat Greek wedding the world had ever known.

"I agree," Leah said.

"I now call upon a witness."

"I witness," the Lady said.

"It is done. May you embody pure love and always remember—the more you rebond with your Timeless Self, the greater the power drawing and keeping your beloved near you."

The Secret Master stepped backward, an irresistible impulse drawing my gaze to the Lady. A smile that was loveliness itself graced her face. A white cushion with yellow fringe rested on her outstretched arms, and two glowing white spheres were descending toward it. The spheres reached the cushion and turned into two babies in luminous swaddling garments.

"These souls, high initiates both, are waiting to be born through you," the Lady said. "This was the prophecy Mataji gave you, Leah dear. Was it not?"

Leah nodded.

"Will you accept them, then? Will you nurture them and teach them the Mysteries? Will you protect them from all that is impure and unholy?"

"We will."

"And so it shall be," the Lady said.

Leah and I basked in the supreme happiness that charged the atmosphere.

"Let us bow," the Secret Master said. "The Timeless Self desires to speak to you."

We all knelt, as the holy voice reverberated throughout the celestial temple.

"I AM that I AM.

"I AM the Sun of Life, beaming my light rays into your heart.

"I AM the Torch of Divine Fire, transforming every limitation in your world.

"I AM the Cosmic Treasure House, bestowing limitless gifts upon your being.

"I AM yourself above. You are myself below.

"Remember me. Accept me. Heed me.

"Take refuge in my Divine Embrace.

"Look to me for all your needs and wield my power.

"Claim my perfection and expand it on Earth.

"Become free to serve life in my Name, free to serve life in the Name *I AM that I AM*."

# THREE WAYS TO CONTINUE THE JOURNEY . . .

1. **Connect and share.**
   Send your questions to the author. Share with others how you felt about the story. Read what other people have to say. Vote for your favorite chapter. And more.

2. **Go behind the scenes.**
   Read fascinating interviews with the book's characters and the author. Discover the secrets woven throughout the novel. Check out the hero's journey, the mythic structure the novel is based on, and see how soul wounds can be healed through the transformative power of story.

3. **Remember your unconditional soul identity.**
   Master Theo asked Diokles to "straighten up his spine and pick up the pieces of his broken self-esteem" (page 26). Having an identity others find acceptable is a powerful survival drive. Conditional soul identity leads to conditional self-esteem, and thus insecurity and unhappiness. Unconditional soul identity leads to unconditional self-esteem and the corresponding peace of mind, freedom from manipulation, and inner joy. You are welcome to access a free download and learn how to transition from conditional to unconditional soul identity.

**For instant access to all of the above, go to www.QuestForTheLostNameSecrets.com**

*Also, you can meet the author at the Conscious Life Expo in Los Angeles (twice a year) where he is one of the speakers along with Gregg Braden, Dannion Brinkley, and Dan Millman.*

# ABOUT THE AUTHOR

George Makris is a practical spirituality teacher and the founder of the Timeless Self Movement. His life-long goal is to assist people to become inspired, empowered, and free.

George was born to a wealthy family on the island of Cyprus in the eastern Mediterranean. When he was ten years old, the family lost everything due to a war. Beset by fear and feeling abandoned by God, he spent his early adult years trying to make sense out of life. In an attempt to find solace and answers, he studied Neoplatonism, psychology, and the world's mystical traditions. By learning to open up to the power from above, and by the Grace of God, he overcame his fears and found inner peace.

George is known for his constant affirmation of everyone's unconditional soul identity as expressed through these words: "You are loved. You are worthy. You are powerful. And all is well."

He graduated with highest honors (*summa cum laude*) from George Washington University where he received a bachelor's degree in business administration and a minor degree in psychology. He went on to obtain a master of science in business education from Montana State University, where he wrote his graduate thesis on business planning.

Over the years, he has held a number of positions, including corporate trainer, vice president of a statistical software company, vice president of a manufacturing company, as well as strategic advisor to CEOs.

George lives with his wife, Karen, on a quiet piece of land in Montana, along with their cat, golden retriever, the deer, an owl, and a roaming pair of eagles.

...

## ABOUT THE PUBLISHER

The mission of the Timeless Self Institute is to help people overcome their problems, manifest their goals, and serve life through unique knowledge, spiritual skills, and belief transformation.

In addition to traditional courses, the Institute offers *accelerated spiritual training*™—a method using an interactive, Internet-based platform that takes spiritual learning to a new level.

**For more information, please visit**
www.TimelessSelf.com.

...

# Lost Name Glossary

*For a more extensive and detailed glossary, please go to*
*www.TimelessSelf.com/Glossary*

**Adult Self.** The most conscious self-state and the one people identify with the most. One of the key functions of the Adult Self is to "wear the mantle" of the Timeless Self and "bear its aegis," and to work with the other self-states under that authority.

**Akasha.** The subtle energy field upon which records of the past are kept.

**Anavasis.** The mystical ascent to the level of the Unmanifest where individual identity is temporarily suspended and the seeker experiences all existence as One Self.

**Aura.** The energy emanation around each person.

**Belief.** An energy pattern that resides in one's energy field, consisting of a mental form empowered with feeling. A "right belief" is a pattern of perfection. A "false belief" is a pattern of imperfection.

**Belief genesis.** The creation of a belief. The interpretation of experiences and outer stimuli is one of the major ways beliefs are formed.

**Belief transformation.** The removal of a false belief by raising its energetic frequency.

**Bhajan.** Devotional Indian song.

**Chakras.** Energy centers anchored in our subtle energy body.

**Cosmic Ocean.** The seemingly empty space everywhere that is filled with points of primordial energy.

**Creating.** The spiritual practice of building a mental form and empowering it with feeling, with the intention to manifest an outcome.

**Deeper Mysteries.** High-level initiations. They are Baptism by Water, Baptism by Fire, Deep Purification, Crystallization of the Light Body, and Grand Regeneration.

**Divine Embrace.** The deeply felt experience of divine love.

**Divine plan.** A mission or work assigned to an individual before birth.

**Ego.** The synthetic ego (as opposed to the divine Ego) is the conglomerate energy field of a person's negative thoughts and feelings, the central consciousness of his or her false beliefs.

**Elements.** Fire, air, water, and earth understood as forces of nature.

**Energy follows free will.** It is a well-known principle that energy follows attention. Similarly, energy follows free will. For instance, by its very formation, a false belief locks up fragments of free will, which in turn draws to it some of the flow of the primordial energy coming through the silver cord.

**Energy magnetizing.** The spiritual practice of drawing primordial points of energy from the Cosmic Ocean in order to create more effectively.

**Ethereal body.** One of the energy vehicles of the Soul.

**Free will retrieval.** The process of releasing locked-up fragments of free will from false beliefs, defense mechanisms, and survival drives. The more one reclaims his or her free will for conscious use by the Adult Self, the greater the creative potential.

**Gnosis.** The experiential knowledge of the Divine.

**Great Forgetfulness.** The energy veil that keeps people from remembering their inner reality, and in particular the Timeless Self. "Alethia," the Greek word for "Truth," translates as "No Forgetfulness." Thus, according to the ancient Greeks, to discover Truth is simply to remember.

**Great Geometer.** An ancient term for God.

**Hierophant.** One who reveals the "hiera," literally the holy objects, and metaphorically the spiritual secrets, to the initiates.

*I AM that I AM.* The Name of God revealed to Moses.

*I AM* **Mind.** The mind of the Timeless Self.

*I AM* **State.** A state of bliss, an energetic frequency above the turmoil of the world.

**Initiate.** A spiritual seeker who has undergone initiation and has partaken of the Mysteries.

**Initiation.** The process of preparing, passing a test, and receiving the ensuing empowerment.

**Inner planes.** Levels of existence beyond the material world.

**Instinct.** The self-state responsible for protecting the physical body from harm. Fighting, fleeing, or freezing (playing dead) are typical survival responses the Instinct employs to perform its job.

**Invoking.** The spiritual practice of calling upon a higher power. Invoking can be employed to create or to transform.

**Katavasis.** The descent of the seeker to places of suffering, including planes of lower vibrational frequency, with the intent to alleviate misery.

**Karma.** The law of cause and effect.

**Kundalini.** The shakti power coiled in the chakra at the base of the spine.

**Light Body.** The energy body created after a seeker passes through the gates of the Deeper Mysteries.

**Mysteries.** Levels of initiation that can lead seekers to liberation.

**Out-of-body experience.** The act of consciously going out of the body and entering some level of the inner planes.

**Perfection transforms imperfection.** The principle which states that an energy pattern of high frequency can transform an energy pattern of a lower frequency.

**Points of primordial energy.** Unmanifest energy permeating space that one can magnetize and harness for creating.

**Power of the Timeless Self.** The great creative potential of the Timeless Self one can access and liberate to overcome problems, manifest goals, and serve life.

**Practical spirituality.** The process of liberating spiritual power to manifest desired outcomes.

**Sacred geometry.** The use of architecture, mathematics, and proportion to harness cosmic energies and create auspicious environments.

**Secret Temple of the Heart.** The spiritual place within the heart where the Timeless Flame resides.

**Self-states.** Points of consciousness within a human being—the Adult Self, the Soul, the Instinct, and the ego. Each of the self-states has its own set of beliefs and priorities, and reacts differently to external stimuli.

**Silver cord.** The thread of life through which the primordial energy flows from the Timeless Self to the self below.

**Soul.** The emanation of the Timeless Self in the matter spheres.

**The One.** See Universal Timeless Self.

**Timeless Flame.** The divine spark. A mystical flame anchored in the Secret Temple of the Heart.

**Timeless Love.** The deep and unfathomable love shared between twin souls.

**Timeless Self.** The divine Ego, the God Self. The Timeless Self is each one's divine being above, connecting to them through the silver cord.

**Timeless Self rebonding.** The spiritual practice of uniting with the Timeless Self by degrees. A good starting point is simply to place the attention on the Timeless Self and send love and adoration.

**Transforming.** The spiritual practice of raising a lower energetic frequency to a higher one.

**Twin souls.** Also known as twin flames. The complementary beings of the divine polarity created out of the same energy core.

**Universal Timeless Self.** The Absolute, the Unmanifest, the Source of all that is. What Neoplatonic philosopher Plotinus termed "the One." The One who is Nothing and Everything. The One who has neither beginning nor end. The One who is birthless, deathless, and boundless.

...

## Acknowledgments

To my parents, our children, and my big Greek extended family. Thank you for the love, the laughter, and our years together.

To Agathi, my sister, and Stelios, her husband. Thank you for being my guardian angels.

To all my spiritual teachers. Thank you for helping me discover my true self.

To Teresa Kennedy. Thank you for your help with story development.

To Margie Lawson. Thank you for showing me the nuances of the written word.

To Dave King, my editor. Thank you for your calming presence, your amazing ideas, and fine work.

To Kate and Simon Warwick-Smith. Thank you for your hard work and support.

To Kathi Dunn. Thank you for the beautiful cover.

To Marius Michael-George. Thank you for your positive attitude, your paintings, and for teaching me that an author is also an artist—a sculptor of words.

To Christophe Lambert. Thank you for your deep insights and for being there during the tough times.

To Paula Kehoe. Thank you for your great dedication to this project and your relentlessly cheerful spirit.

To the initial reading group. Thank you for all your comments and help.

And to my first editor, confidant, pillar of strength and so much more, my wife, Karen. Thank you.